MW01131135

SHOT GIRL

Jack is a retired cop who knows and respects firearms. A recent victim of gun violence, she is confined to a wheelchair, getting physical therapy in a rehab facility, and teaching handgun safety and Second Amendment history to the elderly residents.

A thousand miles away, a very disturbed individual with a modified 9mm pistol, a thousand rounds of ammo, and a singular obsession—to make history as the biggest mass murderer ever—decides to make that active shooting fantasy a reality.

It has been said the only thing that can stop a bad guy with a gun is a good guy with a gun.

Jack is about to find out if that's true.

SHOT GIRL by J.A. Konrath

America has 300 million guns. This is the story of one of them.

SHOT GIRL
A Jack Daniels Thriller

J.A. KONRATH

SHOT GIRL
Copyright © 2019 by Joe Konrath
Cover and art copyright © 2019 by Carl Graves

This book is a work of fiction. Names, characters, places and incidents are either
products of the author's imagination or used fictitiously. Any resemblance to actual
events, locales, or persons, living or dead, is entirely coincidental. All rights reserved.
No part of this publication can be reproduced or transmitted in any form or by any
means, electronic or mechanical, without permission in writing from the authors.

May 2019

AUTHOR'S NOTE

Between starting to write this novel and completing it, the media has covered over a dozen active shooting tragedies. Not just in America, but worldwide.

This book is fiction. I've made up the perpetrators, incidents, victims, reporting agencies, statistics, and news stories.

But it should still scare the hell out of you.

"A well regulated Militia, being necessary to the security of a free State, the right of the people to keep and bear Arms, shall not be infringed."

THE SECOND AMENDMENT

"Throw up your hands! I want your guns!"

VIRGIL EARP

JACK

"According to the best estimates, there are more than one hundred thousand victims of gun violence in the US every year." I lifted my wheel brake and rolled out from behind the table, pausing for effect. "I'm one of them."

I heard no gasps from the group of a dozen, four of whom sat in wheelchairs of their own. Two of the residents, Mrs. Garza from building F16 and Mr. Shoop from B9, flirted in a highly disturbing way, licking and manipulating their dentures, and I might as well have been invisible to them.

Mr. Karakakus from E2 had his eyes closed. Asleep. Or possibly dead.

Mrs. Addelbaum from C41 smiled at me, but I had a suspicion it had nothing to do with her interest in my talk, and a lot to do with her believing I was her daughter, Clarissa.

I locked eyes with Mary Streng from B65, who also smiled appreciatively at me like I was her kid. But in this case, I actually was her kid. Her fifty-three-year-old ex-cop partially-paralyzed kid, wondering once again why the hell I agreed to do this.

A strong and surprisingly cool-for-August Gulf Coast breeze tousled my hair, and Mrs. Marden lost her floppy sunhat and didn't seem to notice as it went somersaulting through the piles of zinnia, hopping the fence into the physical therapy pool.

My mother gave me a thumbs up.

I glanced down at the notes on my iPhone, but I'd given this lecture many times and only needed a reminder of my place before continuing.

"Any time you hear a gun statistic, you need to regard it with skepticism. There are too many factors and agendas on both sides of the gun ownership debate, and no mutually agreed upon data collecting body that can ... do you have a question, Ms. Conseco?"

Ms. Conseco, E55, put down her hand. "Is this the sexual positions group?"

"That's after lunch, Ms. Conseco. This is the gun handling and safety group."

She nodded, smiling. Then she raised her hand again.

"Yes, Ms. Conseco?"

"What time is it now?"

"It's five minutes after nine, dear."

"Are they going to teach us reverse cowgirl?"

"I'm sure they'll cover it."

"How about the clapper?"

I had no idea what the clapper was. "Sure. Probably." Sensing I was losing the room, I cut to the chase. "Who wants to hold a gun?"

Three-quarters of my audience raised their hands. The holdouts were Mom, Mr. Karakakus (who remained asleep or expired), Mrs. Ramos from C28, who was halfway through a disturbingly large plate of BBQ ribs that required one hundred percent of her concentration, and Mrs. Shadid, from Building B, who sat with a poster in her lap. On it, she'd bedazzled the words GUNS KILL PEOPLE with enough glitter to be seen from orbiting satellites.

Mrs. Shadid acted as our conscientious objector, and I'd promised to give her some one-on-one time later to discuss, in her terms, "Why all guns should be destroyed and all people who use guns are evil."

Really looking forward to that talk.

I had my .38 tucked warmly under my left thigh and managed to lift my leg just enough to free it without too much pain or difficulty.

The geriatrics who noticed *oohed* and *ahhed* appropriately. For the gun, I guessed, not for my feeble motor skills.

"This is a Colt Cobra thirty-eight caliber +P. It's a double action revolver, and it holds six cartridges. You pull back the release to free the cylinder to load and unload it."

"What is +P?"

My mother, the plant. She knew exactly what +P meant, but felt compelled to ask questions when I didn't explain something to her satisfaction.

"Plus P means it can accept overpressure rounds, which have a higher internal pressure than a standard .38 cartridge. They have a higher stopping power and velocity."

"And what's double action?"

Thanks again, Mom. "A single action revolver fires when the hammer is manually pulled back into a cocked position. Double action can be fired by just pulling the trigger."

"And what's—"

I gave Mom a *hush up* look, and she nodded and smiled and pulled an imaginary zipper across her mouth.

"Mr. Fincherello, can you tell me the first rule of gun safety?"

"Shoot the head," he crowed.

Titters from the elder gallery.

I gave a polite, tight-lipped smile. When public speaking, never let your audience know how much you hate it.

"The first rule of gun safety is always treat a gun as if it is loaded. Never take anyone's word for it. Always check for yourself. Mr. Fincherello, what's the proper way to hand someone a firearm?"

"Just how I like 'em. Butt first!"

More giggles. I swear, geriatrics were more immature than my five-year old daughter, Sam.

I took the leather pouch out of the compartment beneath my seat and found the key. Then I removed the trigger lock—two metal pieces that fit over the trigger and trigger guard, preventing the weapon from being fired—and did a quick double check of the Colt, swinging out the cylinder to make sure all six chambers were empty, closing it before the hand-off to Mr. Fincherello.

Though he enjoyed his role as class clown, Mr. Fincherello had paid attention, and he checked the cylinder for bullets even though he'd just seen me complete the task.

"Ms. Conseco, what's the second rule of gun safety?"

"Never point it at anything you don't intend to destroy."

"Very good, Ms. Conseco."

"Will we learn the bullfighter?"

"I don't understand, Ms. Conseco."

"In the sex position class?"

"I'm sure they'll go over it." I had no idea what that one was, either.

"Can I dry fire this?" Mr. Fincherello asked.

"If you can tell me the last two rules."

"Only put your finger on the trigger when you are ready to shoot."

"Good. That prevents accidentally pulling it. And the fourth?"

"The fourth is … uh … um … "

"Always know what's behind your target." Mom to the rescue. "Shooting isn't like you see in the movies. People miss what they're aiming at. A lot. And if you don't hit what's in front of you, you'll likely kill what's behind it. With certain kinds of ammo, you can go right through what's in front of you and still kill what's behind it."

Like me, Mom was a former cop. But she hadn't won as many shooting trophies as I had.

"Thanks, Mom. Go ahead and pull the trigger, Mr. Fincherello."

He respected the first rule and avoided pointing the weapon at any of the attendees, though when one of the nurses, Marlotta, walked by, he made a vaudeville show of considering it. Thankfully, instead of dry-firing at Marlotta, he opted for the truck parked on the street to the west, the driver unloading storm windows for our retirement-slash-nursing-slash-rehab facility.

Mr. Fincherello sighted on the side panel and pulled the trigger three times.

"Now try thumbing the hammer back, Mr. Fincherello. What happens to the trigger?"

"The trigger moves in."

"That lowers the trigger pull weight from about nine pounds to about three and a half pounds. It's a shorter pull length, and much easier on your finger."

Mr. Fincherello dry fired three more times, thumbing back the hammer each time.

The wind kicked up again, and someone screamed.

I startled at that; something that had become normal for me lately. Pre GSW, my neurosis of choice had been insomnia. Since my gunshot wound, the sleeplessness had gotten worse, but I'd also been flirting with symptoms uncomfortably close to post traumatic stress disorder.

Panic attacks. Jolting at loud noises. Hand sweats. Dry mouth. Paranoia.

Taking a bullet can damage the mind as much as the body.

The scream had been delivered by Mrs. Ramos; the strong gust had upended her paper plate of ribs, which now decorated her yoga pants and Velcro kicks.

"I love this," Mr. Fincherello declared, holding up my Cobra as if it was a trophy. "Where can I buy one?"

"This is the United States of America," I told him. "You can go out and buy one right now."

"*There are no dangerous weapons. There are only dangerous men.*"
ROBERT A. HEINLEIN

"*All we ask for is registration, just like we do for cars.*"
CHARLES SCHUMER

GAFF

B4 we get into my story, you need background deets.

My story doesn't really start until tomorrow, anyway.

I'm Gaff.

Sup.

Here's truth.

The fake media thinks that violent videogames can make you kill people IRL.

Dead. So dead.

Like some head glitching scrub on Fortnite finna shoot up a school for realz.

As if.

Videogames don't make killers. Truth.

The National Research Study Initiative on Videogame Violence estimates that over a billion people play games involving some degree of violence. How many of them go on shooting sprees? NRSIVV could only connect 12 spree shooters from the last two decades to rated M games. Twelve out of a billion isn't a connection. It can't even be called a statistic. Compare that to the very real statistic that every single active shooter of the last fifty years has drank milk.

Should we ban cows bcuz drinking milk leads to mass murder?

Correlation ain't causation, yo.

It's like those scrubs who think porn leads to rape. That's cray. Some dude addicted to porn won't have any juice left to rape no one.

Those trolls at Good Christian Women and Men United Against Pornography want you to believe that everyone who watches a spanking video is a serial killer in training, and that anytime sex is videoed it degrades women.

Bye, Felicia.

Like every person in the world with Internet access, I've seen porn.

How many people I raped? Zero.

GTFO—get the fuck out—Good Christian Women and Men.

Why do all these teeks want to blame crimes on stupid shit? The problem isn't movies or music or games or the internet or porn or immigrants or Muslims or the poor or the rich or drugs or whatever political party isn't yours.

Truth. Some people are bad and want to do bad things.

Sorry not sorry.

People suck and life is pain and it's better to be the hunter than the prey.

Plus, killing is dank.

That's a guess on my part. I haven't killed nobody.

#NotYet.

But I think about it. Constant.

When I was a shawty I saw this old TV show about Cleveland Hooper. Hooper climbed to the top of a water tower in El Pancho, Texas, near a state park. He had a Winchester M14 rifle and shot 38 people, killing 18. The year was 1966, and the M14 was bolt action.

Every time he fired he had to load the next bullet.

Extra.

The TV went into deets how he pinned down a lot of people, shooting one guy four times, just plinking him in the same leg over and over trying to get others to come help him.

People tried. People died.

Dope.

Raw.

Off the shits.

It took ten minutes b4 the crowd got woke, twenty-eight minutes for 5-0 to respond, and one hour sixteen minutes b4 a police sniper finally took Hooper out.

While we watched the TV, my moms kept saying, over and over, how terrible it was.

"Terrible! So terrible! This is terrible!"

I thought it was high key.

I was seven.

When I was twelve, the Rathlin Massacre went down. You heard of it. August 10, 2009, in Rathlin, South Carolina, teenagers and BFFs Gregory Taylor Schneider and Tully Huffland walked into Rathlin High School wearing commando outfits and ski masks, carrying two giggled-out Glock 21s and four hundred rounds of ammunition. They weren't expert marksmen like Hooper. This was point and click.

Spray and slay.

They offed six teachers, eighteen students, and wounded thirty-four others. Police took nine minutes thirty-eight seconds to arrive on the scene, shot both dudes. Schneider died, GSW to the dome, but Huffland survived, and is now serving twenty-four consecutive life sentences.

Schneider and Huffland called themselves the Suburban Eliminators. I've read five ebooks about them. Like the fake media, the books tried to blame their parents, and bullying, and gun control laws, and violent videogames, and death metal music, and drugs, and splatter movies.

But Huffland always denied all that BS. Everyone knows his famous quote.

"I did it for lulz."

I got that shit tattooed on my forearm.

My moms went ballistic. Not bcuz of the ink; she never seen it. I keep it hid, cover it with make-up when I'm sleeveless. Moms went nuts bcuz of the massacre. Kept me out of school for over a week, blinds drawn and praying her rosary over and over. When I finally went back to seventh grade, she made me carry around a twelve-pound cast iron skillet in my backpack.

"If someone starts shooting, hold it in front of you."

"How about I just get a gun. Then I could shoot back."

"Guns are the problem! Don't you ever let me hear you talk that way again!"

Can't even.

In high school, I hit puberty late, didn't have a growth spurt until I was fourteen. But during my pre-pube years I tried to pick a fight with anyone I could.

For the feels.

When I was a kid, my moms was known as a *helicopter parent.* Always hovering around me, making sure I didn't get hurt. Signed me up for a katrillion activities, and my moms went to every one.

When I fell during peewee soccer practice and skinned my knee, she cried louder than I did, then went on a crusade to force everyone to wear knee pads.

When I came in fourth place during a cross country meet, Moms gave the whole district an earful about how everyone who participates needs to get a ribbon.

Moms went postal when they wouldn't let me into high school bcuz my vaccines weren't up to date bcuz vaccines caused autism. I was forced to get the boosters, and then walked around with a thermometer in my mouth for the next month bcuz if I showed the tiniest symptom Moms was ready to sue the school district, the doctor, the AMA, the vaccine manufacturer, and all the corrupt politicians that made it a law.

I didn't get sick. She acted all disappointed.

Now y'all might think this made me salty or something.

Stay in your lane.

I grew up feeling nothing. Pops died when I was two years old so I had no one to look up to. No neighborhood kid was ever good enough to be my friend. But Moms never loved me neither, so I didn't get why she always scared them off.

#Confusing.

As a kid, I didn't know what it was to win. Or to lose. Or to pay for the consequences of my actions. If I got a C on an assignment, Moms went jihad on the teacher. If I got into a fight I started, Moms always victim blamed.

But I don't blame her for what I am.

Wanting to shoot a bunch of people has nothing to do with anything my moms did or didn't do.

I want to do it for the same reason I got into fights.

To feel something.

High key.

Hitting someone felt good.

Getting hit felt good.

I didn't care about the kids I fought. Some of them were okay.

No offense, bruh. Bite or get bit.

A school counselor, who didn't think my fighting had anything to do with R rated movies, too much sex on TV, the threat of legalized cannabis, or role-playing games and first-person shooters (which I didn't even play, bcuz Moms forbid it), recommended I take an MMA class for kids.

I 4realz loved it. Went five times, did pretty good, until a bigger kid gave me a black eye, and Moms hired a lawyer and sued the kid's parents and my instructor.

To be honest, none of it matters. Maybe, in the future, someone will write a book about me. Try to show I'm a product of my effed-up era. Grew up learning to read on a smart phone. Got my lulz trolling noobs on social media bcuz no accountability online. Just an overprotected and entitled teen who don't understand hard work bcuz the baby boomers and gen Xers deitsched the world and why should I have to do anything difficult bcuz I'm a special snowflake and there's no real equality and SJWs blame me for my white privilege.

#WTF.

#LULZ.

#ACTIVESHOOTER4EVS.

There have been over a thousand active shooting incidents worldwide in the last fifteen years, 95% of them in the US of A. Only 4% were done by women.

Endemic exclusive misogynist sexism. Yet another unfair case of guys having all the fun.

I'm a plural. Generation Z. We're called plurals bcuz we be plural-istic; a generation who accepts everyone, the full spectrum of gender identification, religion, color, appearance, language, beliefs.

People are people. So why should active shooters all be white dudes? #ChangeTheGame.

Of course, we all knew the big daddy of active shooters was Reginald Archibald Lorenz, who rented a penthouse suite in Grover, Pennsylvania overlooking Reinhold Stadium during MoshMania. From the twenty-third floor, only two hundred meters away from the outdoor concert, he opened fire with an AR15 equipped with a bump stock to simulate fully automatic fire. Lorenz wasted 66 people, wounding over 600 others. He had 3000 rounds of ammo, and barricaded himself into his hotel room using cement bags he brought up four @ a time using the bellman's cart.

Pretty dope, but Lorenz went out like a bitch, blowing his own dome off while the cops were still trying to blast their way in.

Bad end.

Trash.

I'd never kill myself, no matter how many people I offed, bcuz that means feeling guilty or having serious mental problems, and homie don't play that.

When I do my thing, it'll be different. I'm not going to get caught and go to jail. I'm not going to get head-glitched by 5-0.

And I'm not taking the bitch way out and eating my gun.

I'm going to get away with it.

So I can do it again.

The biggest problem with the shooters I mentioned, and all the shooters since Cleveland Hooper made it America's greatest spectator sport 53 years ago, is those bruhs only did it once.

Eff that.

I'm going to be the first mass murderer who does it a whole bunch of times.

For the lulz.

I am woke and extra and savage and shook and all that other dumb-shit my plurals say bcuz we need our own language bcuz we don't fit in nowhere with nobody.

I turn eighteen tomorrow. According to the bitch ass law, ima adult. I got money saved up from my shitty job serving shitty fast food to shitty people.

Been saving for two years.

Been saving all for this moment.

Bye-bye job.

Bye-bye school.

Bye-bye Moms.

I'm out.

Mic drop.

Already got an apartment lined up.

Gonna sign that lease.

Then I'm gonna buy a gun.

Then I'm gonna kill more peeps than 9/11.

Thank you, next.

"Happiness is a warm gun."
JOHN LENNON

"We cannot let a minority of people—and that's what
it is, it is a minority of people—hold a viewpoint
that terrorizes the majority of people."
HILLARY CLINTON

JACK

"Tropical Storm Harry has been upgraded to Hurricane Harry. Category 3. It just hit Tobago."

My hands on the parallel bars, holding up ninety-percent of my body weight while my rubbery legs struggled to keep the other ten-percent from collapsing, I had zero desire to talk to my mother about storms.

Especially storms named Harry.

"I thought you were here for moral support, Mom." It came out gruntier than I would have liked.

She made a *pfft* sound. "I didn't coddle you as a baby. I'm not going to start coddling because of a little spine injury."

Little spine injury? "I got shot in the back. My T11 vertebra cracked in half, the nerve holding on by a thread."

"And I was in a coma for months after a serial killer brutalized me. Did you hear me whine?"

"You couldn't whine. You were in a coma."

She made another *pfft* sound. "Wasn't your third operation supposed to be the one that fixed everything?"

I nodded. But my doctors had said the same about my second operation. And my first.

"So the problem isn't your back. The problem is you aren't trying hard enough."

"I'd like to see you balance on your hands on this bar."

"I wouldn't need to. I'd use my legs." She squinted at me. "Are you doped up?"

"No." The pain was bearable, and I weaned off the Tramadol weeks ago. "It's not the pain. It's paresthesia."

"Your doctors said you should be regaining mobility."

"Tell that to my legs."

My mother tilted her head down, talking to my legs. "The doctors say you should be regaining mobility."

Smart ass.

My biceps shook, sweat soaked me, and I had no confidence in holding my bladder. When I did physical therapy with Phin, my husband, and our daughter, Sam, they encouraged me with equal amounts praise and good-natured ribbing.

They tried so hard to be supportive.

It was miserable.

But not as bad as Mom and her world's lousiest pep talks.

Maybe I shouldn't be doing rehab at the retirement home where she lived. But Mom left her last home because of me, seeking out this place, where we could be together.

"Let's do it, Jacqueline," she'd prodded. "It's only twenty minutes from the beach."

We hadn't been to the beach once.

"I chose to do my recovery here with you because I thought we would bond," I huffed and puffed.

"You're not lifting your toes. You're going to trip."

"Think you'd be able to walk when half the feeling in your legs is gone?"

"You're not walking, Jacqueline. You're balancing on your hands and dragging your lower half behind you like an alligator tail."

I gritted my teeth, tried to get my damn feet to listen to my brain.

"They're predicting Hurricane Harry hits the mainland in six days."

Mom was back to squinting at a cell phone.

"Seriously? You're on your phone?"

"Sam calls it phubbing."

"What?"

"Phubbing. It's pluralspeak."

"Speak English."

"Plurals are the generation under millennials. Grew up with smart phones and the internet and instant access to everything. They use their own lingo, mostly when they text. Phubbing is when someone is snubbing you to use their phone."

"Where'd you learn that?"

"It was trending on Twitter."

"So why are you phubbing me?"

"I can watch a YouTube of a dog playing with a sea lion, or I can watch you pretend you're trying your best on those handrails. I'm opting for the dog and sea lion. Maybe if you were trying, I'd pay attention. But you'd rather give up than try."

"Maybe if you helped me."

"The woman I raised wouldn't ask for help. She'd help herself."

I felt my face get tight. She raised a white eyebrow.

"Are you getting angry, Jacqueline?"

"You don't get it."

"I get physical therapy. I remember it well. I remember trying."

I closed my eyes.

"C'mon, Jack. Get angry. Or start crying. Show me something, anything, other than you desperately trying to hold it all together."

"I need my chair," I told the nurse. She was staring at her cell phone, too.

Another phubber.

Was my struggle really that boring?

I thought about the day I'd gotten shot.

I thought about Herb.

I thought about the Cowboy.

I thought about the bullet hitting my back and staring, amazed, as it burst out of my stomach, the blood spraying everywhere like slow-motion red fireworks.

I remembered the Cowboy's face.

I remembered the pain.

I remembered the lack of pain.

My arms began to give out, and my whole body shook.

My mother scowled. "You don't need your chair, Jack. You need a kick in your ass. A kick in your ass that your husband isn't giving you for some reason."

I didn't know I'd pissed myself until I smelled it. The nurse finally put away her cell and came up from behind me with my damned wheelchair. She helped me sit down, then left to go get a towel.

"I can't do this."

"You wet your pants. So what? You can have some of my protective undergarments. I've got some cute ones with pink roses printed on them. Mr. Garza in C17 thinks they're sexy."

I shut my eyes. I wanted my mother to leave.

Actually, there was something I wanted more than that.

I wanted to quit.

My mother, the mind reader, put her hand on my sweaty hair. "You want to give up."

"I just need a break, Mom."

"From what, Jack? What do you need a break from? Your mother? Your husband? Your daughter? From physical therapy? From teaching gun safety classes? From life?"

I didn't answer.

"Where's your Colt?"

I stared at her. "Why? You going to put me out of my misery?"

My lame joke didn't register, and her face pinched with even more pity.

"Is that what you want?"

"Of course not."

"What is it you want, Jack? Because I can't tell anymore."

"I want to walk, Mom."

"Then get off your lazy ass and get back on those bars."

I did not get off my lazy ass. Instead I looked outside, into a windy, overcast Florida sunset, partially blocked by the nurse standing there with a towel, waiting for my mother to stop yelling at me.

"Where's your Colt?"

Why did she keep asking me that? "Where's yours?"

"Locked up in my gun safe. Now answer my question."

Semi-curious where she was going with this, I told her. "Compartment under the chair."

She reached over, opened the caddy door, pulling out the Cobra. "Why isn't the trigger lock on it?"

"I forgot to put it on after class."

She scowled. "Do I have to remind you that you have a five-year-old in your house?"

"I was going to lock it up before I got home."

"What about here? I don't want to talk trash about my elderly co-habiters, but there are at least a dozen residents here with the mental capacity of a lounge chair."

I fished the gun lock, the key still in it, out of my pocket. "Knock yourself out."

My mother took the trigger lock. "Ammo?"

"I unloaded it before class. All six are in the pouch with the snap caps."

Mom took the leather pouch. "Bring any other ammo?"

"For what? We're in a retirement home. Do I need a box of cartridges to break up a riot at the tiki bar?"

My mother, hunched over with a back so curved it made me want to mainline calcium, squinted into my under-seat compartment. "What else have you got in there?"

"A pony. Because you never bought me one when I was a kid."

She took out my first aid box. "What's in here?"

"The big red cross on the top doesn't give it away?"

Mom opened it anyway, rifling through the assorted bandages, sutures, pill packs, and various gear. Besides the standard emergency crap, the box also held some prepping stuff. I got into prepping a while ago, after a particularly disastrous incident in Spoonward, Wisconsin made me paranoid enough to carry around certain essentials. Such as an emergency mylar poncho, a Swiss Army Knife, a multitool pliers, a tube of sunscreen, waterproof matches, a tactical flashlight, candles, energy bars, QuikClot. All the essentials.

She put the kit back, then unzipped the leather pouch and peeked inside.

"Now what, Mom? You load the gun and offer it to me, daring me to do it?"

She replaced the gunlock on the trigger guard and put the .38 in the pouch and zipped it closed. "I'm keeping it, because you're obviously clinically depressed."

I closed my eyes. "I'm managing."

"Well, you're doing a shitty job. You don't want to talk to me. I bet you aren't talking to Phin. When was the last time you talked to your squad?"

"My squad?"

"Your peeps. Your fam."

"Stop talking like Sam."

"Your friends, Jack. When was the last time you talked to Herb?"

I haven't spoken with Herb Benedict, my old partner back from my Chicago PD days, for over two months. "A week, maybe."

"Bullshit. How about Harry?"

"Hurricane Harry?"

"Not funny. You know who I'm talking about. Harry McGlade can be hard to take, but he's the oldest relationship you've still managed to keep."

"There's you and Dad."

"Your father is an asshole."

"Dad's not an asshole."

"Is he here, standing in a puddle of your piddle? When was the last time you talked to him?"

"I dunno." It had been a while since I talked to anybody. People call, leave messages, send texts and email. I ignore them.

"What's talking supposed to do, Mom? Will it help my legs work?"

"Before these can work," she tapped my knees, "you need to get this working," she tapped my forehead.

That's stupid.

"That's stupid," I said.

"You're jelly of my wisdom."

"Jelly?"

"Jealous."

"I'll never let you see Sam again if you keep using that plural crap."

"I'm down. You want some of my Zoloft?"

"You're on Zoloft?"

"I'm in my seventies, I wet my pants, and my daughter got shot and is in a wheelchair. Of course I'm on Zoloft."

I forced a smile. "Who gave you the prescription? Dr. Agmont?"

He was the main shrink at the home, notorious among residents because he looked like a male model.

She nodded. "You'll make an appointment?"

"I will."

"When?"

"Whenever you want."

"Now."

"Fine. Give me my gun back. I feel naked without it."

Mom smiled. "Nothing wrong with feeling naked every once and a while."

My mother had no idea how wrong she was. But she did put the gun pouch back under my chair.

I nodded to the nurse through the window, and she came back in.

Mom was already on her cell phone, calling Dr. Hottie.

I stared out the window.

Palm trees were really starting to sway.

It was going to get a lot worse before it got better.

"A fear of weapons is a sign of retarded sexual and emotional maturity."
SIGMUND FREUD

"Outside of the killings, D.C. has one of the lowest crime rates in the country."
MAYOR MARION BARRY

GAFF

So my story really begins today.

I woke up when my cell alarm rang—6:15 A.M. so I'd have time to catch the school bus—checked my email, went to the bathroom and pissed and shit and showered and brushed my teeth, got dressed, found my Moms holding a birthday cake with eighteen candles on it, and when she started to sing to me I grabbed that stupid AF cast iron pan she had made me carry around for the last six years, and smashed her in the face as hard as I could. She went down, and I flattened out her skull and brains until it looked like a stomped Halloween pumpkin.

Okay, I didn't do that 4realz.

I've thought about doing that, lots of times. But that would be whack.

Srsly, Moms dead in the kitchen, who is 5-0 gonna blame?

I'd be the number one prime first numero uno suspect. And unless I wore gloves and a full rain poncho, her DNA would be all over me and my forensic evidence would be all over her and I'd be locked up b4 I could even buy a gun.

Trill.

Any dummy can kill one time. The key to getting away with killing a bunch of times is all about one thing.

Planning.

Not saying none of my peeps didn't plan. Look @ Salvatore Persimmons, who killed 17 of his co-workers on December 13, 2012. Bruh worked @ a postal factory that set up all this security swerve bcuz another worker got stressed and shot his supervisor a month earlier. So

Persimmons, in a move that can only qualify as genius, mailed three guns to himself then intercepted his own package @ work.

Shaking my head lit.

His planning was tight, but dude broke every rule.

Let's go over Gaff's Eleven Rules.

One, don't do a small crime b4 the big crime.

Persimmons beat the eff out of his wife b4 going to work. I mean, he kicked her ass so bad she needed plastic surgery. When he left for his job, she called the cops, so they were already en route when he unpacked his arsenal and started fronting his displeasure @ his workplace environment.

Two, don't kill people you know.

4realz, bruh killed co-workers. Even if he got away, someone would recognize him.

Three, don't kill people in front of cameras unless you're wearing a disguise.

Persimmons had no disguise, and there were cameras. You prolly saw the footage on the news, from ten different angles.

#StupidAF.

Four, don't shoot any place where people shoot back.

Persimmons did okay here. He was actually smart bcuz his workplace was a no gun zone. You never see any active shooter walk into a police station, or a sporting goods store, or a gun show, bcuz they'd get taken down quick. Best places to kill a lot of people have no security, and you're the only one packing.

Five, don't announce you're going to kill a bunch of people b4 you kill a bunch of people. Lots of channers these days post shooting plans b4 the Big Event, then strap on a GoPro camera and live feed. You know how fast the first responders get there when you're streaming your murder spree on Facebook? I savvy cred and clout. I don't savvy getting your high score cut short by 5-0.

Bcuz; six, the cops will eventually show up. If that's part of your plan, okurrr. If it's not, don't make it easy for them to find you or stop you.

Seven, wear protection. If peeps be shooting back @ you, rock the Kevlar, yo.

Eight, don't leave evidence. Fingerprints on empty cartridge casings come back to convict. Don't touch nothing without gloves, don't bleed on anything, don't let no one see your face, don't leave footprints.

Nine, don't overstay your welcome. Persimmons was still trying to shoot his boss when 5-0 came in and dropped him with extreme prejudice. Bruh never even returned fire.

Where's the fun in that?

Ten, make sure you have two escape strategies, in case one gets effed up. That means knowing the layout of the place you're going to hit. It also makes it easier to maximize kill count.

Efficiency, bruh. Case the place. Learn the floorplan. Know all the hiding spots where the screaming losers are going to cower, hoping you pass them by.

Don't pass no one by. You want the speed run high score, every point counts.

There's an eleventh rule, but I don't want to dish about it now. Maybe later.

So here's how the start of my story really went down.

I set my alarm for two hours early, got up and packed up my clothes and laptop, took a bunch of food from the kitchen and put it in a garbage bag (no birthday cake, eff you Moms), grabbed the car keys, and left a note on the counter.

TODAY I'M 18, AN ADULT WHO CAN MAKE MY OWN DECISIONS.
I QUIT SCHOOL AND QUIT MY JOB.
I'LL TAKE THE CAR AS MY BIRTHDAY PRESENT.
I'LL CALL YOU IN A WEEK AND LET YOU KNOW WHERE I AM.

Then I restored my cell phone to factory specs, erasing everything, left it on top of the note, and bounced.

The ride was a POS white suburban Toyota Camry. The solo time my moms let me drive it was the one time I used it to pass my driver's test.

I sat in the driver's seat, had a wicked little fantasy about going back into the house and bashing her beeatch face in while she slept, decided not to risk it, and then drove away from my old life.

I didn't want to use the car GPS in case it could be tracked, so I'd already printed out directions @ school.

The drive time from Oakdale, Ohio to Katydid, South Carolina would take about ten hours.

I had half a tank of gas, a bag of food, nineteen thousand seven hundred and thirty-eight dollars in my bank account, and three hundred and six dollars in my money belt.

The gun show happened in two days.

Time for my life to really begin.

#HellsYeah.

"Woman must not depend upon the protection of man, but must be taught to protect herself."

SUSAN B. ANTHONY

"We do not need guns and bombs to bring peace, we need love and compassion."

MOTHER TERESA

JACK

I cleaned up in my Mom's room, borrowing a pair of her sweatpants, sticking my dirty clothes in a plastic bag for housekeeping to launder.

Mom was immune to my shame, phubbing me for YouTube dog tricks.

I wheeled downstairs to catch my ride.

My husband, Phineas Troutt, pulled in front of the Darling Center and I rolled up to our van as he got out and opened the side door and pulled out the chair ramp.

Wind tousled my hair, raising goosebumps on my bare arms. I still wasn't used to the smell of Ft. Myers, especially when a storm was moving in. Salt water and seaweed and static electricity. So different from my home, Chicago.

But Chicago wasn't my home anymore.

Phin gave me a kiss on the head. "How was work, dear?"

I didn't tell him that it wasn't really work, because I wasn't getting paid for it. Ironic, to be volunteering at the same place we were paying out the ass for my physical therapy. We were whipping through our savings because we didn't have insurance because we were living under fake names. I attracted dangerous maniacs like nectar attracts bees, and unlike Phin's psychotic brother, Hugo, who was locked away in a Supermax prison, I still had killer stalkers leftover from my old police job who were out there somewhere, hunting me.

Long story.

I didn't tell him that I pissed myself during rehab, just like I pissed myself a few months ago, all over the bed and all over him, the last time we had sex.

I didn't tell him that my mother thought I was depressed and was forcing me to see a shrink.

I just said, "Fine. Where's Sam?"

"Sleepover at Taylor's house. Her mother called to make sure it was okay to watch *Frozen* because it's rated PG."

The last movie we watched with Sam was the uncut version of *Aliens.*

We were probably terrible parents.

Phin pushed me up the ramp, and I didn't try to fight him; sometimes I insisted on getting into the van by myself. Today I was too tired. I locked my wheels in place and he closed the door and walked around me and plopped into the driver's seat.

"Did you think this is how it would be?" I asked.

"What do you mean? Married to the greatest woman on the planet?"

I hated when Phin tried to cheer me up. My husband was a hard ass, and some of my favorite memories of us are when we had fist fights; actually full contact where we tried to knock each other out.

Sounds dysfunctional. With us, it was more like flirting.

But that was back when I could actually stand toe-to-toe with him. When we were equals.

Now we were a victim and a caregiver, and both of us sucked at it.

"Why the pissed-off face, Jack?"

Did he actually want to start an argument? I perked up.

"Have you noticed? I'm in a wheelchair."

"It's hard not to notice, because you bring it up all the time."

Here we go. I'd been waiting for this. "What are you saying?"

"You're letting it define you."

"Says the guy who has been dying of cancer for how long? Like twenty years?"

"I'm in remission. And I never let it define me."

I snorted at that. "Of course you let it define you. You used it as an excuse for all the shitty things you did."

Phin didn't reply. Which irritated me, because we both knew his checkered past was the only thing helping us get through our current financial crisis. Phin had hidden money from his criminal days. I pretended not to know about it, even though I found the hiding place in the garage when we moved to Florida.

One more thing we didn't share.

If the key to a successful relationship was communication, our marriage would be over by the end of the week.

"Whatever you say, Jill."

Jill was my fake Florida name. Phin was Gil. Jill because of Jack and Jill, and Gil because it was a part of a fish, like Phin.

"How about you answer my question, Gil?"

"Fine. I'll answer your question. Did I think this was how it would be? No. I married an exciting, tough, funny, strong, smart woman who made me feel like I had a future."

"And now that woman's crippled, and you want out."

"Wrong. Now that woman has given up, and I want to shake the shit out of her."

"So do it, Gil. It would be better than you trying to sound like a goddamn Hallmark card all the time. You're such an asshole."

I wanted him to slam on the brakes and shake me. Or kiss me. Or both.

Anything other than the tsunami of pity and fake cheer and relentless encouragement that had invaded our marriage.

But instead Phin turned on the radio.

"... Harry is hammering the shore of Tobago with three-foot swells, and all coastal residents are being evacuated as the winds reach upwards of one hundred and thirty miles per hour."

"I don't want to listen to the radio."

Phin turned it off rather than fight about it. Asshole.

We drove for a while in silence. When he turned down the street we lived on, I felt myself bridle.

"I don't want to go home."

The idea of Phin and I spending a night without Sam, pretending to be happy, was too much to deal with.

"Dinner?"

"Not hungry."

"Movie?"

"Nothing good is playing."

I had no idea if that was true or not. I hated watching movies in my wheelchair. Everyone else had reclining theater seats, and I was crippled and uncomfortable and aware of it every single second of the running time.

"Want me to drive around Sarasota randomly until you figure out what it is you want?"

"I want to get drunk."

He seemed to consider it and then said, "I know a place."

I'm a Chicago girl, so I'm spoiled on good places to eat and drink. Florida didn't lack for decent restaurants, especially seafood. But bars were a different animal. In my home town, we had taverns where adults could hang out without dealing with crowds, college kids, or tourists. Especially tourists. Real gin joints, with good beers and honest pours.

I hadn't found a suitable substitute in the Gulf area yet.

How did Phin find one?

After my injury, I'd begun taking sleeping pills. Insomnia and I have always been dance partners, but it took the lead after I got shot. Physical pain, mental pain, emotional pain, existential pain; I'd never sleep again without Zolpidem. On the plus side, it knocked me out and didn't give me a grogginess hangover. On the minus side, it was a memory eraser. I couldn't remember anything about ten minutes after taking my nightly dose, and the next morning I didn't even remember falling asleep.

And sleep was an unawakenable coma.

Could Phin have been sneaking out at night while I was knocked out? Prowling local bars? Looking to get laid, because he wasn't getting it at home?

Would Phin do that?

I had no clue. A year ago, I would have said no way. Phin is loyal like our dog, Duffy, is loyal. And he'd never leave Sam alone with me after I took a pill.

But ugly doubts crawled into my skull and twitched.

I stared at him in the rearview mirror, and he saw me looking and grinned.

Was he a lying asshole?

Or was I the asshole?

I'd been dealing with some jealousy issues prior to getting shot. Phin hadn't done anything to prompt my insecurity. Some of it was circumstantial; leaving my job, changing our identities, becoming a mother, getting older. My husband was younger, fitter, more attractive. He didn't have gray hair or crow's feet or stretch marks. I don't want to get into ageism or body shaming or a culture that worships youth and beauty and disregards women over fifty. But the billion-dollar cosmetic industry was doing well, and even though high heels are the stupidest invention ever I still own over a hundred pairs, even though I'll likely never walk again in anything taller than a flip-flop.

Does Givenchy make anything with Velcro laces?

So my self-esteem circled the shitter prior to my partial paralyzation. Add ten months of being a whiney, self-loathing burden, and I wouldn't blame Phin for finding something on the side.

To show how far into a hole I'd fallen, Phin sleeping with other people wasn't even the thing that bothered me. Neither was the deceit that came along hand-in-hand.

What really freaked me out is that he might leave me for someone better.

He could lie. He could cheat. I could deal.

But I'd die if he left me.

Add abandonment issues to the neurosis pile.

Phin pulled into a parking lot, which was about half full, mostly with older model American cars and pick-up trucks.

I squinted at the glowing sign on the building.

COWLICK'S.

The W didn't light up.

"Is this a cowboy bar?"

"I don't know. Never been here."

"How'd you find it?"

"Yelp."

I felt a twinge of worry, and couldn't tell if it was my old cop instincts saying "don't go into a unfamiliar shitkicker bar" or my new insecurities saying "people are going to stare at you."

Phin parked, then reached for my leg braces.

"No way."

"They have a pool table. You need to stand for pool."

I shook my head. "I don't care. I hate those things."

"They make you look like *RoboCop*."

"They make me look like Forest Gump."

"Only from the neck up."

I searched Phin's eyes. He was trying.

"If I have a few beers wearing those I'll fall over."

"What's the worst that can happen? You hurt your back and become paralyzed?"

"You're a dick."

But I liked Phin busting my balls a lot more than I liked him pitying me. I guess I could meet him halfway.

I endured the indignity of Phin helping me into the braces, fitting them around my gym shoes, cinching them at the ankle, calf, knee, and thigh.

It irked me how much I liked Phin touching my thigh.

"Spring assist or not?"

The joints on the braces had three settings. Locked, which made them rigid, loose, which required me to keep my muscles flexed or else they'd bend, and spring assist, which was sort of halfway between the two, keeping some tension and giving me a bounce when I flexed.

"Spring assist."

He adjusted the settings. "Chair or crutches?"

Ugh. I hated the forearm crutches more than the chair, but they'd give me more support while I stood. If we were actually going to attempt a game of pool, getting in and out of my wheelchair after every shot would exhaust me fast.

"Crutches."

The front door had three stairs leading up to it.

What the hell? Wasn't there a federal law about wheelchair accessibility?

Stairs were my nemesis. Even when I was in Full Metal Cripple mode. I couldn't lift my body weight with my legs, and became overwhelmed with fear that I'd fall and hurt my spine again.

But rather than take my hand and help me balance, my husband scooped me up in his arms, leg braces and all.

He smelled good.

God, I missed him.

Phin set me down, propping me against the side of the van, gave me my crutches, and we began the awkward, painful, excruciatingly slow trip to the front door of Cowlick's.

My husband walked alongside me, eyeing me the way he used to eye Sam when she'd graduated from crawling to toddling.

"Ready to catch me if I fall?"

"No. Ready to laugh at you and post the pics on Instagram."

Good answer.

We eventually made it, and Phin held the door open for me, and I took a step inside and smelled the stale beer and heard the clackity-clack of pool balls and actually felt a tiny bit excited.

Then I had a closer look around and the excitement vanished.

As I'd hoped, it wasn't a tourist bar where out-of-towners brought their kids after a long day mini golfing at Smuggler's Cove, and it wasn't a college spring break hangout where frat boys did tequila shots.

But, as I'd feared, it was a shitkicker bar. Drunk, loud locals, blowing off steam after a long week of middle-class work. My kind of people, if the vibe was right. But this vibe was off. Too many men, not enough women. Lots of wallets on chains. Lots of direct staring when I came in, with some snickers as guys exchanged jokes about the handicapped old lady.

Or maybe I was just being overly sensitive. I hadn't been a cop for a long time. Maybe my cop-sense was malfunctioning.

"I'll grab drinks," Phin said, heading for the bar.

I lumbered to the empty pool table and tugged the triangle out of its hidey hole and placed it on the table; the universal symbol that we were playing next.

"Hey there little lady, that's our table."

I turned, found a guy standing way too close. Not just personal space close, but threatening to topple me over close. He had a handlebar mustache, wore jeans and an old Nirvana t-shirt, and I couldn't tell if he was a redneck or a hipster. It didn't matter, because I could tell he was a bully. His eyes were narrow and he smelled like whiskey and mean.

"You already have a table." He was playing with an equally desirable specimen of manhood, this one in denim bibs, on the pool table to the left.

"Yeah, but my buddies are coming."

"Sign on the wall says NO SAVING TABLES."

"That sign don't apply to me."

And then something really strange happened.

I was afraid.

Fear and I went way back. I had so many life or death situations during my career that I couldn't even remember them all.

But my fight-or-flight adrenaline response usually prompted action. It gave me a surge that sharpened my thoughts and supercharged my reflexes and slowed down time so I could make critical decisions fast, usually with beneficial results.

But standing there, staring at this bully, I didn't act.

I froze.

I couldn't move. Couldn't talk. Couldn't even breathe.

My brain went into overdrive, and I thought a dozen thoughts at once.

I can't fight back. I'm crippled.

Where's Phin?

I hate that I need Phin.

Why didn't I take my wheelchair? I have a gun in my wheelchair.

What am I so scared of?

What if he hits me and I'm paralyzed forever?

What if he kills me?

Would that be so bad?

How could I be afraid of this stinky little drunk man?

I've fought monsters.

I've beaten monsters.

But I'm no longer that person.

"Is there a problem?"

Phin, coming up from behind. Two beers in one hand. Two shots in the other.

The bully turned and sized Phin up. He didn't seem impressed.

Big mistake.

"You with the crip?"

"That's my wife." Phin's tone remained even, but I saw his eyes go dead.

My husband wasn't a sociopath. He loved me and Sam, and he hurt when we hurt.

But Phin had a special ability to turn off empathy if the situation arose, and it was a scary thing to witness.

"Your wife is on my table."

I knew what would happen next. Phin would set down the drinks, freeing up his hands. He'd give the guy a chance to back down. Then he'd insult the guy, provoking him to swing first.

Then my man would beat the ever-loving shit out of him.

Except...

That was a bad idea. A really bad idea.

What if Phin got arrested? We were living here under fake names. We got our IDs from Harry McGlade, and they were the best that money could buy. They'd hold up to a priors search at a traffic stop. But if Phin was brought in, fingerprinted, and our prints were run through IAFIS, things could get really messy.

Or what if Phin got hurt? What if, while he was kicking this redneck hipster's ass, someone broke a pool cue over my husband's head? I couldn't stop it. Phin could wind up in the hospital.

I couldn't take care of Sam alone.

I couldn't even take care of my own bladder.

I need to stop this.

I tried to say something, and it came out in a squeak.

Phin looked at me, raised an eyebrow.

"I want to go," I said, not recognizing the weak, cowardly voice.

"We came here to play pool. I just bought drinks."

"I just want to go." I felt my eyes get glassy. "Please."

Part of me wanted him to object. To man up, tell me to back off, and then feed this bully his teeth.

But Phin didn't do that. He nodded at me, took my elbow, and walked with me out of the bar.

"Thanks for the drinks!" The bully hooted after us.

It took five minutes to walk back to the van.

It was the longest five minutes of my life.

When I was finally inside, my brakes locked, I found my voice.

Time to test him. To see if I can push away the man I love because I'm a scared piece of shit and deserve it.

"Why didn't you punch that guy?"

"You said you wanted to go."

"That's not the reason. Tell me the real reason."

He shrugged. "You're being stupid."

"You ran away, because you knew I didn't have your back."

"Of course you had my back."

He was wrong. I didn't have his back. But I didn't want to pass up this chance to harm our marriage even more.

Full passive-aggressive mode activated.

"You refuse to argue with me. And now you just backed out of a bar fight."

"You said please, you wanted to go."

"Bullshit. You thought I'd get hurt. You ran away, because you can't deal with me being in a wheelchair."

"Jack, the only one who can't deal with you being in a wheelchair is you."

The tears came, which pissed me off even more because I hate crying. "You know something, Phin? If that shithead hit me, it would have hurt less than you being afraid for me. I don't want your worry. I don't want your pity. I'm sick of you trying to be strong enough for the both of us. I don't need a caregiver. I need a partner."

"Then start acting like a goddamn partner."

We didn't talk for the rest of the night. When we pulled into the garage, Phin got out, opened the side door, lowered the ramp, and went inside. Duffy the hound dog bounded out, leaping up to me, putting his big, stupid face in my lap.

I cried into his floppy ears.

"A sword never kills anybody; it is a tool in the killer's hand."
LUCIUS ANNAEUS SENECA

"You don't spread democracy with a barrel of a gun."
HELEN THOMAS

GAFF

I've never driven out of state b4, but I had my destination in mind. I'd discovered it on the Internet months ago, and it was a two-hour drive from my old house.

Slawton, West Virginia. The Deerkill Hunting and Fishing Warehouse.

Walking inside gave me twinges. The good kind of twinges, where everything seemed clearer and realer and exciting, like right b4 I got into a fight.

Fire.

The place was ginormous. Big as a Costco, tall ceiling, row after row of merch.

I passed the boats and fishing crap without looking.

I passed the archery and target crap without looking.

I passed knives and camping crap without looking.

I did stop to look @ the guns.

#Candy.

I wasn't there to buy a firearm, but I'd never seen one IRL. They looked fake and real all @ the same time, rack after rack of rifles, handguns small as a credit card and so big I wouldn't be able to hold them with one hand.

Dope.

I couldn't buy one. FOMO; fear of missing out. All fifty states adhered to the FFL to FFL law. If you are from another state, the only way to buy a gun is from a Federal Firearms Licensed dealer who has to ship it to another FFL dealer in your state. You can't just grab it and go.

If I'd wanted a rifle, I could have bought one in Ohio. No waiting period.

But I didn't want a rifle. I wanted a handgun, and both Ohio and West Virginia wouldn't sell handguns to anyone under 21.

Wubalubadubdub.

Didn't matter. I was @ Deerkill Hunting and Fishing for something else.

Even with the research I'd done, when I found the aisle I got all overwhelmy. Some elderly dude in his forties wearing a red Deerkill shirt came up to me.

"Lookin' for a vest?"

I nodded. If asked why, I had a story planned out. I just joined the Army, and as a gift my parents want to buy me body armor. Apparently some soldiers bought their own gear.

But Old Dude didn't ask me why. "Soft or hard?"

He was asking if I wanted a weave, like Kevlar, or something solid, like steel or ceramic.

"Soft." I tried to remember the rating I wanted. "IIIA."

He nodded. "That's good. Will stop anything up to a .44 mag. No rifle protection, though."

"I was thinking something with trauma plates."

"Smart thinking. It's what law enforcement wears. That'll stop about 93% of what's coming at you. In an urban setting, that's about 80% handguns, 9% shotguns, 9% rifles, 2% machineguns. In a military setting, that's all reversed, plus add explosions to the mix."

"I know. I looked it up."

"Any fiber preference? Kevlar? Twaron? Codura?"

"No preference. But I have a budget."

"How much?"

"Under eight hundred."

"Doable. Color preference?"

"Black."

He nodded, then walked up the aisle and took a vest off a hanger. "This is a Montag Shellmax. Shirt tails in rear and front. Might be a little long on you, but its wider in the chest so you'll be more comfortable. Complies with requirements for 2005 Interim and NIJ 0101.04. Front and back pockets for 8x10 trauma plates. Water and stain resistant, inner moisture wicking system to keep cool. Want to try it on?"

Hells yeah.

Old Dude helped me into it, and I was twinging like a fiend.

Felt like I could charge through a plate glass window.

"Looks good on you. In your price range, too. On sale for $679."

"I'll take it."

"Trauma plates are extra."

"Got them in ceramic?"

"Course we do. Front and back?"

"Yeah, both. How about ballistic helmets?"

Old Dude smiled. "Right this way."

He showed me a smaller model that fit my head. Black, an above-the-ear model (highly unlikely I'd get shot in the ears), with a chinstrap, level IV rating.

Sweet.

Twenty minutes later and twelve hundred dollars poorer, I was back on the road.

Six hours beyond that, a sign welcomed me to Katydid, SC. I consulted my Google maps to find the apartment.

My new landlord was a fat AF guy named Marko who had more hair growing out of his ears than I had on my whole head.

Literally.

He looked @ me funny and breathed through his mouth when I gave him the cash for the first month of rent and the damage deposit.

"You okay?" he asked as I signed the lease.

There were a lot of ways to read into that. "Why?"

"The blinking. You keep blinking your eyes funny."

My blepharospasm. I can't go a whole day without someone making fun of the fact that my eyelids sometimes spasm and close and I can't control it.

"It's eye dystonia," I said. "It's a somatic disorder."

"Is it contagious?"

"Naw."

Marko didn't follow up with more questions. No one ever does.

Garbage.

"The ad said utilities are included," I confirmed.

"Water and gas are. Cable, internet, and electric aren't."

"The electricity is on now." The overhead ceiling fan and light whirred with a mildly annoying buzz.

"You gotta get it switched over to your name, Guthrie."

I didn't like that he used my first name. Too familiar. Creepy.

We stood staring @ each other for a few seconds. Dude wouldn't leave.

"Anything else?"

"No. Welcome to my building. It's my pride and joy. I built it six years ago, and I'm really choosy with my tenants. It's good to have you here."

He held out a chubby hand. I shook it.

Moist and limp. Like holding a newly killed frog.

I broke the handshake first, and Marko grinned @ me and waddled away.

The small studio apartment I rented was on the ground floor—key if you need to make a quick exit—and had pile carpeting that smelled like shampoo, a bathtub with a clear plastic shower curtain and a giant mirror on the wall, and a gas stove.

I'd never used a gas stove b4, but after playing around with it I figured out you press the dial in to get the piezo electric switch to spark, lighting the gas.

Fire. Literally.

I started my laptop and searched around for a WiFi connection. Six of them within range, none of them public.

B4 I ran my password cracker or checked the hacker databases, I began with the first hub and tried the obvious passwords.

123.

1234.

SHOT GIRL • 55

12345.

123456.

1234567.

12345678.

password.

qwerty.

Blink182.

abc123.

123123.

I began to laugh when the last one was accepted.

Srsly? 123123?

Yeet LOL. This scrub deserved to have all his data erased and his credit cards swiped.

Laterz.

My first job was Googling to find the local power company, and set up my new electric account using automatic withdrawal from my bank account.

Other utilities?

Naw.

I didn't need a phone, landline or cell. Didn't need Internet, thanks to neighbor 123123. Didn't need cable.

So I unpacked. Food in the fridge and cabinets. Kept my clothes in my suitcase. Set up the few personal items I'd brought along next to my sleeping bag.

A Powertac 1300 lumen tactical flashlight.

A sick ex-library copy of *Blood Pact of the Suburban Eliminators: The Rathlin Massacre School Shootings* by Homer Schorrington.

A Spec Ops XX736 spring-assisted folding knife with a high carbon steel tanto blade.

A Victorinox Hercules Swiss Army Knife.

Three bottles of the different meds I take.

And my lucky charm; a Zippo lighter with an etched Marlboro design on it.

I picked up the lighter and thumbed open the top.

I liked the sound, so I did it ten or twenty more times. Then I spun the flint wheel over and over and over, watching the sparks. It didn't light bcuz it had no fluid.

Fiending, I went into the kitchen—my kitchen—and found a pack of American cheese and a can of tomato soup. I ate a slice of cheese and spent a few minutes stabbing the soup can with my folding knife, trying to open it bcuz I'd forgotten to take a can opener. I managed to jab it a few times through the top but there was no way I'd get the whole lid off.

I couldn't microwave the can, bcuz everyone but scrubs know you can't microwave metal, so I looked through the cabinets for a bowl and then remembered—derp—that I didn't have any dishware.

So I started my stove, got a medium flame going, took off the paper soup label, and put the can directly on the burner, figuring I could heat it up a little then drink it from the holes in the top.

I ate more cheese, then made a list of shit I needed.

Can opener.

Food.

Plates. Bowls. Forks. Glasses.

Pillow (how'd I forget my frakking pillow?).

I looked around the empty apartment. Did I need furniture?

I had a computer. Didn't need a TV.

Maybe a desk and chair?

Naw. Floor is chill.

Stool, for the breakfast bar?

Waste of money. I could eat standing up.

What else do I need to adult?

Lighter fluid.

Marlboros.

There was a whistling sound, and I freaked for a second, then looked in the kitchen and saw my can on the burner was erupting steaming tomato soup in all directions. I ran to it, got squirted on the arm—savage level legendary pain—and I slapped the can off the flame and it fell onto the floor, continuing to spit my dinner everywhere.

Can't even. The struggle is real.

I ran my burned arm under cold water, added paper towels to my grocery list, then walked out of my apartment and headed to the car to go shopping.

Halfway to the store I remembered I didn't turn the stove off.

That should be no big deal, right? It's just a flame. What's the worst it could do? Burn the building down?

#WhoCares.

#NotMyBuilding.

I had my cash in a money belt around my waist. Only thing irreplaceable was the Marlboro lighter. But that was a lighter. Meant to be heated up. If the apartment burned down, the firefighters would probably find it intact.

No need to turn back.

I got to the market, some ginormous department grocery superstore that sold food and car tires and TVs and flowers and booze and books.

Shopping was brutal. The layout of the store didn't make sense. Everything was too far away from everything else, and there were too many choices.

I bought the shit I recognized. Same soup. Same cheese. Same lunch meat. Same bread. Same cereal. The milk looked different than the stuff my Moms bought, but milk is milk, right?

What's the difference between 2% milk and whole milk?

Was 2% like just a tiny bit of milk, the rest water?

I got the whole milk.

Plates and bowls and silverware were hella expensive, and they sold it in packs. I didn't need a set of eight bowls and dinner plates and salad plates and mugs. I didn't need sixteen forks.

I thought about buying microwave food that came in its own trays, but there were too many choices, and I didn't recognize any brands.

Hold up ... fast food comes with forks and napkins. I could just buy a burger or a pizza and use those.

I put back the roll of paper towels. Then I looked @ pillows.

Okurrr. The feather pillows like I had @ home were killer expensive.

I got a cheap one. Finna be fine.

Prolly.

The store bill was monster, over fifty bucks. And a whole bunch of people stared @ me while I took off my belt to take money out.

Note to self: keep some cash in wallet.

I didn't get the squares there bcuz I forgot so I stopped @ a gas station and went into the shop while I filled up the tank.

The guy behind the counter looked like one of the dickasses @ my old school, sides of his head shaved and pimping a pencil-thin douchestache.

"Pack of Marlboros."

"What kind?"

"Marlboros."

Bruh rolled his eyes. "Reds. Lights. Medium lights. Ultra-lights. Menthol. Smooth. What kind?"

Hell if I knew. "Smooth."

He handed over a pack. The blue cover design looked like my lighter. "I also need lighter fluid."

"What kind?"

"I got a Marlboro lighter."

"Plastic one? Or a metal one, like a Zippo?"

"Zippo."

He gave me a yellow bottle. I waited for him to ask for ID, and was ready to show him my Driver's license to prove I was 18 today.

The dickass didn't even ask.

Which was good. I didn't know if gas stations could trace your ID when you showed it to them, and I didn't want Moms tracking me down.

"You got a car?"

"What?" Why did he want to know that?

"A car."

"Why should I tell you?"

Another eye roll. Griefer punk. "Which pump, kid?"

Oh. "Pump six."

"Fifty-eight sixty-one."

Woes.

"Gas was only forty-bucks."

"Smokes and fluid, shorty."

Shorty? I should smack his dickass.

I paid and got the hell out of there.

Then I got lost.

I didn't want to use the GPS bcuz it might be trackable, and I left all my printouts in the apartment. To make it worse, the bright lights @ night made me blink more than usual, making it harder to see.

My hands started to shake a little, and I remembered I didn't take my meds today.

Doctors, shrinks, teachers, counsellors, and my moms all thought I needed them for some made-up diagnosis, but I always knew they were trash.

I looked up what they said about me.

Functional neurological symptom disorder.

Borderline personality disorder.

Passive–aggressive personality disorder.

Alexithymia.

Mood.

I was prolly shaking bcuz I was withdrawing from the pills. I needed to throw that shit away, yo. Get my headspace clear.

I turned around, tried to find the department store again.

Couldn't find that, either.

I got angry. Angry like I used to get angry, all hate and rage and out-of-control shit, and I punched the top of the dashboard, over and over and over until the top of it cracked.

Stupid cheap POS foreign cars.

I finally saw a billboard I recognized from earlier, and then remembered how to get back onto the expressway, and that's when I noticed my knuckles were bleeding.

Giggle to myself.

I got to the apartment and brought in all the groceries. Building didn't burn down, bcuz the stove was off.

Weird. Swore I left it on.

I ran my hand under cold water, looked for a towel.

Day-am. Forgot towels.

I wrapped an old tee shirt around it, picked up the tomato soup can, and used my new can opener to open it up. There was only half left. The other half was hardening on my kitchen floor and walls, and I didn't have any towels. Or cleaning supplies.

I also forgot to get a bowl.

Hold up ... I didn't forget. I could order food that came with stuff to eat with.

So I put the can in the fridge (I should also get some plastic wrap or tin foil) and then found a local pizza place online and typed in my order. Under special instructions I wrote *extra napkins and plates and forks*.

I wanted to shower, but had no towels (or shampoo, or soap), so instead I went to YouTube to learn how to fill my Zippo.

Easy. y/y.

Plus the Zippo is OG. Started making them back in 1932. First lighter that could be operated with one hand. Wind proof. Lifetime guarantee.

Sick.

I opened up the pack of Marlboros, using my knife bcuz the cellophane on the box was extra AF, and took a big sniff.

Didn't smell familiar.

I dug a square out and hung it on my lip. Then I went into the bathroom and stared @ myself.

I looked bad ass. High key.

I fired up the smoke, then took a big pull.

#Smoking.

My lungs felt like they'd been set on fire then stomped on, and I started to cough so bad that I had to turn around and puke in the john.

#Smokingsux.

I threw the cig in the toilet, spat, and right b4 I flushed I thought I heard someone giggling.

Voices?

Was I hearing voices?

Weak.

Moms and all the docs I saw used to ask me that a lot, and I never heard any fakeass voices.

Except for Mr. Bloodlust, who tells me to kill people.

j/k.

Lulz.

I never heard voices. A few years ago, b4 I was on meds, I took a whole bunch of tests to see if I was schizo, and I passed them all.

Only voice in my head is my own.

But, 4realz, that giggling sounded legit.

I began to look around my bathroom, wondering if someone was watching me, looking for cameras and bugs and shit, and then there was a loud buzzing sound that sounded like the oven buzzer.

I went into the kitchen. Stove was still off.

WTF?

Another buzz, and it was coming from the speaker next to the door.

Doorbell. It's my doorbell.

I looked through the peephole, saw the pizza guy, and he gave me the za and a bag of stuff and I gave him money and a two dollar tip and I sat on my sleeping bag and ate pizza until the taste of smoke was gone.

Then I counted up my stash.

Eight forks. Eight plates. Twenty-two napkins. And bonus, six wet wipes, a dozen parmesan cheese packets and small plastic cup of red pepper.

Score.

I put everything away and turned out the lights.

Freaky.

Too dark. Too quiet. Too strange.

Wack.

I put the lights back on and crawled into my sleeping bag.

It was my first day ever on my own.

Pretty good day.

Tomorrow I had to get my new driver's license.

Then, the gun show.

That will be lit.

Literally.

"A woman who demands further gun control legislation is like a chicken who roots for Colonel Sanders."

LARRY ELDER

"Two million felons have tried to buy a gun and, because of the background check, have been denied."

JOE BIDEN

I woke up in an Ambien haze, still groggy.

Phin wasn't in bed. I checked the time.

9:41 A.M.

I smelled sweat, dragged my naked butt out of bed, struggled into a robe, and flopped into my wheelchair.

When did I take off my clothes?

My last memory was taking my sleeping pill and climbing into bed and turning my back on Phin to read my Kindle.

Had I wet my pants again, and Phin took off my clothes?

I patted down the mattress. Didn't feel any damp spots.

Was he trying to protect me?

Maybe I needed to accept my mother's offer of diapers.

I looked around for a note—Phin sometimes left a note when he went somewhere—and then vaguely recalled he was picking up Sam at 9:30.

I rolled into the hallway, called for Duffy.

The dog didn't answer.

Paranoia kicked in, and I called again, louder.

Duffy woofed at me, and came bounding over, half-climbing into my lap.

"Where were you?"

He didn't answer, but he had coffee grounds on his snout.

"You were eating garbage," I deduced.

My body might be shit, but my cop instincts weren't completely gone.

Duffy woo-wooed, rubbing coffee on my robe.

I gently pushed him off and rolled into the kitchen. My calico cat—about fifteen years old and too mean to die—was picking through the mess Duffy left on the floor.

"Good morning, Mr. Friskers."

He gave me an *oh great, you're still alive* look, then stuck up his nose and sauntered off, like he was the king and I was a filthy peasant who offended him.

I considered leaving the mess for Phin, recalled his comment that I needed to start acting like a goddamn partner, and then got a fresh garbage bag from the cabinet under the sink and began to pick up Duffy's buffet spread.

Halfway into it, I found a box of condoms.

An empty box of condoms.

All twelve were gone.

I remembered buying that box, more than six months ago. We'd only used one, and then my peeing incident made me too insecure and ashamed to try again until I was fully healed.

So where had the other eleven gone?

I knew the answer. Even though I'd been hoping I was wrong.

He was cheating.

I couldn't blame him. A marriage was a contract. I hadn't been keeping up my end.

But hell, Phin, couldn't you hide the evidence a little better?

I finished gathering up all the garbage, once again ashamed to be crying, and then wheeled into the bathroom and wrangled my worthless body onto the shower seat.

On top of being partially paralyzed, I'd gained a few pounds, making me feel even less attractive.

Or maybe the lack of self-esteem had less to do with my belly and more to do with my philandering husband.

My fault.

For marrying a younger guy.

For not taking care of his needs.

For getting shot.

I did actually blame myself for getting shot. My cop past always caught up with me and hurt the ones I loved, because no good deed goes unpunished. Even worse, I'd turned my back on a loaded gun.

Nice lack of situational awareness, Jack.

I turned on the water, shrieking because it came out cold, enduring it until the heat came, then dumping baby shampoo on my body and scrubbing myself as best I could.

I shaved my legs, wondering why I bothered.

I cleaned my body okay.

My conscience remained filthy with shame, regret, jealousy, and self-loathing.

I shuffled out of the shower like a crab, folding my robe around myself, rolling into the bedroom and beginning the arduous, lengthy, depressing task of dressing.

My closet; crammed full of designer shoes and suits and dresses by Kate Spade, Manolo Blahnik, Vera Wang, Calvin Klein, Jimmy Choo, Oscar de la Renta, Dior, Michael Kors, Armani, et al.

Today's ensemble; a white Dave & Buster's tee, black Wilson sweatpants, mismatched cotton socks, and light blue Converse All Stars with hook and loop straps.

Once upon a time, I prided myself on dressing smart. Purse matched shoes. Creases were sharp. Heels were high. I looked good from every angle. Dressing well, like competitive shooting and my judo blackbelts, was a hobby that helped me define myself.

These days, I dressed like a crippled panhandler. The only accessory I lacked was a cardboard sign. Current hobbies included whining a lot, trying not to wet my pants, and wistfully recalling the days I could walk unassisted.

Loser.

Loser loser loser.

Phin bought devices to help me dress; sock aids and shoe funnels and a claw hand extension to grab things off the floor. But I figured out if I just laid on my back on the bed I could reach all my parts without gadgets.

It took me about eight minutes of huffing and panting to put on everything, including my oversized granny panties, and just as I finished, Duffy barked. A second later the burglar alarm beeped as it disarmed, then the garage door opened.

I ran a quick brush through my damp hair and then put a smile in place.

Be upbeat, Jack. Don't let your little girl see you down.

I didn't have to fake it. When Samantha came running into the bedroom yelling, "Mommy! Mommy!" my spirits automatically lifted.

My little angel's face looked like she'd been beaten bloody, and even though she tried to hug me I held her at arm's length while trying to understand what I was seeing.

"Me and Taylor drew on each other with marker," she explained.

"Did Taylor's mom and dad try to wash it off?"

Sam sighed. "They tried. But I think this is on forever. Do I look like Optimus Prime?"

Some little girls liked princesses. Sam liked Transformers.

"No. You look like a five-year-old drew on you in marker."

"Taylor can't draw. I drawed, I drew, on her better."

"What did you draw on Taylor?"

"Wolverine. I did the beard perfect. Taylor is jelly of my mad skills."

"Stop teaching Grandma to talk like that. It's freaking me out."

"LOL, Mommy."

"She actually did a pretty good job with the beard." Phin, from the doorway, smiling like he wasn't a cheating, lying son of a bitch.

We produced a damn good kid, though.

"Looks like bath time, with extra soap," I said.

"Can't I just go swim? The chlorine will get it off."

I looked at Phin. We had an above-ground pool, and I couldn't supervise when Sam went swimming. Too high up for me to see.

"It's too windy, and Mommy has to go to work in an hour," Phin said. "Why don't you two play some GameMaster?"

Right after my injury, Phin had picked up a used video game system so Sam and I had something to play together while I was in a recumbent position. Aside from a brief period during my teenage years when I frequented arcades, I'd never cared much for videogames. But the Game-Master grew on me, and we had several favorites.

"Block Attack?" Sam asked me. "Or want me to kick your butt at City Fighter?"

"City Fighter. I'm feeling lucky."

My lucky feeling was unfounded, and Sam kicked my butt at City Fighter. She'd memorized many of the complicated button combinations needed to pull off devastating knockout moves, whereas my style was to just mash the controller and hope something special magically happened.

Probably a life lesson there.

After my fifth loss in a row, Sam started to ease up to let me win.

"Play your best, Sam."

"But you're getting pwned, Mommy. I'm trying to make it fair."

"Life isn't fair. Making things easier on people just makes it harder for them later on."

"So stop sucking."

I didn't stop sucking. So we switched to Block Attack, where I was a bit more competitive. The goal was to line up blocks of the same color, fitting them into a growing wall. A more calculating and cerebral game than City Fighter. A game where old age and thinking ahead could beat youth and fast reflexes.

Even so, we were pretty evenly matched.

As I focused on the game, and lived in the moment, my mood improved. My daughter and I giggled a lot. Made fun of each other. Yelled in anguish when appropriate.

Just like it used to be, when I was whole.

The hour went by fast, then Phin interrupted. "Time for Mommy to work."

"Can I come with you, Mom? Visit Grandma in the pool?"

I thumbed her bangs off her red-colored forehead. "Not today. Pool is closed because a storm is coming."

"Hurricane Harry?"

I nodded.

"Is that named after Uncle Harry?"

"No." Though it wouldn't surprise me if McGlade somehow had something to do with it.

"Harry Junior chews his toenails. It's gross."

"Uncle Harry does that, too."

Sam giggled. "Can I have some string cheese?"

"Sure."

Sam bounded out of the room, Duffy on her heels because she dropped food all the time.

Phin stared at me. He had a lovey-dovey look in his eyes that made my stomach turn.

"The GameMaster 2 comes out in a few days," he said. "Sam really wants one."

This was the third time Phin had brought this up. Money was really tight, and we couldn't afford a non-holiday splurge. Especially for a new gaming system that cost five hundred bucks.

"I thought we discussed this. We can get it for her birthday."

"It can be an early birthday gift."

Why did he have to make me the bad guy? "I heard they're sold out everywhere."

"What if I told you I was on a waiting list? All the VideoTowns in the country are opening early on release day. The one in town is opening extra early."

"And where do we come up with the money for this?"

Phin didn't answer. One more thing he wouldn't admit to.

I decided to go full provocateur. "Duffy got into the garbage again."

"My fault. I didn't put the lid on tight enough."

I watched him closely. "It was spilled all over the kitchen floor."

"Sorry. Thanks for cleaning it up."

Phin didn't react, and didn't say anything else.

Do I tell him? That I saw the condom box?

"Can I have some bacon?" Sam ran into the living room and stood between us, holding a package of bacon.

Phin scooped her up. "We can make it after we drop Mom off at Grandma's."

I rolled over to the TV, putting our GameMaster controllers in their charging stations.

When I killed the power, the windows shook. I looked outside, saw the palm tree in our front yard sway like an invisible giant shook it.

We'd been in Florida long enough to live through three tropical storms, but Harry would be our first hurricane. When we bought the house, it had storm shutters already installed, an impact-resistant garage door, and a back-up generator that ran on propane and provided power to half the circuit breaker. Only thing missing was roof straps, but the private owner we bought it from assured us that he'd never had a problem with the roof, even during the worst storms.

But I did have some concerns. We had ten trees on our property. And that above ground pool. And you couldn't talk to a single Florida resident without them telling stories of Irma or Andrew or Charley or Ivan or Jeanne.

None of those stories were happy.

Phin came in, holding the van keys. "You ready?"

"Did you clean out the gutters? If they're full, the house could flood."

"We're the highest house on the block. If we flood, it won't be because of the gutters."

"Can you do it anyway?"

He shrugged. "Sure."

I went for it. "Also," I said, "we're out of condoms."

"Fine. Anything else?"

That's all he had to say? Really?

I lifted my brake up and rolled past him, heading to the garage, not letting him see me cry.

"*The only misuse of guns comes in environments where there are drugs, alcohol, bad parents, and undisciplined children. Period.*"
TED NUGENT

"*I'm active in PAX, which is a gun awareness organization. We treat gun safety as a public health issue.*"
MANDY PATINKIN

GAFF

So the cheap pillow I bought was rekd. Got up with my neck and back effed.

Done.

I fiended a bed. Or one of those foam memory mattress thingys.

Plus waking up in pain, I had that garbage dream again, the one where I sorted my sock drawer.

Matching socks.

Folding socks.

Putting the balls of socks in rows according to color.

#SocksSocksSocks.

In the dream, Moms screams @ me, saying I'm doing it wrong, but I keep on going and don't care what she says and then when I finish I look in the mirror and I'm a robot.

Bonked.

I pissed, hit the kitchen for snax, grabbed all my gear, then headed for my car to visit the superstore.

Marko, my sus super, was walking in the parking lot with one of those plastic Costco tubs of candy, like five gallons of sour worms. I tried to flake, but he cut me off.

Traphouse.

"Hey, Guthrie. Want some candy?"

For breakfast I had dry cereal bcuz I'd left the milk I bought back at the store, forgetting to grab the bag when I left.. And I loved gummy worms.

"Kay."

He opened the lid, and I stuck my hand in and grabbed one.

"You can have more than that. Look how much I got. I'll never eat it all. You like sour candy?"

I nodded, grabbing more and stuffing my face.

"How was the first night in your new crib? Dope?"

Marko had a creep factor, but him trying to talk like a plural was extra.

"Off the shits," I said.

"You know how to work everything. Like the gas stove?"

I nodded again.

"Take a few more."

"I'm set."

"Take some for the road. You got your computer with you. You going to school? To work?"

I didn't answer. I didn't like Marko pretending to be my bestie. And he kept looking @ my mouth as I ate the candy.

I grabbed more gummy and bounced. "Gotta blast."

"I hate to see you go, Guthrie. But I love watching you leave."

Whatevs that meant. I walked away, feeling his eyes crawl all over me as I headed toward the car.

Edgelord.

In the daylight I didn't have no problem finding the department store. I bought a gel foam mattress, a better pillow, two towels, shampoo and soap, a fireproof glass bowl that I could eat out of and heat stuff up, aluminum foil, a bottle of cleaning spray.

What else did I need? I used to keep notes on my cell phone, but I gave that up so Moms couldn't track me.

I wandered around the store, feeling myself get overwhelmed, feeling all the stuff on the shelves waving @ me, screaming for my attention, feeling ready to just get the eff out of there without buying anything, and then stopped in front of a huge cardboard display.

GAMEMASTER 2: THE ULTIMATE GAME MACHINE!

The drawing of the Gamemaster 2 had legs and arms and a big yellow cape, flying through the air.

BS. I knew the console couldn't fly, and didn't have arms and legs. #FalseAdvertising.

A big sign stuck to the display said TOMORROW!

I waited 4evs @ the electronics counter for some kid my age to come by.

"Sup."

"You still taking pre-orders for the G2?"

"No way. All reserved. Maybe we can get you one for next month."

"How many pre-orders you have?"

"Over six hundo, bruh. Fire. City Warriors 2 got a perfect 10 from *Gaming Jerk Magazine*. We got merch."

He pointed to another cardboard display. Rave masks of CW2 characters. I grabbed one of Blorkta, a half-man-slash-half-angler-fish who had a mouthful of wicked blue needle teeth.

#Perfect.

Tomorrow will be a good day.

I paid for my swag, then got in the bucket and headed for the DMV.

Time to become a legal resident of South Carolina, yo.

I done the research online, knew I needed my old Driver's License, Birth Certificate, Social Security Card, and two proofs of residence. One was my lease. The other might need some finesse.

Finding the place was easy. I parked, saw the big NO WEAPONS sign on the door; a silhouette of a black gun in a red circle with a line through it.

One of SC's many gun laws.

I knew them all. And other laws as well.

#Google.

#BillofRights.

Inside the crowd was low key. Smelled kind of like school. People and paper and anxiety. I spent nine minutes in line, each minute thinking about how the previous minute felt, thinking about thinking about minutes, then thinking about thinking about thinking about them, and then got to jaw with an old lady who worked there.

"Just moved here from Ohio. Need a new driver's license."

"Welcome to South Carolina."

Whatevs.

I gave her all my credz, and old lady got frowny. "I need two proofs of residence. Y'all got mail yet at your new place? Utility bill?"

"Yo, I don't get paper bills. Pollution messes up the planet. Pay direct online."

I took my puter off sleep to show her my new electric company account.

"I don't know if we can accept proof of residence on a computer."

Finesse.

"They do it all the time in Ohio. I thought South Carolina would be, you know, progressive."

She looked @ my Ohio license. "Do you have some kind of eyeglass restriction?"

Day-am. My blepharospasm.

I thought about a book my school counsellor told me to read, donezo by this clout chaser named Carnegie. How to Win Friends and Shit. Truth, I didn't have friends, bcuz people were bonked, yo. I didn't know what any of them wanted, or why they acted all unpredictable and salty.

This Carnegie bruh broke it down so you could fool cats and get your way. Smile and listen and make them feel good.

"Don't need glasses," I told the old lady. "Just dry eyes. Inherited. You know, you remind me of my moms. She's all smart and has a good job and she's got pretty hair like you."

"Is that so?"

I couldn't tell if the old lady was feeling it or not. Sometimes it looked like every person I met wore a mask.

"You got kids?"

"Two kids. Four grandkids."

"What they call you? Gramma? Nana?"

"Mama. They call me Mama."

I smiled so big I thought my face would crack. "That's what I call my moms. Mama. Mama lost her job, bcuz of the cancer. All her hair fell out. I came to SC to work, bcuz you prolly know the jobs in the Midwest all suck."

"I'm sorry to hear that—"

"Guthrie. Name's Guthrie. People call me Gaff. You know, like the fishing hook?" I tried to go from looking happy to looking sad, but it was hard to do without a mirror so I wasn't sure I got it right. "You seem real good at your job, Mama, and you can turn me away if you want to, but with my gen it's all about online docs. We don't do paper. Your family sends you email, right?"

"Of course. I have the email. I have the Google account."

"Google is hype. Same as paper mail, right? And you're using a computer right now, right? Well, check my info on the website. You can see the address matches my lease. The electric company don't send me a paper bill bcuz I pay online. Never gon get a paper bill."

"This really isn't the way we—"

"I get it if you say no. You got all the power here. You can turn me away. I'm just a kid trying to adult."

"Pardon me?"

"Trying to be an adult. Trying to help Mama."

She stared @ me. Could go no. Could go yes. Might as well flip a coin.

Then she stamped a piece of paper and handed it to me. "Bring it to line C to take your picture."

Savage level legendary.

I brought the paper to line C, and while I was waiting I counted the people.

Sixty-eight. And prolly no concealed carry bcuz of the sign on the door.

But there were cameras. And it was a DMV, so cops could come in @ any moment.

I finna stick with my OG plan.

I got my pic, waited some more, then got the license.

My pic didn't look like me. Or maybe it did.

Random.

Still warm from the machine, I put it in my wallet and then went back to the car and tried to remember where I was headed next.

Right. The gun show.

I moved to South Carolina for several reasons.

The Carolina Hunting Show Spectacular was one reason. One of the biggest gun shows in the country, running for three days, starting today.

Another was bcuz South Carolina law allowed eighteen-year-old residents to buy handguns.

And I was now a resident.

Snap.

#WelcomeToSC.

"They that can give up essential liberty to obtain a little temporary safety deserve neither liberty nor safety."
BENJAMIN FRANKLIN

"I think we ought to raise the age at which juveniles can have a gun."
GEORGE W. BUSH

JACK

I wheeled myself out of the van, my daughter the Transformer gave me a hug goodbye, and Phin kissed me on the head, like I was a child.

Rolling back into Darling Center, I came across Mrs. Shadid, who appeared to be waiting for me.

"I was waiting for you."

Instincts confirmed. Or how would Sam say it?

Instincts on fleek.

Mrs. Shadid skirted the tail end of her seventies, and age had shrunk her to roughly the size of a garden gnome. Today she wore a silver hijab with a Nike swoosh, matching her silver hair and glasses. Her outfit was a silver and purple cloak, or maybe it was a dress, and the wind was whipping it back and forth, outlining her bony body.

"How can I help you, Mrs. Shadid?"

"I don't like you teaching everyone here about guns."

Straight to the point.

"Are you saying that having information is a bad thing?"

"I'm saying that having guns is a bad thing."

I phubbed her, checking my phone. Still forty minutes until my class.

"Would you like to get some coffee, talk it over?" I asked, hoping she'd say no.

"Very much."

That's what I get for hoping. "Let's head to the cafeteria."

The wind had gotten so bad that when I hit the handicapped button for the automatic door, it stayed open behind us, blowing and shaking. Mrs. Shadid had to grab the handle and put her weight on it to close the damn thing.

"This will be my first hurricane," she said.

"Mine too. Where are you from?"

I was expecting someplace in the Middle East. She answered, "Rockport, Iowa."

Good call, Jack. Lump me in with all the other casual racists who think that any American with an accent is a foreigner.

I should demand more from myself.

But that's a song I've been singing for a while.

"I'm from Chicago."

"I could tell. Your accent."

Touché.

The Darling Center cafeteria had tolerable coffee. It wasn't an exotic dark roast as sold in overpriced specialty shops, but it wasn't the mud I used to drink all the time at my old job. My ex-partner Herb Benedict truly believed that suspects who wouldn't talk under interrogation would confess to killing Lincoln if we forced them to drink more than a cup of our District coffee.

I missed the coffee. And Herb.

Mrs. Shadid drew two cups from the stainless-steel coffee urn and placed them on a tray with some artificial sweetener and artificial creamer. When I reached into my purse for cash, she graciously waved me off and paid at the counter. We found a table next to an indoor Buccaneer palm tree, which gave me a full view of the café and its two egress points. I did a quick scan of the crowd, and the only mildly suspicious subject was a teenage boy in a leather jacket, his hand jammed in his pocket.

He was too young to be retired, and too healthy to need rehab.

Maybe visiting grandparents.

I kept him in my peripheral vision as Mrs. Shadid doctored her coffee with carcinogens. I sipped mine black.

"Chicago," she mused while stirring her brew. "Doesn't that city have the most gun murders per year?"

Apparently we were getting right to the point.

"It depends on how you look at it. In 2018, the Chicago area had over 1500 firearm homicides. That's about 8 per 100,000 people. New Orleans had fewer deaths, but 16 per 100,000. So Chicago had the most, but not the highest percentage rate."

"Is that where you were a police officer? In Chicago?"

"No." I didn't like lying, but I was living a fake identity for a reason. I didn't want anyone to know who I really was. "Milwaukee."

"I've read that there are 40,000 gun deaths every year."

Statistics were ridiculously hard to come by, for three reasons.

One, gun lobbyists and privacy advocates felt it wasn't in the citizens' best interests for the federal government to know their business, so we had no federal department or system for compiling statistics.

Two, the organizations that did accrue this data did so in different ways, such as morgue searches, newspaper stories, obits, hospital records, police reports, and polls, and none told the whole story.

Three, a lot of gun incidents, both crime-related and self-defense related, went unreported.

I used to teach shooting classes at a local firing range, so I tried to keep up on my numbers because students always asked. Still, I had no real way of knowing if the numbers I Googled were accurate.

"Forty thousand seems about right."

"That's unacceptable."

I nodded. "I agree. But to put it into perspective, that's about the same amount as people who die in car accidents. And over half of the firearm deaths are self-inflicted. Some were in self-defense. Some were law officers performing admirably in the line of duty."

"And some were cops shooting unarmed minorities."

I winced at that. "Unfortunately, yes. That's a problem, and it's worth discussing why it's a problem and how to fix it. As far as statistics go, one innocent person dying by the hands of someone sworn to uphold the law is one person too many. It can't be tolerated."

The teenager hadn't moved. He still had his hand in his pocket. He still seemed out of place.

"How do we fix that?" Mrs. Shadid asked.

"Honestly? I see it as a multilayered problem. We need a higher police presence in high crime areas, and the majority of the cops should come from the neighborhoods they patrol. We need more money pumped into education and social services in low income areas. We need the police to know and interact with their communities in positive ways. We need to end the war on drugs and legalize, regulate, license, and tax drugs and prostitution. Take away dealing and pimping from the gangs, there won't be as big a need for guns. And of course, we need to make sure the police we hire aren't racists or bigots or mentally unstable, and make sure they get regular training and counselling so they don't slip into the *us vs them* mentality. Cops are supposed to protect and serve. They aren't a military unit deployed into a war zone."

I was missing some points, but that was the brunt of my grand plan that will never happen because things are far too broken.

A girl can dream, though.

"None of those things you proposed has to do with getting rid of guns."

The teenager in the leather jacket continued scanning the area. His eyes met mine, and he stared a moment longer than socially acceptable.

I liked to rate threat levels according to colors. Sitting in bed, watching TV, with nothing suspicious going on, was a green. Seeing someone run into a bank with a shotgun was a red.

Based on this teen's appearance and behavior, he had graduated to yellow.

"I don't think getting rid of guns is possible," I answered. "The USA has too many."

"What about preventing guns from falling into the hands of criminals? And children?"

I glanced back at Mrs. Shadid. "There are a lot of laws already on the books that do this. New guns are sold with locks so children can't fire them, like the trigger lock on my .38 that I showed everyone yesterday. Many states have laws about keeping guns locked, or in a safe."

She frowned at me. "The PLCAA."

This woman came armed with information. The Protection of Lawful Commerce in Arms Act prevented gun manufacturers from being held accountable for crimes committed with their products, signed into law in 2005 after dozens of lawsuits. In 1998 in Chicago, Mayor Daley sued gun manufacturers, as did a mosque in Rockport, Iowa after—

Oh.

Oh, boy.

"Mrs. Shadid, were you in Rockport in 2012?"

Her eyes became glassy, and she nodded. "I was there."

"In the mosque?"

She nodded again.

When I realized who I was arguing with in a debate about gun violence, I knew I'd made a huge mistake.

This talk wasn't going to end well for either of us.

"It's shocking to me that it's easier to buy a gun at
Wal-Mart than it is to buy my record."
MARILYN MANSON

"Gun bans don't disarm criminals, gun bans attract them."
WALTER MONDALE

GAFF

O ff. The. Chain.

Everywhere I looked, guns.

Real guns.

Fire.

After paying ten bucks admission, getting a red stamp on my hand, and being asked if I had any firearms on me and saying no—why would you bring a gun to a gun show?—I walked into the Saucer County Fairgrounds and was swallowed by guns. Guns on tables, with steel cable locks stringing them together through their trigger guards. Guns on makeshift wire racks, hanging on hooks. Guns in glass display cases. Guns on racks, guns in boxes, guns everywhere.

Guns guns guns.

#HellaGuns.

I'd never touched a real gun b4. Never even been close to one.

Being surrounded by so many @ once made me feel like …

Well …

It made me feel.

I walked up to the closest table, which was topped with AR-17 rifles. I'd done my research, so I knew what they were, but seeing them IRL was dope.

I trailed my fingers along the picatinny rail, and it was like I'd grown taller.

"Can I pick it up?"

The dealer was talking to someone else, and he gave me a casual glance and nodded.

I raised the rifle, the cable running through the trigger guard giving me enough room to bring it to my shoulder and peer down the sights.

Turned on.

There was a plastic zip tie around the trigger, looping up behind the charging handle, so it couldn't be fired.

Still, my hands shook.

"Looks good on you." The dealer grinned @ me.

"How much?"

"Six hundred, comes with two mags and a case."

A fair price. But it didn't suit my needs. I needed something concealable, to use up close.

I set the gun down. "I'll think about it."

I moved along.

The next vendor sold flintlock pistols. No interest.

The next, shotguns and hunting rifles. No interest.

The next, revolvers. I reached for a nickel-plated revolver that was almost as big as a rifle, and the vendor barked @ me. "Hey!"

I froze.

He jerked a thumb over his shoulder, @ a sign stuck to a wire cubby. ASK BEFORE TOUCHING.

"Can I pick this up?"

He nodded.

Like the AR-15, this had a zip tie around the trigger, going up over the hammer. I grabbed the gun, shocked by how much it weighed.

#HoldingBricks.

"That's Dirty Harry's gun," the vendor said.

"Who?"

"Movie. Before your time."

The gun was too big, too unwieldy, too heavy. Shooting it would hurt like crazy. I set it down and moved along.

One row over, I heard a few men in a heated discussion, and I got in closer bcuz it sounded interesting and familiar.

"Iver Johnson Cadet 55-A," said one guy with a big belly.

"Caliber?" asked a guy in a red flannel shirt.

"Twenty-two," answered the man, wearing a baseball cap. "Sirhan Sirhan. RIP, RFK."

Big Belly said, "Okay, his brother."

Flannel Shirt answered, "Too easy. Carcano Model 91/38, courtesy of Lee Harvey Oswald."

Baseball Cap snorted. "Only the most famous assassination in history. Give us a harder one."

"Martin Luther King," said Big Belly.

"Remington 760 Gamemaster, wielded by James Earl Ray," answered Baseball Cap. "I said a hard one."

"John Lennon."

"Charter Arms .38 Special, Mark David Chapman."

"Gandhi."

"Father or daughter?"

"Father."

"Beretta .380 ACP."

"Okay, who did it?"

All three remained silent.

"Nathuram Vinayak Godse," I said. I must not have said it loud enough, bcuz they looked @ me but didn't acknowledge I was right.

"Okay, easier one," said Flannel Shirt. "Garfield."

"Who? The cartoon cat?"

"James Garfield, you dumbass. The 20th President of these United States of America."

Big Belly and Baseball Cap didn't answer.

"British Bulldog," I said, louder this time. "Forty-four caliber."

The three men looked @ me again.

"Nice one, kid," said Flannel Shirt. "Who killed him?"

"Charles J. Guiteau."

The three men began to laugh. I didn't understand why.

"It was Guiteau," I insisted. "July 2, 1881. Garfield took two months to die."

Flannel Shirt leaned closer to me. "Okay, smarty pants. Yitzhak Rabin."

"The Prime Minister of Israel, shot on November 4, 1995, by Yigal Amir."

"Weapon?"

I went through the files in my head and found the right one. "A Beretta 84F."

Big Belly and Baseball Cap hooted. Flannel Shirt checked his phone. "Goddamn, that's right. Kid is some kind of goddamn savant."

"Is that the blinking thing? Some kind of autism?"

"I got one for you," I said. "Selena."

"Whozzat?"

"Selena Quintanilla-Pérez. The Tejano singer."

Big Belly snapped his fingers. "I saw a movie on her. With J-Lo."

"Taurus Model 85," I said. "Thirty-eight caliber. You guys just do assassinations, or do you also do active shooters?"

Flannel Shirt squinted @ me. "What do you mean?"

"Like the Crewmill Shooting in Mason, Montana, 2001. Seventeen dead. Can you name the rifle and shooter?"

No one answered, so I said, "Britt Sigmundson. Used a Dawber Arms .30-06. Every kill a headshot. The lady had mad skillz. Women can kill, too. Just as well as men."

Big Belly took a step away from me.

"Or how about William Phillip Martingale?" I asked. When no one answered, I continued. "Burger Barn shootings in Chicago, over a decade ago. Got eleven at the Burger Barn, and ten more at Thomas Jefferson Middle School. Used two Dilton 76ETX 9mm semiautomatics. The kids were all point blank range. Everything he aimed at, he hit. Cray cray."

Flannel Shirt said, "This conversation is over."

Whatevs. Couldn't hang with the big dawg so he dipped. "Are you a private seller, or do you have an FFL?"

I knew I'd pass a background check bcuz I had no background @ all, but I really didn't want a seller to take down any of my info or put me into the National Instant Criminal Background Check System. Shit like that could be brought up later.

"I'm private," he said.

"Can I see that Gen 4 Glock 21 you have in the case?"

"Not interested. Move along."

"I have cash."

"What part of *move along* don't you understand, kid?"

WTF was this d-bag's prob? Wasn't he here to sell guns? Big Belly and Baseball Cap stared off into the crowd like life wasn't happening right in front of them.

Griefers.

#NoClue.

#KillEmAll.

I left the booth, moving along to the next one. Took me a few minutes, but I found another guy selling Glocks.

"FFL or private?" I asked.

"FFL. You even eighteen?"

I searched for the next one. Found a lady with a whole display of semi-automatics. After confirming she was a private seller, I asked to see a Glock 19.

"You here with your parents?"

"I'm old enough."

"Can I see an ID?"

I hesitated, then handed over my new Driver's License. She studied it like she was preparing for an algebra test.

"Guthrie, are you a convicted felon or is there any legal reason you can't own a gun?"

"Naw."

"Any history of mental illness? Depression? Anger issues? Schizophrenia? Do you take any medication?"

Was she allowed to ask that? Bitch was looking @ me like she was my moms, all concerned and shit.

"Do you take any medication?" I clapped back.

She ignored my question. "Have you ever gone shooting?"

"Plenty of times," I lied.

"Have you ever taken a gun safety class?"

"Sure."

"Have you ever fired a Glock?"

"Sure." What's with all the damn questions? Private sellers were supposed to be chill.

"Where's the safety switch on a Glock?"

I pointed @ the weapon in the glass case. "On the other side. Near the top of the grip." That's where safety switches always were.

The lady frowned. "Glocks don't have a safety switch. They've got one in the trigger, and two internally. I don't think you've ever fired a Glock. Or a gun. Or taken a safety class."

Whatevs. Plenty more vendors out there. I let her talk to the hand, and bailed, wading deeper into gunland.

"Hey, dude, you looking for Glocks?"

I turned around, saw a guy talking to me. I'm not good with ages, but he didn't have no grey hair, no wrinkles. He wore a hoodie with a college logo on it, but it looked wrong on him. Like a costume.

"You selling Glocks? Got an FFL?"

"I'm private. You into polymer frames?"

"Sure."

"Ever hear of MGC?"

"Merican Gun Company," I answered. "Established 2004. Manufactured in Montana. Frames are made of composite carbon fibers."

He smiled wide. "How'd you know that?"

"I know a lot about guns." Except that Glock safety thing.

#MyBad.

"Dude, you are on brand."

I got the same funny vibe from this cat as I did from my landlord. #StrangerDanger.

"It's OK." He winked. "I'm cool. I heard you talking at that woman's table. What a bitch, huh?"

"She's here to sell guns, wouldn't even show me one."

"I know, total bitch. Hey, you want to check out some Mericans? I got a few models. Brand new."

"Where's your booth?"

"No booth. Didn't want to pop for it. I sell my firearms so cheap, I can't afford overhead. Know what I mean?"

I nodded, even though I didn't know what he meant.

"What kind of Mericans you selling?"

"Got all four models. Nine mil. Forty-five. Forty. Three-eighty."

"Extended magazines?"

"Dude, you really know your guns. How old are you?"

"Eighteen." I added, "I just got my South Carolina driver's license."

"Good for you, dude. You in high school? Where do you go?"

I wasn't sure what that had to do with anything, so I wasn't sure how to answer.

"Hey, dude. I get it. Not my business. I hated school. Couldn't wait to get the hell out of there. Wished I could blow it up, you know? Anyway, it's good to meet you."

He stuck out his hand. I took it, squeezing hard, like one of my old therapists taught me. Strong handshake, eye-contact, don't look away bcuz then people don't trust you.

But I did look away. Dude's hand felt funny, and I stared @ it.

He laughed and held up his hand. Bruh wore a bunch of gold rings. Like ten of them, on all four fingers. "Like my bling, dude?"

I squinted @ them, seeing each one had letters and a logo on it. "MGC?"

"Yeah. Merican gives them to their top sales people. Eighteen karat gold. Cool, huh?"

"You work for Merican? I thought you were private."

His smile faded, just a little. "I'm like a special salesman. Usually I deal with gun shops and sporting goods stores. Big accounts, y'know? Where they order hundreds at a time. But I sometimes sell from my personal collection. It's totally legit."

I didn't care if it was legit or not, as long as I didn't get in trouble. "It's cool."

"So you want to take a look? Got them in the trunk."

"Yeah," I said. "Show me what you got."

"I've got an idea; how about you don't blame all gun owners for the actions of a few?"
JEANINE PIRRO

"Ending gun violence isn't political. This is personal."
JOE KENNEDY III

So, Mrs. Shadid survived an active shooting.

No wonder she protested my safety classes. In my experience, people whose lives were personally affected by firearms went two ways. They armed themselves, or they became anti-gun advocates.

I understood, and sympathized, with both mindsets.

The Rockport Islamic Center shooting took the lives of eighteen people, and it made headlines long after the bodies had been buried. The survivors filed a class action suit against the manufacturer of the semi-automatic rifle used in the massacre. It was the first of its kind, and kickstarted modern public awareness of gun issues.

I reached out and put my hand on hers. "I'm so sorry."

Mrs. Shadid pulled away. "I don't want to talk about that. Let's stick to the debate. What about smart guns?"

Mrs. Shadid was referring to the fingerprint ID technology where the firearm could only be used by the owner.

"I'm all for smart guns. But I will tell you, my life has been saved by people who have used a gun that wasn't their own. I think smart guns are a good way to reduce gun trafficking and sales and accidents, but I don't think they'll solve the bigger problem."

"You gun people always do that."

I glanced at the suspicious teen in the leather jacket. He still fiddled with whatever he had in his pocket.

"Do what?"

"You say a minor improvement won't solve everything, so why even bother?"

I gave her my attention again. "I can point to dozens of minor improvements over the years. The Gun Control Act regulated interstate commerce. The Undetectable Firearms Act criminalized firearms that don't have a detectable amount of metal in them, so we don't have guns that bypass metal detectors. The Gun-Free School Zones Act, self-explanatory. The Brady Act, requiring mandatory background checks. The Federal Assault Weapons Ban. All are improvements. The question remains; have these improvements made the USA safer?"

"Of course you don't think they have, because you're against gun control."

I held up my palms. "Whoa, there. I'm all for gun control."

Mrs. Shadid squinted at me. "During your first class, you talked about the importance of the Second Amendment and how you fully support the right to bear arms."

"Sure. And the law supports it, too. That Amendment was incorporated in 2010, when the Supreme Court ruled to protect that right from the actions of state governments. It means state or local governments can't ban guns. But the court also ruled that the right to bear arms is not unlimited and can be regulated. There are hundreds of federal and state laws that regulate firearm sales, types, modifications, and locations they can be carried."

"And you're for regulation?"

I nodded. "Anyone with any common sense doesn't want guns anywhere near schools. Or on airplanes. To paraphrase Ronald Reagan, there is no reason to own a fully automatic AK47 for self-defense, or for sport."

The teenager had moved to a spot closer to the register, which he kept staring at. His hand still in his pocket. My threat level remained at yellow, but the yellow kept getting brighter.

"I thought one of the points of the Second Amendment was so citizens could protect themselves from the tyranny of their own government. And to form a militia."

This lady had really done her research.

"That was probably one of the original points." I shrugged. "Or maybe it was the main point. But this is far beyond the government forcing you to house soldiers in their standing army to fight foreign invaders, or restricting your guns so it can implement a totalitarian regime. Those things have happened in history, but they are unlikely to happen anytime soon in the United States. If they did, the Second Amendment isn't going to protect us. When the Constitution was written, black powder muskets took fifteen seconds to load and fire a single shot. These days, the government has tanks. They have drones. They have MOABs, and long-range hypersonic missiles, and LRAD sound cannons, and smallpox in a freezer. If our government really wanted to turn on its citizens, do you think anyone could hold off the full force of our military with a stockpile of handguns and rifles? Ten million people armed with revolvers can't beat radiation poisoning from a dirty bomb, or weaponized anthrax, or an airstrike from an F-16."

I sipped my coffee. Mrs. Shadid added more artificial cream to hers. A small lizard scurried up the trunk of the palm tree, disappearing into the fronds. The teen pulled his hand out of his pocket in a quick motion, and I tensed up—

—and saw he held a smart phone. He began to Facetime someone.

My threat meter dropped back to green.

"You brought up dirty bombs, so what about those? If you're comfortable with citizens owning firearms, why stop at guns? Why not let everyone have a nuke?"

I'd heard this argument many times. "First of all, that's just a thought experiment. It's not ever going to be a reality. Second, I'm all for laws that regulate weapons. I don't feel that violates any rights. Citizens shouldn't have dirty bombs. No one should."

"So why do the gun lobbies and organizations want to destroy all gun laws?"

A good question, but one I'd also heard. "It might seem that way, but I don't think they do. Does the majority of our populace really want armor piercing bullets that can punch through body armor? Or the ability to carry a fully automatic rifle with a fifty-round magazine on the train to work? Or for a convicted felon with a history of violence and mental illness to walk into a convenience store and five minutes later walk out with a 9mm? Of course not. But those gun groups have to take a hard stance and defend everything, because losing on any issue is a slippery slope."

"What do you mean?"

"The Gun-Free School Zones Act is a good idea. But some were against it. Gun groups worry that if guns are banned from one place, other places will follow. We can all agree on no guns in schools, or near schools. But what's next? No guns in any public places where children are present? No guns in your vehicle on public roads that go past schools? No guns in your house if you have kids? Is it plausible that we can go from gun-free school zones to gun-free neighborhoods?"

"No. That's a big jump."

"It's not. Chicago did it. A handgun ban in the 1980s, eventually overturned in the courts. Just last year they had a ban on any firearm within 1000 feet of any public park. Also overturned in the courts. There's a federal ban on assault weapons, and that one hasn't been overturned. Each state has its own laws on open and concealed carry, and they're all different, and they don't transfer from state to state."

"I don't think I'm following your point."

"My point is that gun rights are restricted all the time. Gun advocate groups feel like they have to fight for armor-piercing pistol ammunition because they fear that all ammunition will be banned. Slippery slope, and there's a lot of precedent to support it. You fight for something you know you won't ever get, so you can keep the thing you really want during the negotiation process."

Mrs. Shadid frowned. "But this is about more than just the type of weapons that are allowed. It's also about who is allowed to buy weapons."

"The Brady Act requires background checks for mental illness and criminal records."

"Do you agree with that?"

"Yes."

"So why would gun lobbies fight that?"

"Same slippery slope argument. What happens if a guy with a cluster headache goes on a killing spree? Can the Brady Act be amended to ban anyone with a headache from buying a firearm? What about veterans with PTSD? Can we tell those who have served our country, using firearms to do so, that they aren't allowed to have firearms as civilians because their service compromised their mental health?"

As the words left my mouth, I realized how much that statement might apply to me. Happily, Mrs. Shadid didn't pursue that direction.

"That's paranoid," she said.

"There are over a dozen federal laws controlling firearms, and hundreds more on state and local levels. Those gun lobbies and organizations keep pushing for the right to bear arms, and more and more regulations keep getting passed that limit that right. That's not paranoia. It's history."

"You mentioned the assault weapon ban. But that man in Pennsylvania, the one in the hotel room with all the rifles who shot people at an outdoor concert, he shot seven hundred people. He had assault weapons."

"Do you remember the class where I explain the difference between automatic and semi-automatic weapons?"

Mrs. Shadid nodded. "Fully automatic is where you hold the trigger and it keeps firing. Semi-automatic is where you have to pull the trigger each time."

"Right. The Reinhold Stadium shooter technically had semi-automatic weapons. But he used an aftermarket product called a bump stock. It uses recoil to sort of throw the trigger against the shooter's finger. The accuracy suffers a lot because the rifle is shaking, but it allows a shooter to fire hundreds of rounds per minute. Because the mechanism is different, it got around the legal ban. There are other things that can do the same thing. An auto sear—"

She interrupted. "What's the point of making laws if there are ways around them? Like the gun show loophole?"

Businesses with a Federal Firearms License were required to do criminal background checks on every gun sale, either in their shop or at a gun show. The private sale exemption was a way around that. I own a .38. If I wanted to sell it to Mrs. Shadid, I could, without a background check. To make it even scarier, an FFL holder is allowed to sell a weapon from their personal collection as a private sale, without having to run a check. In rare cases, you have a gun shop owner who goes out of business, so all of his stock becomes part of his personal collection. Then he could sell hundreds of guns without a license or an NICS.

That extended to Internet purchases, depending on state laws.

Lots of things scared me when it came to guns.

But the loophole scared me most of all.

"Close the loophole," I said without any hesitation. "Congress voted to close this in February of 2019. We'll see what the Senate does. I hope it passes. Private sellers should have to go through a licensed dealer, who would get a percentage for the trouble. It will take longer, and it's more expensive, but law-abiding gun owners should accept it as a cost for their right to bear arms. Just like we accept the recurring costs for owning cars and property."

"But you said it yourself. Fixing this won't fix the problem. No matter how many laws are passed, the gun violence problem in this country won't go away. What are we supposed to do, Jill?"

A memory came back, unbidden. "When I was in grade school, I was bullied. An older girl, taller, heavier. Knocked my books out of my arms when we were in the hallway. Pushed me around on the playground. Threw mud at me on Halloween, ruining my costume. I told my mother about it. She said I had two choices. I could let her take care of it by talking to my teachers and confronting the girl's parents. Or I could take tae kwon do lessons and deal with her myself."

"What did you do?"

"I took the lessons, stood up to her, and gave her a black eye. Then her parents complained to the principal, and I got expelled." I shrugged. "This country has a problem. There are no easy answers. And we can't depend on anyone else to do the right thing. Not our politicians or judges or police officers. Not our friends and neighbors. And certainly not those who want to do us harm."

"What are you saying?"

"I'm saying, Mrs. Shadid, that we live in a country where bad people have guns. We need to do whatever we can to try and stop that from happening. Until we come up with the solution to keep guns out of the hands of criminals, there is only one way to level that field."

"That's the answer? Arm yourself?"

"I don't like it, either," I admitted. "But if you don't defend yourself, who will?"

"It's not a gun control problem; it's a cultural control problem."
BOB BARR

"I'm a Texan—my idea of gun control is hitting
what you aim at and nothing else."
BLAKE FARENTHOLD

GAFF

his is the Merican XCQ-TER9, holds thirteen plus one 9mm rounds. Polycarbonate frame, striker fire, fiber optic tritium sights, threaded barrel for the attachment of a compensator, curved and rounded body so it doesn't snag on clothing. It's the best handgun currently available for personal defense." The guy winked. "Or offense."

"Can I hold it?" I asked.

"Of course."

He picked up the firearm, pulled the slide back to make sure it wasn't loaded, and handed it to me, butt-first.

The gun fit my hand like I'd been born holding it.

"Feels sexy, doesn't it?"

I never understood sexy. Puberty came @ me, and my body changed accordingly, but I never had those urges my health-ed teachers talked about. Pornography, even the really weird stuff, didn't do anything for me. Get laid? I'd rather watch YouTube vids of screws being cast @ a metal factory. Most satisfying video evah.

But the Merican was sick AF.

The grip felt perfect. Effortless. Weight nice. So much lighter than that magnum I'd held earlier.

I raised it up, peering down the sights, which winked @ me bright green.

I aimed @ a car.

Imagined it was a long line of people.

"Can I dry fire?"

"You can pull the trigger. Won't fire without a magazine inside."

I squeezed the trigger. It felt loose. No click.

"Do you got mags?"

"A'course."

"High capacity? Extended?"

"MGC doesn't make aftermarket mods for its firearms. That could be misinterpreted by the ATF and those anti-gun asshats. But I know a few booths at the show that could set you up with drum magazines. High capacity, fifty to a hundred rounds each."

"A compensator is for tip-up, right?"

"Partly. It also suppresses the sound, like a silencer. But, sure, a compensator can balance the recoil, especially if the weapon is giggled-out."

WTF?

"You can put a giggle switch on this?"

"You know what a giggle switch is?"

#HellsYeah.

"You put it on the end of the slide, replacing the back plate. It makes the gun fully automatic."

"You know a lot, dude."

"I thought those were illegal."

"It's a gray area. I may know a seller that has one."

"Here?"

He nodded. "They're expensive. And you wouldn't want to get caught with it, especially installed on the Merican. But by itself, it's just a harmless little hunk of metal. A paper weight. You can buy them online, from China, for cheap. A'course, you gotta wait six weeks for shipping. Some folks don't like to wait."

I switched the Merican to my other hand. I can use both hands the same.

Grip felt good.

Felt right.

I aimed @ another car.

Imagined people running away. Bleeding. Screaming.

"How much?"

"You got a caliber in mind?"

"Tell me about them."

"The XCQ-TER3 is a .380. Plusses; smaller, lighter, easiest trigger pull. Three-eighty is the kind of bullet James Bond uses. Assassins like it for the head shot. It'll enter the skull but not have enough energy to exit. Instead it bounces around inside, scrambling up the brain. Quietest of the four. Ammo is the cheapest. Grip is easier for smaller hands. Minuses; not much power. If the target is behind cover, it may not penetrate. No aftermarket drum mags. Shorter barrel means less accuracy."

"Does it have a giggle switch?"

"None of these firearms come giggled out. Paperweights are aftermarket. But, yeah, some are out there. A little hard to find."

"What about the .45?"

"XCQ-TER4 is the biggest and baddest in the family. Plusses; stopping power. Penetration. It'll kill the target in front of it, plus whatever is behind it. Minuses; much heavier, and louder. Ammo is expensive. Gives your hand a real workout after you fire off a box or two."

"And this one?" I held up the Merican in my hand.

"You're holding the XCQ-TER9. The 9mm and the .40 are similar. Both have their propogandists. They're more powerful than the .380, not quite as powerful as the .45. Nine ammo is cheaper than the .40, and a little lighter. More common. The forty is a heavier bullet. Rule is; bigger bullet, bigger hole. But it has a harder recoil. If I were shooting, say, two hundred rounds, I'd rather shoot the nine."

"Giggle switches and drum mags?"

"Available for both."

"Silencers?"

"We need to call them compensators. Silencers are in that legal gray area. Again, available for both. But more options with the nine."

"What about laser sights?"

"Like a dot target? All four models have the same Pics—Picatinny rails. Pretty much any sight will fit any of them."

The XCQ-TER9 sounded like the best option.

Plus, now that I held one, I really didn't want to give it back.

"How much?"

"That one in your hand, with a case, lock, manual, hex wrench, two seventeen round mags, and some cleaning brushes...four hundred bucks."

I'd done my research. That was cheap.

"Is it used?"

"It's brand spanking new. But I dig the vibe I'm getting from you. And I'm a salesman. I sell you this gun, you tell all your friends about it, they buy it at retail price at local shops, and I make more money in the long run. Make sense?"

It would make sense if I had any friends. But for four hundred, I couldn't pass this up.

"Do you take cash?"

"It's America." He smiled. "Cash is king."

I turned away and opened my wallet, taking out enough. I handed it over.

"Thanks, dude. You're now the proud owner of a Merican XCQ-TER9."

"Don't you have to check ID?"

"Are you eighteen?" He looked @ me like he didn't care what age I was.

"Yeah."

"Then we're cool."

He was also supposed to ask if I had a criminal background. I didn't push the issue.

"Do you believe that we have a right to privacy?" he asked.

I nodded.

"Even from the government?"

Another nod.

"I believe that, too. We already got the NSA up in our grill every time we fire up our WiFi. Two adults, doing a private firearm transaction, doesn't need government interference. We don't even need names. I don't know you, you don't know me. It's better that way. Agreed?"

"Yeah."

"Now you were asking about aftermarket mods, right? Drum mags? Compensators?"

"And the giggle switch."

"A'course. Put your Merican in your car, meet me by the entrance. I'll introduce you to a few cool dudes."

"I will teach my children weapons and warfare, so they might teach their children science and law, so they might teach their children art and literature."

GREEK PROVERB

"We have to face the fact that meaningful gun control has to be a part of homeland security."

JEH JOHNSON

JACK

After a short but pensive silence, Mrs. Shadid asked, "Did you need more coffee?"

I stared into the bottom of my empty mug. "If I have another I'll be jittery."

"Is that a yes or a no?"

I checked my phone.

Still ten minutes until my class. I agreed to more caffeine.

"It's a yes. Thank you."

She went for refills. When she brought mine back, I sipped it quietly, contemplating the best way to wrap up the conversation.

"Thanks again for the coffee and the conversation, Mrs. Shadid. I hope I got you to understand that at least a few people who support the Second Amendment aren't crazies who want every child to have an automatic weapon."

"I already knew that, Jill. People like you don't worry me. I'm worried about the crazies."

Me too. "We could continue this later, if you like."

"I'd like that. But I don't believe I'm going to attend your class today. I'm not in the mood to see another gun."

"No guns today. My mother is bringing her Kevlar vest. We're going to talk about body armor, and everyone can try it on."

I regretted the words the moment they left my lips. Besides discussing body armor, I also meant to discuss what to do during an active shooter situation.

Mrs. Shadid, of all people, probably didn't want to hear that.

"Maybe some other time."

Whew. Dodged a bullet there.

No pun intended.

Mrs. Shadid left ahead of me. I searched the tree for our lizard friend, and found him perching on a palm frond, judging me with his beady black eyes.

"Storm is coming," I told him. "Make sure your family is safe."

He scurried off.

What did animals do during hurricanes? I took a quick imagination break, picturing the lizard grabbing his lizard wife and lizard kids and hopping into a tiny Prius, heading north.

Drive fast, little dude.

I rolled out of there. One benefit to being in a rehab/retirement/nursing facility was the wheelchair accessibility. Ramps and automatic doors were everywhere. Somewhere in the last couple of years—maybe it was generational, or maybe a social media side-effect—chivalry sort of vanished. In my mother's time, people stood up when a woman entered and left the room, pulled out her chair at the dinner table, held out their arm to hold when strolling.

When I was younger, boys paid for dates, and bought flowers and candy.

I didn't miss much of that. But since being in a chair, I missed men who held doors open for women. One time I couldn't get into a shop because I couldn't get the door myself, and a dozen guys walked past, oblivious.

But that was probably sexist of me, because women walked past, too.

Maybe I didn't miss chivalry so much as regular old human compassion.

I hit the door button and it whirred open, letting in a blast of wind that actually blew me backward a few inches.

I thought about something Harry once said. My ex-partner, semifriend, and occasional co-worker Harrison Harold McGlade was more well-travelled than I. He liked to boast he'd been to all fifty-five states, counting the commonwealths Puerto Rico, Samoa, Guam, the Northern Mariana Islands, and the Virgin Islands. When my family was looking to disappear, I made the mistake of asking Harry which was the best state to live in.

"The state of intoxication," he'd said. When I didn't laugh, he answered for real.

"Every single one of them wants to kill you," Harry told me. "They're either too populated, making them hotbeds of crime and communicable disease and car accidents, or not populated enough, so if you trip and bang your head you'll bleed out before the nearest ambulance gets there. Every state has animals that bite and gore and sting and trample. Or they have natural disasters; earthquakes, wildfires, volcanos. Or floods, tornadoes, hurricanes, tsunamis, lightning storms. Or they have temperatures so low they'll freeze your eyes in your head, or so hot you'll run out of sweat. I wouldn't grade any state in the country higher than a C."

"So what's the best place to live?"

"Canada."

"What if I want to remain a US citizen?"

"Depends on your needs. Mine is strippers. I've got a spreadsheet if you want to see it."

That killed our conversation. So Phin, Sam, and I moved near my mother.

Chicago had crime, and killer traffic, and bitter cold, and some wicked storms. Florida had heat, and alligators, and tourists (which some think are the worst thing of all), and hurricanes.

I lived in the Windy City, where you had to keep a tight hold of your car door so it didn't bend when a gust hit it. But I hadn't ever experienced anything like the wind when I rolled outside. It damn near knocked my chair over.

My pocket buzzed, and I set my brakes and checked a text from Mom.

CLASS SWITCHED TO REC ROOM in B. CAN'T FIND VEST.

Building B was Mom's building, just fifty meters east—

—directly into the wind.

According to recent weather reports, we were still two days away from Hurricane Harry hitting shore, but the head-on gusting was so strong it blew tears straight back across my temples, into my ears. After wrestling with my wheels for twenty meters, my arms straining, I considered letting it blow me back to the cafeteria and calling an orderly for help.

I might as well just ask for diapers, too. Because if I'm giving up, I should give up fully, not just half-assed.

But I didn't quit. I muscled through, my hair whipping around so hard it hurt my roots, and finally got to Building B, where Mrs. Shadid was struggling to pull closed the automatic door.

"Mrs. Shadid!" I yelled above the whistling. "Don't shut it!"

Mrs. Shadid must have seen me because she halted her attempts until I wheeled in. Then I pulled up close, added an arm to help her, and we managed to get the door shut.

I blew out a breath. Then another.

Damn… when was the last time I had an actual work out? Not just trying to walk, but actual cardio and strength training?

Add that to my list of reasons to hate myself.

"So, you decided to come to the class?"

"What? No. I live in B62. You're having class here?"

"In the rec room. Moved because we didn't want residents getting blown into the Gulf."

She nodded, and began to walk the familiar hallway. Familiar, because my mother lived in this building, and also familiar, because all six apartment buildings in the Darling Center, named B through G, looked the same. Each had an identical layout in the shape of a right angle L, every apartment with a view of the center pool/lounge area. Ten apartments per floor, six floors per building. If Mrs. Shadid was in B62, that would put her on the sixth floor, just down the hall from Mom.

The circular layout of the village, and the similarity of the buildings, made it confusing to navigate. Especially since the residents were sixty-five or older. To compensate for this, the buildings were all clearly marked with their respective letters, and signage abounded.

Besides the apartments, the six resident buildings each had a smaller recreational room with tables and chairs, a vending area on each floor, and a center lobby with sofas, chairs, tables, and a television, usually used for visiting with families.

The seventh building in the complex, Building A, housed the cafeteria and kitchen, security office, gym, rehab facilities, medical clinic, laundry, and large community rooms for meetings, bingo, movies, etc.

There was also an eighth building, called H, to the west of the others, reserved for residents with later stage dementia.

Because this retirement village only housed the elderly, I couldn't live here even if I wanted to. But they did allow some adults over fifty into their rehabilitation programs.

I barely made the age cut-off. Yay me.

I followed Mrs. Shadid down the hall, to the middle of the building, and we got into the elevator.

"I thought you were in the rec room," she said.

"Gotta help my mother find her body armor."

I pressed 6.

We didn't speak as we went up. Not an icy silence, but not exactly friendly, either.

When the door opened, Mrs. Shadid waited for me to roll out. I headed for B65. When I got to Mom's door, I lifted my hand to knock, then instinctively looked back down the hall.

Mrs. Shadid stood in front of B62, unmoving. Not going into her room.

What was she waiting for?

Odd.

I rapped my knuckles, and Mom answered.

From my peripheral vision, I caught Mrs. Shadid opening her door just as I rolled inside.

"Morning, Mom."

My mother didn't look too hot. "Morning, dear."

"You okay?"

"Yeah. Tired. Looked everywhere. Can't find the vest."

Something was off about her. Her voice, kind of slow. As she walked away from me, her gait wobbled just a bit.

I didn't press it, and took a look around my mother's room. I knew some residents had large apartments with three bedrooms, and others had just a studio. Mom had two bedrooms, one of them set up for Sam when she stayed overnight.

Like hotels, the Darling Center had maid service, room service, and laundry service. Unlike hotels, it also had doctor service, nurse service, and orderly service. Every room had several panic button intercoms that would immediately summon help in case of a fall or medical emergency, and the bathrooms had railings and raised toilets. The bedrooms were also set up to accommodate medical or hospice care, with extra electrical outlets, wall IV hooks, and adjustable beds that could be fitted with railings.

This was my mother's third or fourth retirement home. She moved here expressly because I'd been shot, and their rehab program was one of the best in Florida.

She also liked the bars here. A lot. And the Darling Center slung booze like a typical Florida resort; frequent and cheap and full service. It had a tiki bar, a night club, a music lounge, and drink carts, beer runners, and shot girls who prowled the pool area. Mom even played shot girl for a Caribbean party a few weeks ago, wearing coconut halves for a top and delivering Jamaican rum shots to every senior waving five bucks.

Sizing up Mom, I wondered if maybe she'd been hitting the rum early.

Or, in her case, late. Her bedroom door was closed, but I could clearly hear someone snoring from inside.

"Mr. Camerotti?" I asked.

"Mr. Camerotti dislocated a hip. That's Mr. Feinstein. His Viagra wouldn't wear off so he kept me up all night."

Maybe that's why she was walking funny.

I didn't like to question my mother about her sex life for three main reasons; it was none of my business, she went into way too much detail, and I envied the fact that her love life was so much better than mine. So I stayed mum.

"Did you check the bedroom for the vest?"

"I did. I think it's in one of the closets."

I rolled to the nearest closet, opened the door, and frowned.

It was crammed full, every shelf overflowing, stuff practically spilling out.

"Is your other closet this organized?"

"It's worse. This place is smaller than my last one, and I don't have enough room."

I eyed some of the items jam-packed in there. "I see you have two typewriters. Planning on writing a book?"

"Typewriters are coming back. Don't judge."

"And several dozen VHS tapes of *Columbo*."

"You bought those for me, twenty years ago. That club where you got one tape a month in the mail. Haven't gotten around to watching them yet."

"You can probably get the whole series on Blu-ray, and it would take up a lot less space. Do you even have a VCR?"

"It's in there somewhere. I think in the box with all the old *Life* magazines."

"Should I worry that you've become a hoarder?"

"I'm not getting new stuff. I just don't like parting with the old stuff. If you're talking about hoarders, there's a rumor we have one on this floor. I heard two maids talking. Stuff stacked to the ceiling, they said."

Retirement home gossip was another thing I never questioned Mom about, because she could go on and on and on, yakking about people I didn't know and never would.

It reminded me of high school. Except with more sex.

I decided finding the vest wasn't worth digging through all of her crap, and I closed the door, having to push on it because; jam-packed.

"I'll look for it later. I can fill the time with active shooting info." I made a face. "If there is anyone even here, in this weather. Why am I bothering? Even with a full class, more than half of them don't care."

My mom looked at me funny.

"What?" I asked.

"You think you're doing this for them?"

"Who else am I doing it for?"

She continued to stare, and reality sunk in.

"You didn't get me to teach this class because you wanted your friends to know about firearms. You did it to get me to do something."

"Everyone needs to feel useful, Jacqueline. Especially when they feel the most useless."

"There's a word for sneaky women who do things like that. It rhymes with *hunt*."

"We need to reclaim that word. And pussy, too. Why is calling someone a pussy equal to calling them weak? Pussies can take any penis you throw at them, pump out babies, and last a lifetime without needing erectile dysfunction pills. They're tough and resilient and provide pleasure for those who own them and those who want to use them. We need to take pussy back. It should be a compliment. Someone is brave or strong, they should be called a pussy."

"No argument here."

"Women call each other sluts and bitches, don't they? As a term of affection."

I nodded. "Yeah. And we're late for my class, slut. Do you need to say goodbye to Mr. Feinstein before we go?"

"I said goodbye to him earlier this morning." Mom offered a lopsided smile. "That's why he fell asleep again. Pussy power. Maybe I should get one of those pink hats."

"Maybe you've already got one, buried in the closet somewhere under a stack of LPs."

"LPs are also coming back. Seems like everything old and considered obsolete is coming back these days."

Sure.

Everything but me.

"I don't have to be careful, I've got a gun."
MATT GROENING

"Yes, people pull the trigger—but guns are the instrument of death. Gun control is necessary, and delay means more death and horror."
ELIOT SPITZER

GAFF

The stamp on my hand let me back into the gun show, and I followed the XCQ bruh through the rows and rows of gun sellers until we got to a table that had a big sign with the word PAPER WEIGHTS on it.

On the table were an assortment of brass knuckles, arranged on newspapers. The man standing behind the display was Asian, maybe ten years older than me, bare arms covered in tattoos.

"Dude here just picked up an XCQ-TER9," said the XCQ guy to the tattoo guy. "Looking for a paperweight."

"I got a perfect one right here for you." Tattoo picked up one of the knuckle dusters. One that had spikes on two of the knuckles. "Two hundred."

Two hundred bucks for a cheap chunk of crap metal? Str8 trash.

#HellsNo.

I started to say something, and XCQ guy gave me a nudge. "Pay the man."

Total T-bagging.

So WTF? Bounce?

I tried to read the tattoo guy's expression, but I was shit @ doing that. People all looked the same to me. So I pulled finesse.

"Kinda high, bruh."

Tattoo guy smiled. "No negotiation. My shit is on brand. GOB brand, you know what I'm saying?"

I didn't know what he was saying. But XCQ nudged me. "This is what we were talking about."

Hol up.

Paperweights.

The giggle switch.

K.

I turned away, fished out two hundos, and handed them over. Tattoo guy squatted down, spent some time under the table cloth, then came up with a cheap box with a pic on it of the trash brass knuckles.

I looked @ XCQ, and he smiled and nodded, so I took the box.

Heavy. I gave it a shake, heard a metallic rattle.

XCQ motioned for me to follow him.

"It's in the box with the knuckles. No install instructions, but you got the Internet, right?"

I nodded.

"Should be easy for a smart person like you. You also wanted extended mags, laser sights, and a compensator?"

Hell yaaaas. "And ammo."

"Follow me, dude. We're gonna pimp your nine out so hard it'll crush. Pure GOAT."

He was trying too hard with the slang, but I got his point.

I stuck the box in my pocket and let him lead me to the next booth.

"If someone has a gun and is trying to kill you, it would be reasonable to shoot back with your own gun."
DALAI LAMA

"We can protect the Second Amendment, we can protect our constitutional rights, and we can still do something about this public health crisis that is gun violence in our communities."
SETH MOULTON

JACK

The rec room wasn't much bigger than my living room at home, boasting a few cheap tables, some folding chairs, a TV on the wall, a coffee machine with hotel-level accoutrements, and a wall-length window view of the swimming pool area, which had been closed by staff, all the lounge chairs and sun umbrellas put into storage, a cover stretched over the pool, and the outdoor bar shuttered. The palm trees in the courtyard shook like they were in a mosh pit. The sky was dark.

There were five people waiting for us. Mr. Fincherello, from B41, wearing a green poplin suit over a blue Hawaiian shirt, leafing through a vintage copy of *Mad Magazine* with Jimmy Carter on the cover. At another table, Mrs. Garza and Mr. Shoop were engaged in an extremely public display of affection that seemed to center around passing the same pair of dentures from mouth to mouth. Mrs. Ramos sat across from them, oblivious, fully engaged in a po' boy sandwich half-wrapped in foil. Mr. Traeger, from E33, wore a Darling Center bathrobe, and sipped coffee with an audible slurp.

"I made coffee," he said.

I thanked him and beelined for the coffee cart, pouring myself a mug. The first sip brought me back to my cop days. It tasted like greasy dirt, with a hint of rust.

Reminded me how much I missed my old partner, Herb Benedict.

I checked my phone. Five after. Then I found my notes and looked at my bullet points on active shooter response.

Heh. Bullet points. Maybe I should work that into the talk.

"Good morning, everyone. Thanks for coming. We're going to get started. A lot to cover today. Who can tell me what an active shooter is?"

Mr. Fincherello spoke. "One of those wackos who comes in and tries to kill everybody. Like that guy in Pennsylvania who rented a hotel room and shot up that outdoor concert. Or those kids at Rathlin High School who murdered all those teachers and students. The Suburban Eliminators, I think they called themselves."

"Correct, Mr. Fincherello. Gregory Taylor Schneider and Tully Huffland. A dual shooter situation like that is actually pretty rare. It's usually a lone wolf. The Department of Homeland Security defines an active shooter as an individual actively engaged in killing or attempting to kill people in a confined and populated area. They may have a single victim or group of victims in mind, like a school they attend or their place of employment. But what's happening more often is the locations and victims are chosen at random. The only selection process is; who is nearest and easiest to shoot. Last year, the FBI identified 30 active shooting situations, claiming 90 deaths and over 200 wounded. This year, so far, is on track to double that number."

"You used to be a police officer, am I correct, Jill?"

"Yes, Mr. Traeger. For over twenty years."

"Were you ever involved in an active shooter situation?"

"Yes, I was. It began at a fast food restaurant, and then ended at a school."

"Was that the Burger Barn massacre in Chicago?"

I swelled up with panic. The point of moving to Florida, anonymously, was so no one knew who I was. While I tried to think of what to say, the memories began to jab at me.

The screaming.

The blood.

The children.

The mangled body of Billy Martingale . . .

"Jill and I were police officers in Milwaukee," my mother said, covering my ass and sticking to the story we'd made up. "In the case she's referring to, no one was killed."

Good lie, Mom. I took a deep breath, got myself centered, and reigned in the brief panic.

"We got lucky and stopped him before things got out of control," I furthered the lie, slipping back into my regular speech. "But relying on luck puts you at much higher risk than being prepared and having a plan in mind. Today, we're going to talk about what you do when someone walks in and starts shooting."

There was a clunking sound. Everyone looked.

Either Mrs. Garza, or Mr. Shoop, had dropped their dentures onto the floor.

Mr. Shoop picked them up and examined them, so I assumed they were his.

I sipped more awful coffee, then continued.

"Your first defense is self-awareness. Whenever you're indoors, know where your nearest exits are. Look for two, in case one is blocked. Pay attention to the people around you. Someone acting suspicious. How would you qualify suspicious behavior? Mr. Fincherello?"

"When someone is holding a gun and shooting it at you."

Titters from the geriatrics. Mom also giggled. I gave her a look not to encourage them.

"What else? Mrs. Garza?"

"Someone alone who looks out of place or lost."

"That could be anyone from Building H," Mr. Fincherello said.

More laughs. I wondered how Mrs. Fincherello put up with him.

"Fair enough. But to be serious for a moment, what would be the difference between someone in the dementia ward in Building H, or someone who might actually be an active shooter? Mr. Fincherello?"

I braced myself for another joke.

"Hands in his pockets," he said. "Or a big coat."

I nodded. "Good. Bulky clothing can hide firearms. And someone wearing a coat in warm weather is definitely suspicious."

"Someone who looks nervous or angry," added Mrs. Garza.

"Good. And remember, most active shooters are loners. If you see someone alone, who doesn't look like they have any particular purpose, like going to the bathroom, or buying a candy bar, or texting on their phone, you should pay more attention. I'm not saying that every kid loitering has a gun on him. But if you get that little feeling in your stomach that says, *this guy makes me nervous*, then listen to that feeling. That feeling is fifty thousand years of evolution warning you something is wrong."

"I always thought it was gas," Mr. Fincherello said.

Titters.

Mom was wrong. Teaching this class wasn't helping me feel useful at all. But I persevered.

"Let's say that someone does come rushing in with a gun, what's the first thing you do?"

"You beat the little punk down," said Mr. Shoop.

Mr. Shoop was a proud veteran, stationed in Cambodia during their civil war. Which may have been where he lost his teeth. He'd hinted at that once or twice.

"Attacking the shooter is an option, Mr. Shoop. But only as a last resort. You don't know how much firepower he has. You don't know how good a shot he is. You don't know if he's alone. If you are in public, and someone is shooting, the first thing you should do is run."

"I can't run," Mr. Traeger said. "My top speed is shuffle."

I smiled at that. "I mean get away, as fast as you can. Immediately. Don't wait for the change from your bar bill. Don't search for your sandals and floppy hat. And don't waste time trying to argue with others about how serious the situation is or isn't. Get to the nearest exit, pronto."

"Shouldn't we help others?"

"Yes and no, Mrs. Garza. If someone is in a wheelchair and needs help, certainly you should help push. But don't waste time trying to convince everyone they need to come along. And if someone next to you is shot and cannot get up, leave them there."

"We don't leave the fallen behind," Mr. Shoop said, folding his arms across his chest.

"An active shooting situation isn't war, Mr. Shoop. A shooter is looking for targets on their feet, not on the ground. Trying to drag someone out of there will slow you down, and could get both of you killed. And if you move someone critically injured, you can make their injuries even worse."

"That sounds cowardly."

I shrugged. "Take it up with Homeland Security. I'm reading from their pamphlet. Run away, let the professionals deal with the injured."

"What if you can't get away?" Mrs. Ramos smacked. She'd finished her po'boy and was sucking some sauce off her finger.

"If you can't run, you hide. If the shooter is in another room, close and lock the door."

Mr. Fincherello laughed. "Most of the locks in this place are rinky-dink. I was a locksmith for forty-four years. You can get through most of them by loiding with a credit card. Or with a swift kick. They certainly won't hold up to a bullet."

"An active shooter wants to kill as many people as possible, and the average shooting incident rarely lasts longer than a few minutes. A closed and locked door could deter him enough for him to move on. You could also barricade the door with heavy furniture."

Mr. Shoop still seemed irritated. "No offense here, Jill, but you're in a wheelchair. How are you going to push something heavy in front of the door? Or how is Mrs. Garza?"

"Hey! I'm doing Zoomba!"

"No offence intended, sugar lips."

"Doorstops work best," said Mr. Fincherello. "Wedge it under the door. Doesn't even have to be a doorstop. I once spent ten minutes trying to get into this lady's apartment, because her daughter locked her out. Couldn't figure out what was keeping it closed. All the daughter did was wedge a tube of hand lotion under the door. Kicked it in there real good. Folded magazines also work. A clothespin. Or a fork."

"Good suggestions, Mr. Fincherello. Then you should hide. If you can, hide behind something heavy, that fully covers you. And remember to stay quiet. Turn off your phone. Turn off any TVs or music."

"And if running and hiding don't work, can we beat the little punk down?"

"Yes, Mr. Shoop. As a last resort, if you can't get away or hide, you have to attack the shooter with everything you've got. Use whatever you can. Mrs. Garza, what would you use in this room?"

"I'd whack him with the pot of hot coffee."

"Good."

"Coffee machine, too," Mr. Shoop said. "Weighs even more."

"Also good. These chairs could be thrown. You could turn over the tables and hide behind them."

Though they wouldn't offer much cover. And I'd hate to be at the mercy of a gunman with my only defense being a pot of coffee.

But that's why I carry a gun.

"So let's go over it again," I told the class. "If you see someone suspicious, pay greater attention to them. If you see them with a gun, or making threats, get a safe distance away and tell someone in authority. If it's in a restaurant or shop, tell the manager. Or call the police. But don't call the police until you're someplace safe."

I checked my bullet points and continued.

"If you see someone pull a weapon, or start shooting, first you run. If you can't run, hide. If you can't hide, fight back using everything you can, with all your power and aggression. Help others if you can, but don't try to help anyone who is down and can't get back up. Leave them for the responders. And again, don't call 911 until you are sure you're safe. In fact, turn your phone off."

"Why is that?" asked Mrs. Garza.

"Two reasons. First, you don't want to draw the attention of the shooter by talking, or your phone ringing. Second, when the first responders come—and they can arrive on the scene within a few minutes—you don't want to have anything in your hands."

"Because they might think it's a gun, and shoot you."

"Exactly, Mr. Shoop. When you are getting away, make sure your hands are raised and empty, your fingers spread. Try to stay calm and quiet. And don't stop to talk to the police. The first ones on the scene have one priority; neutralize the shooter. More responders will come and help the wounded and take statements."

Was I missing anything? I checked my notes.

"Jill, I have a question." Mr. Shoop again. "What about the *stand-your-ground* law?"

He was referring to applying lethal force against threats or perceived threats, with no duty to retreat. AKA the *shoot first* law. If you're someplace you have the lawful right to be, and you perceive a threat, you could legally preempt that threat with a firearm.

Statistics on stand-your-ground are as hard to come by as all gun stats. But the highest profile cases involved shooting someone innocent, usually a person of color.

"What is life worth, Mr. Shoop?"

He squinted. "What do you mean?"

"An unarmed kid breaks into your house to steal a TV. Someone drunk is banging on your door at 3 A.M. because he got the wrong address. Some pinhead cuts you off in traffic, you honk at him, and he pulls over and gets out of his car and starts banging on your hood. All three perpetrators are in the wrong, and it is reasonable to assume that anyone in these situations would be threatened by them. But does that justify shooting, possibly killing, any of these people?"

"I mean in cases of real self-defense. Where you'll die if you don't protect yourself."

"Those cases are much rarer than you'd think. Everyone knows what *self-defense* means. But very few people know the term *duty to retreat*. It means that if you are in danger, and can get away, you should make every attempt to get away. You don't have the right to harm anyone else."

Mr. Shoop folded his arms across his chest. "I learned otherwise in the military."

"But this isn't the military, Mr. Shoop. And we're not engaged in combat. We're civilians, in peacetime. A guy mugging you wants your money. Is the fifty bucks in your wallet equal to taking his life? I know you're being wronged. But the hassle of getting new credit cards never justifies killing someone's child. And everyone is someone's child."

"What kind of world would we have if everyone ran away?" Mr. Shoop asked.

"A world without any war," said Mrs. Garza, looking up from her cell phone.

Mr. Shoop shook his head. "So who defends the innocent?"

"Charles, we've talked about Cambodia. You were there in '70. Do you know how many wars the United States has been involved with since then?"

"A few. Iran. Iraq. Somalia."

"Twenty-seven," Mrs. Garza said. "I have it right here on my phone, on Wikipedia. I've told you many times that I appreciate your service, Charles, and I'm not going to criticize our country, or our government, or get into how many of these wars can be justified. But twenty-seven wars in the last forty-nine years is too many. Almost three million United States citizens have died in wars. Three million, Charles. Maybe running away isn't such a bad idea."

"I'm not talking about war, Manuela. I'm talking about protecting yourself, right here."

I closed my eyes, considered the events of yesterday, and decided to lay it out there.

"Let me go even further. You're in a bar, someone starts pushing you around. Your smartest option, even though it bruises your ego, is to leave. Escalation is always bad. But you might be tempted to engage. Fight back. Then maybe a few punches are thrown, and you're on the floor. Is reaching for your firearm really worth it? You've got a black eye, a bloody nose, feel angry and scared and victimized. That doesn't mean you have the right to kill the guy."

"Why not? Guy like that is a scumbag, deserves whatever he gets."

"We all feel that way. We make assumptions that a person is bad because they've done something bad." I checked my notes. "The psychological term is *correspondent inference*. Someone cuts you off in traffic, you automatically think they're a bad driver and a jerk. But you don't really know. It could be a guy rushing to the hospital because he's having chest pains. Or maybe he just won the Nobel Peace Prize, but his wife dumped him, and he's so emotionally upset he isn't paying attention to the road. Bad behavior doesn't make someone a bad person. Making a mistake doesn't mean someone deserves to be shot."

Mr. Shoop remained defiant. "So I can't defend myself, but cops get a free pass? How many times do unarmed black kids get killed because some cop perceived a threat?"

"Too many," I said. "One time is too many. We have a gun problem in this country. We also have a lethal force problem. In high-level firearms training, the most important aspect is learning when not to shoot. Going to your local gun range and plinking targets doesn't teach you how to use a firearm. Part of what I want to teach all of you, as these classes continue, is how essential it is to know when you *shouldn't* shoot a firearm."

I couldn't tell if Mr. Shoop was satisfied with my answer.

I wasn't sure I was, either.

Back in Chicago, we had to write a report every time a weapon was discharged. We had rules to follow, and required legal justification to use a firearm. But I knew cops who never really learned how and when lethal force needed to be employed, and others whose judgement was impaired by stress, burnout, PTSD, mental health issues, substance abuse, fear, and bigotry.

Add that to the many, many problems in America.

I looked to my mother for some assistance or moral support, but she seemed oddly disengaged.

"This has been a lively discussion, but getting back to active shooting situations, I want you to remember the big three. Run. Hide. Fight." I looked at Mr. Shoop. "In that order."

He didn't seem convinced.

I wasn't convinced either.

Those were the rules, according to Homeland Security. But I'd had firsthand experience.

In an active shooter situation, there was really only one thing you could do.

Hope you got lucky.

I had no doubt that the Run/Hide/Fight rules could save lives. But like everything in life, there were no guarantees.

But people needed assurances. They wanted to believe they had some control.

I read somewhere that those buttons on crosswalks, that were supposed to make the light change, didn't actually change the light. The lights were on timers, and the button fooled the pedestrian into waiting for the walk signal, which would have come up anyway. I've also heard that the button in elevators to close doors didn't close them. But it made people feel like they made the doors close faster, rather than standing there and being at the mercy of an automatic system.

When staring down the barrel of a loaded gun, Run/Hide/Fight wouldn't do much. Neither would begging, or bargaining, or reasoning.

All you really had was hope. And all you could hope for was luck.

But that would have made for a nihilistic gun safety class, so I stuck to the program.

"This will be the last class until next Monday, so we can all prepare for Hurricane Harry. Thanks for coming today."

There wasn't any applause. There never was.

I considered my mother's reason for me teaching this class. That I needed it, to feel useful.

But instead of bolstering my self-esteem, I felt deflated. And more than a bit hypocritical.

At the bar last night, I wanted Phin to beat the crap out of that asshole.

Hell, I wanted to do it myself.

All these years, I've always thought of myself as the good guy. The protector. The shining beacon of morality that fairly and impartially enforced the law and defended the weak and strived for justice.

But maybe I was just another bully with a badge.

Maybe I shouldn't be teaching firearms safety. Maybe I should re-evaluate my life and teach Zen Buddhism.

Everyone filed out, and I rolled over to Mom.

"Your appointment with Dr. Agmont is in twenty minutes."

"You made the appointment for me?"

"Blame me for loving too much."

"Did you and Mr. Feinstein have breakfast in bed?" I was wondering if mimosas or bloody marys were involved, because she still sounded tipsy.

"Normally you tiptoe around my sex life, and now you want details. What's on your mind, Jacqueline?"

I changed the topic. "Sometimes I'm not sure of the difference between good and bad."

She patted my hand. "You're one of the good ones, dear."

"How do you know?"

"Because someone bad would never question themselves like that."

I wasn't sure Mom was right.

I believed it was a lot more complicated than that. Bad people, really bad ones like murderers and pedophiles and rapists, can do good things. Create art, give to charity, help others, act decent 99% of the time, and only act like monsters 1%. And good people, upstanding members of society who care about their fellow human beings and try to contribute, can make mistakes and be capable of very bad things.

A poor man, out of desperation, could rob a liquor store, which is an immoral and illegal act, but he has mental clarity and a clear motive; he's robbing to feed his family. A spree killer who hears voices that tell him to kill others is a monster, but that monster might be a victim of his own genetics, or abuse, diagnosable as mental illness. Should we, as a just society, blame someone for their actions if their brain chemistry is demonstrably erratic?

I don't know the answer. I've met a lot of terrible people. Mental problems don't excuse their crimes.

But maybe we should be focusing on pre-emptive treatment rather than post-crime punishment.

The line between good and evil is a lot thinner than most people think.

Sometimes all it takes is a push.

"Supporting mental wellness is crucial to any goal of decreasing gun violence in America."
CHARLES B. RANGEL

"Know guns, know peace, know safety. No guns, no peace, no safety."
UNKNOWN

GAFF

"There are two ways to go with extended magazines," the dealer guy said. "Check out this one. Holds thirty-six rounds. But because it's straight, it sticks out of the bottom about ten inches. If you're at the range, no problem; you're standing still and firing at a stationary target, and it's cool to not have to reload. But if you're in a self-defense situation, the extension could get caught on clothing, or bump against shit. Not ideal."

The dealer wielded a semiauto with one of those long mags, and it looked ridiculous. Impossible to conceal, and I wouldn't be able to swing it around without whacking it on something.

Cancelled.

"Going in the other direction, there's the dual drum." He picked up a mag that had curlicues on both ends, like Leia's cinnamon roll hairdo in Episode Four. "Holds a hundred rounds, and because it curls up on either side of the magazine port, kinda like ram horns, it's much easier to aim and maneuver. But when this is fully loaded, it's heavy."

Heavy would be a problem. I wanted to start lifting weights, but I never got around to it, and arm strength wasn't my thing. With a giggled-out Merican, keeping it on target would be hard. I didn't want added weight.

Can't even.

"Now the smart alternative, and what all the competition shooters prefer, is the GOB Donut Drum." When he said it he spelled out the letters G and O and B. "Holds fifty rounds, has a lever to hold back the internal spring for easy loading, and only sticks out five inches from the bottom of the magazine well."

GOB? That was what the other guy said about the paperweight.

"What is GOB?" I asked.

The guy smiled, revealing brown teeth. "GOB. It's a company, specializing in accessories. Good Ole Boy Incorporated. Manufactured right here in the US of A. By Mericans, for Mericans."

I wasn't sure if he was talking about Mericans the people, or Mericans the gun brand. But the Donut Drum was badass.

"What about jamming?" I asked.

"Guns are mechanical. Sometimes they jam. Clear it like you would any other jam."

"How do I do that?"

He didn't sneer @ my ignorance. Props. "Release the magazine, pull back the slide until the bullet or casing falls out, replace the magazine, load the next round."

Made sense. "How much?"

XCQ and Tobacco Teeth exchanged a look.

"It's seventy-five for one, hundred twenty-five for two."

"How about six?"

Tobacco teeth smiled so wide I could see the chaw stuck in his gums. "Six? Sounds like you're getting ready for the zombie apocalypse. For six, I'll do you my preferred special customer rate of three twenty-five."

The guy looked happy as a pig in shit when I gave him cash.

He spat in a cup and said, "Shoot well. That many GOB Donuts, you'll be able to defend yourself against dozens of zombies. Maybe hundreds."

Hundreds would be hella. But they weren't going to be zombies.

I turned to XCQ. "How about laser dot?"

He winked. "Follow me. I know a guy."

"*The fact that you own a gun and shoot to defend
your life is a very American way of thinking.*"
ISABEL ALLENDE

"*No guns but only brotherhood can resolve the problems.*"
ATAL BIHARI VAJPAYEE

JACK

After the meeting ended and goodbyes exchanged, guns were the furthest thing from my mind.

"I don't want to see the shrink, Mom."

"You promised you would."

"I lied to you so you'd leave me alone."

"When was the last time you saw a psychiatrist, Jacqueline?"

When I worked homicide, I had to do mandatory psychiatric sessions every time I shot someone.

So I'd seen a few psychiatrists.

But it had been years since I'd sparred with a head doctor, and I didn't want to do it again. I remember struggling to offer just enough information and emotional feedback to fool them into thinking I was normal and not a barely functioning mess.

"Phin and I are seeing one," I lied. "A marriage counsellor. I didn't tell you because I didn't want you to worry."

"How did that happen?"

"We're going through a rough patch."

Mom tsked me. "How did it happen that you rose to the rank of Lieutenant when you're such a terrible liar?"

"I'm a good liar," I lied.

"That's a lie. You're awful at it. And you're seeing Dr. Agmont."

I changed tactics. "I don't like him."

"Why?"

I didn't want to ping Mom's bullshit detector, so I opted for truth. "He's too handsome."

Dr. Agmont had the dark, chiseled good looks of a cover model for Italian GQ. And to make it worse, he knew how to dress. My husband, for all of his charisma, dressed like a Levi's commercial from 1988. I once bought Phin an Armani jacket, and he looked miserable as a dog in a sweater. I exchanged it for a leather bomber and a subscription to Beef Jerky of the Month, and that suited him fine. Then I spent the leftover money on a pair of Isabel Marant ankle booties that I can't wear anymore because; crippled.

"What does that have to do with him being a good doctor?"

"I don't like being around him. He makes me feel inadequate."

"He's young."

"That's another problem. He's too young to teach me anything about myself."

"*Jung*. As in Carl Jung. He can get to the root of your core complex."

"I don't have a core complex."

"You have an inferiority complex, and your ego is bifurcated be-tween caregiver and hero because of your animus issues."

"I have no idea what you just said. And neither do you."

"It means you feel bad about yourself for a lot of reasons."

Couldn't argue with that. "You really like this doctor."

"He looks like Michelangelo's David, but with a bigger bulge."

I folded my arms across my chest, the universal symbol of defiance. "I'm not going."

"You're going."

"You can't make me go."

She made me go. Physically made me, pushing me through the high winds—which were now complimented by a fierce drizzle that stung like microscopic wasps—over to Building A.

"Just want you to know I'm calling a lawyer to be emancipated from you," I told her after we got inside.

Mom didn't answer. I turned to her, and she looked like a walking corpse.

"You okay?"

"Just cold, and a little unsteady."

"I'm calling a nurse." I began to wheel away, and she pulled my brake lever.

"I'm fine."

"Mom ... "

"I'm fine, Jacqueline. Go to your appointment."

My mother was the strongest person I ever met, and when we locked eyes the strength was still there.

"I'm not ready for this," I said, my voice cracking.

"It's just a little psychotherapy."

"Not that. This. Being responsible for my elderly mother."

Mom smiled kindly. "We're not there yet. I plan on being around to see Sam grow up." She placed her hand on my damp hair. "And to see you walk again. Meet with Dr. Agmont. Call me when you're done."

I wanted to say something, but my words were the truest I'd ever spoken. I wasn't even semi-competent at being a parent to Sam. If something went wrong with Mom, I didn't have the strength to deal with that.

Let alone be responsible for her.

"Can you just talk to a nurse? You don't look good."

"That's not what Mr. Feinstein said."

"I'm serious, Mom. See a nurse."

"I promise. Give Dr. Agmont a big, sloppy kiss from me."

When I took the elevator to A21 I did not give Dr. Agmont a big, sloppy kiss. My resentment at being there had brewed to the point of boiling over, and the last thing I wanted to do was talk to a PhD who looked like a swimsuit model.

When I wheeled into his office, Dr. Agmont was hanging a framed Rorschach inkblot on the wall. He turned and smiled at me, his teeth so white and straight and perfect that he looked like a real-life toothpaste ad.

"Good morning, Jill. I'm adding some decoration to the office. What do you think?"

"Are you asking me what I think of decoration, or what I think the inkblot looks like?"

"Both."

"I think decoration is a way to distract from the mundane, and I think the inkblot resembles a woman in a wheelchair strangling her mother."

Dr. Agmont squinted at the picture. "Most people say *butterfly* or *jazz hands*. But I think I can see it. A concerned mother, forcing her wounded healer daughter to go to counselling."

He sat in his desk chair, crossing his legs, again looking like he was ready for the photographer to start snapping away. His face, his body, his clothing; all impeccable.

I hated him.

Not just because he was prettier than me. But because I had an immediate anti-chemistry with people who had their shit together, and my visceral impression of Dr. Agmont was that he did everything perfectly. I pictured an Ivy League school, maybe with a tennis scholarship, a supermodel wife who also ran her own company, and on weekends they ran couples' marathons to benefit kids with cancer.

Not my kind of people. I liked mine damaged and self-loathing.

We played the not talking game for twenty long seconds, and I broke first.

"So I'm a wounded healer?"

"Your mother told me you teach gun safety classes to residents, when you yourself were injured by a firearm. The wounded healer is an archetype. By trying to help others, you are in fact trying to help yourself."

I folded my arms across my chest, then unfolded them because; defensive. "My mother says I'm doing it to feel useful."

"You could feel useful by volunteering at a soup kitchen. Or teaching origami. You're teaching the very skills that injured you, physically, mentally, and emotionally."

"Physician, heal thyself."

"Am I being inaccurate?"

Thunder cracked outside the window, loud enough to make me flinch. Dr. Sexy Smartypants raised an eyebrow. "Have you ever been diagnosed with PTSD, Jill?"

"No. Have you ever been shot, Doc?"

"I haven't. I can't even imagine the trauma. Do you want to talk about it?"

"No."

He was quiet. I was quiet. A whole lot of quiet went on for about a minute.

"Ever been in a car accident?" I asked, mostly because I was growing uncomfortable at him staring at me.

"Not anything serious. My worst injury was breaking a leg."

"Bad break?" I'd much rather ask questions than answer them.

"They had to carry me down the Southwest face to base camp. Compound fracture, laid me up for two months. Still have eight screws in my femur."

"Mountain climbing?"

He nodded.

"Which mountain?"

"Everest."

Of course it was Mt. Everest.

"Did you reach the summit?" I asked, hoping he didn't.

He gestured with his perfect cleft chin, and I checked out the wall behind me.

Blown-up pic of Dr. Agmont, on top of Mt. Everest, smiling wide. Under his diplomas from Yale and Princeton, and a picture of the Dalai Lama embracing him.

What a dick.

"So getting shot is like being in a bad car accident?"

Sort of. "The trauma is there. The way time slows down. The pain. The memory that won't go away. But car accidents usually happen out of nowhere. They blindside you. Imagine a car accident where the driver is trying to hit you. Coming at you at ninety miles an hour. And the only way to survive is to hit them first. And even if you do ... "

I shrugged, gesturing at my useless legs.

"Do you think about it a lot? Being shot?"

I didn't answer.

"How about nightmares?"

"I take Ambien. That pretty much knocks me out. No dreams, so nothing to psychoanalyze there."

I studied the inkblot on the wall again. I didn't see me and my mother anymore. I saw me pushing a smarmy psychiatrist off a mountainside.

"Why do you think your mother wanted you to come see me?"

"Because I'm an unhappy bitch."

"Do you want to be happy?"

"What I want," I said, "is to not be in a wheelchair."

"It's common for people who are injured to resent life."

"Did you resent life, when the Sherpas were carrying you down Mt. Everest?"

He gave me what he thought was a disapproving look, but all the handsome bastard did was smolder.

"Jill, for psychotherapy to work, the work has to be on you. If you don't want to be here, there's nothing I can do to assist the healing process."

I crossed and uncrossed my arms again. "I need my T11 vertebra healed. Not my psyche."

"There's a mind-body connection. A positive mental outlook can speed up healing time. Conversely, a negative attitude can delay recovery."

He wants to go there?

Fine. I'll go there.

"I can't walk. My husband is probably cheating on me because the last time we had sex—which was months ago—I lost control of my bladder and pissed all over the bed, and him. I don't think we have any money to continue my rehab much longer, because my husband—a career criminal—keeps his finances separate from mine, hiding cash in the garage in the rafters where I can't reach. And because of my old job, there is at least one, possibly several, serial killers actively looking for me. So explain what sort of visualization exercises I can do to improve my mental outlook."

He kept his face neutral. "How is your relationship with your daughter?"

"We used to play tag, hide and seek, go to the beach, swim in the pool. Now our relationship is beating up each other in videogames and me trying not to cry around her because then she starts crying."

He crossed his legs and made a tent with his fingers. A goddamn tent with his fingers. Who does that?

"Videogames can be a healthy, bonding experience. Did you know the GameMaster 2 is being released tomorrow?"

"I'll ask my criminal husband if he has any money left over from his bank jobs."

Dr. Agmont's thoughtful expression dimmed a little. Score one point for me.

"How about your squad?"

"My squad?"

"Your fam. Your posse. Your friends."

Jesus, was I the only one who didn't speak plural?

"I've been out of touch for a while."

"Why is that? When you're at your lowest, that's when you need those who love you."

"What's to love, Doc? I'm a shell of who I used to be. Crippled. Scared. Helpless. I can't keep up a relationship with the man I cherish and live with. How am I supposed to stay connected with my out-of-state friends?"

"Are you on social media? Skype? Facetime? Snapchat? How about a good, old-fashioned phone call? There are lots of ways to connect."

I wanted to connect. My fist and his nose.

I hated that he was smart and good looking and climbed Everest and was trying to help me.

I also hated that he was probably right. My mental outlook was shitty, and reaching out to my squad was a no-brainer.

"You're right," I said. "I don't want to be here."

"I won't keep you. And if you change your mind, my door is always open. But I'd like you to do something for me."

If he said he wanted me to smile, I would have actually smacked him. But instead he said, "Reach out to your friends. I'm betting they need you."

I snorted. "Need me? I can't even help myself. How am I supposed to help them?"

"Wounded healer, remember?" He smiled. "It was a pleasure speaking with you, Jill."

He held out his hand to shake. When I took it, I caught a whiff of sandalwood.

Of course he smelled like sandalwood. I bet when this guy took a dump, it smelled like hot cocoa.

Nothing made you feel worse about yourself than being around someone better than you. I wondered how he had any clients at all.

Oh, right. He worked in a retirement home. His patients had no other choice.

So why the hell did he work in a retirement home?

I took my hand back and asked, "Hey, Doc, if you don't mind me asking, why did you choose to practice here? I would have figured you for New York or LA."

"The elderly have one of the highest rates of depression in the country, and they are the least likely age group to seek treatment. I went where I thought I could do the most good."

I smiled politely at the sanctimonious jerk, then wheeled out of there.

Mt. Everest.

Helping old people.

Smelling great.

Telling me shit I needed to hear.

I really hated him.

Almost as much as I hated myself.

"Remember the first rule of gunfighting … have a gun."
JEFF COOPER

"With the right to bear arms comes a great responsibility to use caution and common sense on handgun purchases."
RONALD REAGAN

GAFF

So who is it?" XCQ asked as we weaved through the peeps.

"Wha?" I didn't understand the question.

"You're obviously concerned about self-defense, and in this crazy world, that concern is valid. So who you worried about? Who you wanna protect yourself against? Islam extremists? Declaring jihad on America. Jews? Control the banks, the media, and Hollywood. Mexicans? Coming here illegally, taking our jobs. Blacks? Don't know their place. Libtards? Special snowflakes trying to take away our God given right to bear arms. Teachers? Poisoning the youth of America with their standardized bullshit. Co-workers? Those assholes don't understand anything, and don't get me started on bosses. Queers? It's Adam and Eve, not Adam and Steve. Those pro-choice dickheads? Killing innocent babies, worst form of birth control ever. Catholics? Got a Pope protecting child molesters, but still wants to lecture us about sin. Cops? Bullies with badges. Wall Street? Took our jobs, ruined our future. Who is it? Who gets under your skin?"

I shrugged. "I don't care about any of that."

"Really?"

"Don't care what any of them do."

"What do you care about?"

The highest body count possible. But I wasn't going to talk about that.

"You got a manifesto?" he asked.

"What's that?"

"You know. Like a mission statement. Writing down all your thoughts about all the things that piss you off."

"Like a diary?"

"More like a declaration. Something you share with the world."

"I don't want to share anything with the world."

I want to blow it the eff up.

"Cool. Not trying to pry or nothing. Just making conversation."

"So who gets under your skin?" I didn't care, but figured we were doing give and take. One of my shrinks said that's how people communicate. Answer a question, ask a question. Made no sense to me, but I wanted a laser sight.

"The anti-gun movement gets under my skin. Bunch of whiny little babies trying to take away our Constitutional rights."

"I thought you'd like those guys."

He snorted. "Yeah, right."

"Every time they try to make a new law regulating guns, don't gun sales go up?"

XCQ stopped and stared @ me. "You with the ATF?"

"What?"

"This some kind of entrapment sting? You got a wire on?"

ATF? WTF was this jag talking about?

"I thought you were showing me laser dots," I said.

He stared @ me a moment longer, then nodded. "Right. Sorry. I get paranoid sometimes. Angry. You ever get paranoid and angry?"

Bruh, you have no idea.

"Dots?" I reminded him. People were so extra.

"Right. Dots. My guy is just a few booths over."

The guy he knew rocked dreads and wore green Air Jordans that matched his dashiki.

"What kind of rail?" he asked.

"Picatinny," XCQ answered. "XCQ-TER9."

"Red or green, mon?"

I looked @ XCQ.

"The tritium sights on your weapon are green. The human eye detects green better than red. And if your target is already bleeding, a red dot might get lost."

"Green," I told the dread guy.

My cost: $50. The box had a familiar logo on it.

Good Ole Boy. Again.

I wondered if XCQ's side bitch was GOB.

#Kickbacks.

Next we looked for silencers, er, compensators. The gun show was starting to burn me out. Too much noise, too many people, too many things moving and talking, too distracting. I must have been blinking more than usual, bcuz as we weaved through the endless piles of booths and tables and peeps, XCQ stopped to stare @ me.

"You cool?"

"Totes."

He nodded, and we found the booth he was looking for. He talked to the seller, but I wasn't really paying attention, trying to tune out all the noise around me. The dude XCQ negotiated with had a mustache, and I focused on his mouth until I could zoom in on what he was saying.

" … no such thing as a real silencer. A bullet is a controlled explosion. Can't silence an explosion. But a suppressor can reduce the sound, especially for subsonic ammo. Even better when wet. This model compensates for tip up, mitigating recoil and helping you stay on target. Besides muzzle break capabilities, it has a flash hider, so you won't give away your position at night."

I understood some of that, but one part really confused me. "Better when wet?"

"It can fire dry and reduce the noise. But if you use an ablative media, it really cuts down on the sound."

"Ablative—?"

"There are lubes, foams, gels. Squirt a little in the suppressor every few rounds. But good old water works fine."

He handed me the suppressor, and I was surprised by the weight.

I was even more surprised by the price.

"Six hundred."

Day-am. That was more than the gun cost.

I squinted @ the tube of metal, finding the logo mark.

GOB.

Go fig.

"That's a lot of money."

"It's a lot of tech," said the mustache guy. "It's not easy to suppress a gunshot. Do you know anything about suppressors?"

I shook my head.

"There are three noises made when you fire a weapon. The mechanical sound of the firearm. Can't really do much to muffle that. The sound of a gunshot is actually muzzle blast, the hot propellant explosion hitting the cool air, which is what the suppressor is for. It cools the hot gasses with baffling, perforations, and wipes. It can also slow down supersonic rounds, so they don't crack when breaking the sound barrier. Follow me so far?"

I nodded.

"Subsonic 9mm rounds are about 150 decibels. Fire one next to your head without ear protection, you'll burst an eardrum. This suppressor, wet, takes it down to 110dB. About the noise of a rock concert."

"That's still loud."

"Guns make noise. But it's all about how far away you are. No suppressor, the decibel level at a hundred meters away drops to 110dB. With the suppressor, from a hundred meters the weapon is about as loud as tapping on some piano keys. You can hear a rock concert from five hundred meters. You can't hear a piano. Big difference."

Still sounded shifty to me.

"My dude here just bought an XCQ-TER9," XCQ said, patting my shoulder. "Can we offer the special client discount?"

The mustache guy rolled his eyes. "Everyone you bring over is a special client, Barney."

XCQ looked pissed. Maybe bcuz this mustache guy wouldn't haggle. Or maybe bcuz he called him by his name.

"I can take the kid somewhere else," XCQ/Barney said.

"Five-fifty. Been a shitty show. Haven't even covered the booth fee yet."

"Five-fifty is a great deal," Barney told me.

I forked over the $550.

"You've got yourself a great set-up, my dude. Great set-up. Now all you need is some ammo."

"I can find my own," I said.

I was certain Barney would take me someplace that only sold GOB ammo, and I was done with this clown and his squad of clown kickback griefers.

"Great set-up, my dude!" Barney called after me as I walked away. "Great set-up! You are buffed AF!"

I wanted out of the gun show, so after one final buy (to follow my ninth rule) I got the hell out of there, locking my purchases in the trunk with the XCQ-TER9, and then heading for the supermarket.

They had ammo. And I had a feeling I'd get a better deal there than I'd gotten @ the gun show.

Fo sho.

"An armed society is a polite society."
ROBERT HEINLEIN

"How many have to die before we will give up these dangerous toys?"
STEPHEN KING

JACK

called Mom. No answer. So I wheeled over to her building, the rain so bad that it soaked me, the wind so bad that it made the rain feel like ice. Getting to Mom's room, I found her in bed, sleeping, blessedly alone.

I didn't wake her, but I did make use of several of her towels and one of her old blouses. Dry enough to think again, I considered Dr. Agmont's suggestion.

I'd had a lot of low points in my life. This might have been the lowest.

Maybe getting in touch with my squad wasn't the worst idea ever, even if it came from a smarmy metrosexual with a handful of degrees.

I fished out my cell phone.

My mother calls my father an energy vampire. He's a nice guy, loving, but talking with him sort of saps the strength out of you. The kind of person where you could put the phone down, come back in five minutes, and they'd still be talking, not even knowing you were gone.

I called him anyway.

"Jack! So wonderful to hear from you! We need to catch up!"

He caught me up on his new boyfriend, his recent bunion surgery, his Roth IRA, his ongoing feud with a neighbor whose dog kept crapping on his lawn, his Netflix queue, his centrist political views (and he actually had an argument with himself about the two party system), his opinions about intermittent fasting supplemented with bone broth, and the problems he encountered while trying to assemble a *Tyssedal* from Ikea, the whole time using enough details to fill a book.

It was an hour I'd never get back.

But it did feel nice to hear his voice.

Dad did inquire about my life, too. Mostly questions about Sam and asking to send more pictures, concerns about Hurricane Harry, questions about Mom, and concerns about how my rehab was going.

Whereas Dad was specific, I kept things vague. Probably not what Dr. Agmont wanted when he suggested I reconnect with my fam, but it was enough for me to check my father off the *must call* list, at least until next week.

Or maybe next month.

I followed that call with one to Herb Benedict, my best friend and ex-partner. Calling Herb was always weird, because the basis of our friendship revolved around solving cases. While I'd spent more time with Herb than I had with my husband, much of it had been small talk and work talk and comfortable silences while on stakeouts.

We didn't get personal too often. Especially on the phone.

At least, I thought we didn't.

"I'm back up to a hundred and eighty," he said.

Herb had recently lost a lot of weight because of a horrible ordeal that I played a big part in. Weight was also a subject he usually didn't want to talk about.

"Bernice's cooking finally catching up with you?"

"No. I do all the cooking. Lots of protein, healthful fats, keeping my carbs under twenty grams a day. My gain is muscle."

That was something new. And strange.

"Seriously? You're weight training?"

"Circuit training, mostly. Did you see my new Facebook pic?"

"I have not." I wasn't on Facebook, for the same reasons I was living in Florida under an assumed name. Putting a pic of myself online carried some serious risks.

My cell buzzed, and I pulled it away from my ear to view the picture Herb texted me.

Whoa. He wore a shirt so tight you could count his six pack, and his biceps were popping.

"Holy shit, Herb. You're ripped."

"I know, right? Who would have guessed there were muscles under all that fat."

"And that beard is … an interesting choice."

"Like Hugh Jackman, in those superhero movies."

Actually, he did sort of look like Hugh Jackman. Which was a real mindjob, because during the decades I'd known Herb, the celebrity he most resembled was Dom DeLuise.

"You look fantastic."

"Thanks. Rough year, so I'm trying to make lemonade out of lemons. Didn't kill me, so it made me stronger. You know?"

In theory, I knew. In practice, I wasn't doing so hot. "Every tragedy is a lesson."

Even if the lesson is to give up.

"How's things going down south? You batten down the hatches for the hurricane?"

"Phin has." At least, he was supposed to.

"Hurricane Harry. Of course it's named Harry. You talk to that jackass lately?"

Herb and Harry McGlade had a love/hate relationship. They loved to hate each other.

"No. I've been focused on the rehab."

"Last I heard, McGlade was in LA. Something high profile. He actually asked if I wanted to work with him on a case. Did he call you?"

"He left me a few messages."

Twenty-nine messages in the last two weeks.

McGlade was a private detective, and we'd been working together for most of our lives. It hasn't always been pleasant, but we shared a bond forged by decades of fighting side-by-side, even though he irritated me.

Harry thought himself to be funny, and every once and a while he was. Thanks to a recent bit of Internet fame his already large ego had gotten even larger.

"He offered me an insane amount of money, but I promised Bernice I was retired. Some sort of plastic surgery case, people getting disfigured. You should think about it. Getting back on the horse."

Screw the horse. I answered, "Huh." The standard non-committal response.

"How's rehab? Walking yet?"

"Getting better every day," I lied.

"How's things with Phin?"

"Better than ever," I lied.

"Sam?"

"She's good." That wasn't a lie.

At least I hoped it wasn't a lie.

Thunder shook the windows and I startled, flinching in my chair hard enough to make my back spasm. I stretched, getting the pain under control, as Herb battered me with questions about Sam, along with a promise to send pictures.

We small talked for a bit about our families, and that segued into how some of our old cop acquaintances were doing.

"You get Tom's Christmas card?"

"Yeah."

Tom Mankowski used to work under me in Homicide. After surviving a particularly nasty attack, he moved to California with his significant other, Joan, and his old partner, Roy. The Xmas card was a picture of Tom and Roy on a boat they'd bought to use for a fishing charter business.

Tom had also called me a few times this past month. He was on my squad list to call back.

The conversation meandered to Herb's new eating habits and workout routine, and my mind wandered, wondering what Phin was doing.

Or, more precisely, *who* Phin was doing.

I interrupted Herb sharing a recipe for lamb chops and asked if he'd heard from Tequila, another old mutual acquaintance of ours.

"Sure. We train together at the gym on Thursdays. We're running a 5k in September."

"He doing okay?"

"He's back to his old self. You know; quiet, intense, sociopathic. I think he's dating someone."

"Really? He told you that?" Tequila was notoriously tight-lipped, but he'd gone through the same ordeal as Herb, and maybe it had changed him.

"No. He barely talks. You know that. But a few weeks ago, I saw him smile. He denied it, but I know I saw it. I'm thinking it's a lady."

Well, good for Tequila.

"Jack, I don't want to sound weird, but it's time for my protein shake. If I don't eat every three hours, my metabolism slows down. Can I call you back in ten?"

Yeah, that didn't sound weird at all. "How about we get in touch next week? I'm on my way to my rehab session."

"Sounds great. Kick some ass. And great catching up with you, partner. My love to Phin and Sam."

"My love to Bernice. And tell Tequila I said hey."

We hung up.

I tried to tune into my feelings.

Did reconnecting with Dad and Herb make me feel better?

Worse?

Anything?

Maybe I felt a little better. A little more connected.

Which made me dislike Dr. Agmont even more.

I wheeled into the bedroom. Mom still slept.

I considered waking her, to talk. Then I remembered she'd been up all night with Mr. Feinstein and his ED pills, and figured I should leave her be.

I paged through my text messages, and decided I'd had enough of reconnecting with my squad. Still had two hours before my rehab session.

Eat?

Mom's fridge didn't contain any ready to eat food, and I didn't feel up to cooking. So I grabbed a fresh towel, stuck it in a garbage bag, and risked braving the storm and heading on over to Building A. The cafeteria pizza was edible. Not deep dish Chicago style, but greasy enough to fill my need.

The rain had calmed a tad, but the wind was insane. Ridiculous, considering Hurricane Harry still wouldn't make landfall for another day. I'd seen big storms on TV and the Internet, usually with some reporter standing in the middle of gale force gusts, yelling above the noise while debris blew through the background. But I couldn't imagine how the wind could get worse than this. It took every bit of my energy to get to the cafeteria, and I knew I'd need Phin's help to get to the van when he picked me up later.

I resented asking him for help.

Lately, I resented everything.

I toweled off in the lobby, trying not to draw too much attention to myself as I tried to get my labored breathing under control.

Naturally, the café had no pizza. I built my own comfort meal with a baked potato, pulled pork, and chili mac and cheese, and found my table from breakfast, next to the tree.

My lizard buddy wasn't around. Maybe he'd actually heeded my warning and got the hell out of Florida before the hurricane came.

I ate in joyless silence for a few minutes, indulging in my uplifting habit of scanning the crowd for threats, and saw Mrs. Shadid come in.

We made eye contact and exchanged the universal *I see you* nod, and she got in the food line.

I hoped she'd had enough of our earlier conversation and didn't want to sit next to me, because I'd had my fill of talking for the day.

Hell, I'd done enough talking for a whole week.

Naturally, Mrs. Shadid came up to me. And, naturally, she had a slice of pizza on her tray.

"May I sit with you?"

Shit.

I nodded. "Pizza, huh? I didn't see any."

"Just came out of the oven."

Of course it did.

We ate in semi-comfortable silence, my chili mac keeping a lid on its pizza envy, and eventually Mrs. Shadid spoke.

"Why should we have guns at all?"

Great. Here we go again.

"Make no mistake about it. Gun control is not about crook control. It's about America control."

DERRICK GRAYSON

"We don't have a gun problem; we have a math problem: ZERO GUNS = ZERO GUN-RELATED DEATHS."

QUENTIN R. BUFOGLE

GAFF

The supermarket had a whole aisle of ammo to choose from, but without a cell phone I couldn't go online and compare different brands. I settled on one that had 147 GRAIN 9MM JACKETED HOLLOW POINT SUBSONIC written on the box. On sale.

From what I remembered about researching hollow point ammunition, it had greater stopping power, but less penetration. That would suit my purpose. And subsonic meant it wouldn't break the sound barrier, so I didn't have to rely on my overpriced suppressor to reduce velocity.

SBD. Silent but deadly.

Buying on sale also made me look less like I was planning a mass shooting, and more like a thrifty shopper stocking up on a good deal.

I bought a whole case of 1000 rounds, for just $179.99 plus tax.

#GodBlessAmerica.

The cashier didn't even ask me for ID.

Eager as I was to load up my new XCQ-TER9 and start shooting, I had prior plans for the afternoon.

Exciting plans.

The third reason I moved to South Carolina plans.

I jetted back to my crib without getting lost, took all my shit inside, and laid my purchases out on my foam mattress.

Sick.

#Sick.

I jonesed to start assembling everything, but instead stuck it all in my suitcase, zipping it up. Then I powered on my laptop and checked for the email I needed.

To: Guthrie Slessinger
From: Fardkork Correctional Center
Guthrie Slessinger,

Your Adult Visitor Application and Background Investigation Authorization Form has been reviewed and accepted, and you are pre-approved and listed in the VACORIS Visiting Module as an approved visitor for Tully Huffland, Offender ID 381341C. Please review attached Form 851-1 General Rules for Visiting Room Operation. For questions and comments, you may contact the Department of Corrections Offender Management Unit.

Tight.

Time to go to prison, yo.

I don't get scared. When I was a shawty, Moms freaked out a lot bcuz I did stuff other kids didn't do. When I was six I slipped through a loose bar to get a closer look @ a tiger @ the zoo. First time I saw a swimming pool I jumped right in and sunk to the bottom. Opened a window and crawled out on the ledge of the twentieth floor of this child shrink she took me to. Went under the kitchen sink and found all these bottles of cleaner, and the caps were child proof so I punched holes in them with a knife so I could taste them all.

Fear didn't affect me. Horror movies were lame. Extreme stuff on the dark net, like RealGoreDeaths or Usher House 2.0, with vids of people being tortured and killed, gave me a little twinge in my gut, sort of like that feeling when you balance on two legs of a chair and almost fall over, but I never got scared by them.

Driving up to the Fardkork Correctional Center gave me one of the biggest twinges of my life. If I was into sex I would have called it sexual.

The guard towers. The razor wire on the fences. The stark, gray, concrete building with bars in the windows…

On brand.

I pulled up to a booth b4 the big gate. Some guard, a wannabe cop in a dorksuit, checked my ID against names on a list and told me where to park. I went to the prison website @ least fifty times, so I knew what I could wear, and what I could bring inside. They had lockers you could rent for a quarter, but I left all the prohibited items in my car. All I had on me were my driver's license, car key, and ten dollars in quarters. Prisoners wore white and black striped jumpsuits, so I wore blue jeans and a green t-shirt bcuz you couldn't wear anything striped. (You also couldn't wear miniskirts or halter-tops, but I was chill there, bruh.)

After parking, I went into the Visitor's door and checked in with a receptionist. I had to go through a metal detector, putting my change and key in a bin that got X-rayed. After walking through, I got a pat down. A guard dog also sniffed me, looking for drugs.

Totes serious.

Then I had to wait for about ten minutes, b4 a different guard told me that Tully had visitation privileges restricted, and I'd only get to see him in a No Contact room.

Sux.

I brought the change bcuz I wanted to share a soda with the dude and buy him a candy bar.

Next time.

The guard led me through a series of hallways and security doors, and then told me to wait in Box 6. I opened the door, and saw a chair and a big glass window, and an old-fashioned phone on the wall, like in the movies. Room smelled like lemon bleach. Tully wasn't there yet, so I sat down and waited.

#NotScary.

I spent a lot of time thinking about my spree, and even with all my planning, I knew there was a possibility I could get killed, or captured.

Death didn't scare me. Death was just death. Like sleep without dreams. I wasn't a little baby who believed in God or the devil or hell or nothing. If I got killed, no biggie.

But I didn't have any 4sure feelings about prison, bcuz I didn't know what to expect.

So far, I wasn't afraid. So far, it was like going to the DMV.

Being locked up was one of the things I wanted to ask Tully about.

A few minutes passed, and then a guard brought in a man wearing prison stripes, his hands cuffed, a chain extending down to ankle cuffs.

I felt a twinge.

Tully Huffland didn't look as big as he did in Internet clips. He also looked a lot older. Barely an adult when he and Gregory Taylor Schneider became the Suburban Eliminators and caused the Rathlin High School Massacre of 2009, he now appeared ancient, like forty years old, with a receding hairline and sunken eyes and a tattoo on his cheek of the number 24.

He sat across from me and stared like a zombie, then picked up his phone.

I did the same.

"You're Gaff. Kid that wrote to me."

I nodded, and for a moment I forgot my list of questions, forgot my list of how to act around people. Routine eventually kicked in, and I said, "Hey, Tully. How you doing?"

"Restricted privileges for two months. Some asshole got touchy feely, and I shanked him in the kidney."

Cool.

"What's it like, being inside?"

"It's like Disneyland. They got all these rides and attractions, and all the drugs you want, and free whores to suck you off."

That didn't sound right. He was probably being sarcastic.

"You look good."

"You sweet on me, Gaff?"

I shook my head. "Just saying you been locked up ten years. You're keeping it tight."

He nodded, then adjusted in his chair, his posture relaxing a little.

"Prison's a'ight. I get by. Miss the pussy. Miss the outside. But it's bearable. Dude can get by, know what I'm saying?"

I didn't really know what he was saying, but I think he confirmed my beliefs. I could handle prison, if it came to that.

We stared @ each other for a little bit.

"You're thinking about it," he said.

I shook my head. "Done thinking. I'm doing it."

After a pause he said, "School?"

"Lots of schools have metal detectors now, thanks to you and Gregory."

Hard to tell, but he seemed to appreciate that. "What's your plan?"

Tully Huffland was probably the only living person that I felt any kind of respect for, but telling him my plan would be stupid. Every time I trusted someone, I got burned. Tell doctors my feelings, and they put me on whack meds. Tell Moms what's on my mind when she asks, and she freaks out.

"You get TV in here?" I asked him.

"Yeah."

"You'll see," I said. "Tomorrow."

He smirked. The smile vanished as quick as it came. "You ever kill anyone, Gaff?"

I shook my head.

"Ever shoot a gun?"

Another head shake. "Just bought one." That made me remember one of my questions. "What's it feel like?"

Tully sat up a little straighter, and he seemed to get bigger all over. "It's loud. Louder than you think. Gotta wear earplugs. Eye protection, too. And it hurts your hands after you fire off a bunch. Makes you feel like you're in a movie or a videogame, know what I'm saying? That kind of rush."

I didn't get a rush from movies or videogames, but I nodded bcuz that seemed right.

"How about the rest?" I asked.

"What's it feel like to kill someone?"

I nodded.

Another smirk. "I can't describe it. When you do it, you'll know. It's like a new part of you opens up, shows you who you really are. Know what I'm saying?"

I waited for more. More came.

"I can tell you this, Gaff. I been in this shithole for ten years. There's stuff to do. TV. Music. Games. Weights. You can read, if you're into that shit. You can even get drugs and booze, and get your willy sucked. But the thing I like most is closing my eyes and ... *remembering*."

I wondered what that felt like. I remembered a lot of my life, but didn't like any of it.

It would be high key to remember something I actually liked.

"So it's worth it?"

"Hells yeah it's worth it. I envy you, Gaff. And I don't regret shit. You know what this is?"

He held the phone receiver to his cheek, pointing @ his tattoo. I nodded, and he put the phone back to his ear.

"Twenty-four victims," I said.

"Twenty-four life sentences," he corrected me. "But I can still get parole. Might take another forty years, but my lawyer said it's possible. One of the things the parole board will ask, is if I'm sorry about what I did. If I regret it. And they'll ask what I want to do when I get out. You know what I'm gonna tell them assholes? That killing those people was the best thing I ever done in my life, and if they let me out I'd do it again in a heartbeat, no questions asked. You know what I'm saying?"

I think I did know what he was saying. I nodded.

A guard came for him, and he smiled @ me. "Good to meet your acquaintance, Gaff. Come back and see me again when I'm off restrictions. I'd be proud to shake your hand."

He hung up and shuffled away.

Fire.

On the way home from prison I stopped @ the supermarket again.

For earplugs.

I also bought some plastic shooting glasses, tinted yellow to reduce glare, a pack of fifty latex gloves.

Gotta have protection, yo.

"In Chicago, which has the toughest gun laws in the United States, probably you could say by far, they have more gun violence than any other city. So we have the toughest laws, and you have tremendous gun violence."

DONALD TRUMP

"You can't put a gun in the hands of someone who represents a danger to themselves or society."

THOM TILLIS

I pushed away the rest of my chili mac and let out a slow breath.

Mrs. Shadid wanted to resume our conversation.

I did not.

But when was the last time I got what I wanted?

"Studies have shown that when there are fewer guns available, there are fewer gun deaths," she said. "Look at Australia."

In 1995, after a spree shooting, Australia passed the National Firearms Agreement law. It put severe restrictions on firearm ownership, created a national firearm registry, and the government bought back almost 700,000 firearms from citizens.

"The NFA significantly lowered the firearm homicide rate in Australia," I said. "But some studies have shown the overall homicide rate wasn't affected. People kill each other at the same speed. They just found other ways to do it."

"I read that it eliminated mass shootings."

"There's no way to be sure the NFA directly influenced mass shootings. Remember that spree shooting isn't a gun problem. It's a mental health problem. In Japan, where guns are scarce, people with that same mentality go on stabbing sprees."

Mrs. Shadid scowled. "You're diverting. You know you can do a lot more damage with a gun than a knife."

"True. But to play devil's advocate, if we take away all guns, what's to stop a disturbed student from stockpiling kerosene and burning down his high school? Do we ban all fossil fuels?"

Which, honestly, I wouldn't object to, considering how oil has screwed our planet and been responsible for countless wars and deaths.

"You keep being provocative, Jill. And going way off the subject."

"Trying to keep things lively."

"Or trying to veer away from the main point. Knives and fossil fuels have specific purposes that don't involve harming others. Guns have a single purpose; to hurt people."

"I'll disagree there, Mrs. Shadid."

"Please, call me Sowa. Let's go back to the Australia law. Wouldn't a US government buyback program eliminate a lot of the guns?"

I eyed her pizza, then picked at my chili mac, raising a lukewarm, bland forkful to my mouth.

"Some. Maybe. In Australia, a lot of people sold broken, unworking firearms back to the government. But do you think a gangbanger, who uses a gun to protect himself from rivals, is going to sell his firearm to anyone, ever? Or the millions of Americans who hunt for sport? Or hunt to eat? Or shoot recreationally? And even if there was a buyback program, we'd have no idea if it had an effect."

"Why not?"

"No one knows for sure how many guns there are in the USA. Three hundred million is an agreed upon estimate, but no one keeps track."

"That doesn't make any sense."

Actually, it did.

"I've heard it said that there are only two reasons why the government would want to keep tabs on gun ownership. To tax them, and to take them away."

Sowa nibbled her pizza. "Sounds like more paranoia."

"Maybe. But every year we need to buy a new license plate sticker. No one likes it. Every year we have to pay property tax on land we own. No one likes it. And since the average gun owner has more than eight firearms, good luck passing a law that registers firearms. Plus, there's the privacy issue. Do you want the government to know everything about you?"

"If you have nothing to hide, who cares if the government knows?"

This was an easy argument to defuse. "Would you like cameras in your house, recording and broadcasting every single thing you do, twenty-four hours a day? Every private moment? Every conversation?"

"Of course not."

"Then you believe a person deserves privacy. We're just arguing over how much privacy."

I pushed my plate away again and studied the room.

A man had entered that I'd missed during my last scan. Thirties, wearing sunglasses indoors, and an ankle-length duster jacket with all sorts of bulges in it.

My threat level kicked up to yellow, and I felt more uneasy about this guy than I did that teen earlier in the day. I considered my .38, under my seat. Locked and unloaded. I'd practiced, and it took me twelve seconds to get my revolver in hand, loaded, ready to fire.

If this guy had an automatic weapon with a large magazine, he could kill all twenty-two people in the cafeteria before I even got my trigger lock off.

"So you think everything is okay with guns in the USA?" Sowa asked.

"What? No. I think everything is messed up."

"What's the solution? Arming everyone?"

I shook my head. "The more guns there are, the more gun deaths there are going to be. That will always be the case with anything. More cars, more car accidents. More skyscrapers, more ice falling off the sides of buildings and killing pedestrians. More hamburgers, more people choking to death on hamburgers."

"So let's restrict guns. Ban all new guns from being manufactured or imported into the US. Supply and demand will make the costs of guns skyrocket, out of the hands of criminals."

"And out of the hands of law-abiding citizens. Remember, there are more lawful gun owners than there are criminals with guns, by a large percentage. Besides, prohibition doesn't work. Look at the War on Drugs. Trillions of dollars spent, and drug use is as widespread as ever. When the regular market doesn't provide, the black market will."

The guy in the duster had wandered over to the buffet line, staring at donuts through the sneeze shield. His long coat was still closed.

"You're doing it again. Objecting to a good idea because it won't solve everything. If that's your attitude, why do anything? Seatbelts and airbags don't save all lives, so why force auto manufacturers to equip them?"

"Fair enough. Let's consider your idea. No more guns made in the USA, no more guns imported. We still have over 300,000,000 guns that already exist in America, which will still be bought and sold and traded and passed along."

"So that's a reason to not restrict gun sales? The laws of supply and demand state that those guns will become more expensive and harder for criminals to get."

"If a criminal wants a gun, he'll find a gun. New guns will be smuggled in from other countries. Guns will be created on 3D printers. Or maybe guns will be replaced by something else. Muggers with sulphuric acid. Homemade bombs. Chainsaws. There will always be people that want to harm others, and they'll always find a way."

I knew that all too well.

"You're back to saying we shouldn't do anything because nothing will fix everything."

"I understand your argument, Sowa. I'm not saying that. Something needs to be done. There will never be a solution that solves America's gun problem. But I believe legal firearm ownership can be regulated much better than it is now."

She leaned in closer. "How so?"

"In the case of firearms, people should be required to pass a test and get a license the same way they need a license to drive a car. The laws on the books need to be enforced. Guns should be registered, and every transaction should require a background check. In the case of two private sellers, they should still go through a licensed firearm dealer, and there should still be a waiting period between purchase and delivery. Gun manufactures should be required to disclose how many guns they've sold. Gun safety should be taught in schools."

Mrs. Shadid chortled. "You want to give children guns? That's insane."

"You're saying it's okay to put a sixteen-year-old behind the wheel of a one ton vehicle that goes a hundred miles per hour, but it isn't okay to teach one how to handle a gun?"

"Teaching gun safety just encourages gun ownership."

"If it's good people owning guns, how is that bad?"

"It would also teach bad people about guns."

"The bad people learn anyway," I said. "They seek guns out. And they use them against good people. It isn't a coincidence that most active shooting situations happen in gun free zones. If a mugger, or rapist, suspects that a possible victim is armed, will they risk going through with the assault? What if it was something as simple as a red bandana that reads I'M ARMED? If that even became somewhat widespread, it wouldn't matter if the person was armed or not. They'd be avoided by predators."

The duster guy began to stride quickly across the room, and I was surprised enough to reach for my compartment under my seat just as I saw the smile on his face as he embraced an older, shorter version of himself while semi-shouting, "Dad!"

Here to visit his father. Which was more than I'd done in quite some time.

My threat level dropped back to green.

"How about suicides?" Sowa asked. "More guns means more people killing themselves."

"Actually, it means more people killing themselves with guns. In Australia, gun suicides plummeted after the National Firearms Agreement. But other types of suicide, like hangings, rose in direct proportion. At least, according to one study. Another study refutes it."

Sowa pushed her half-eaten pizza away. "I've seen that same problem. One article says one thing, another says the opposite."

"The problem with most studies is bias. Those who fund these research projects often have agendas. We pass laws in this country based on big business and moral outrage and the corruption in our political system. We should be using science and facts. But that's less likelier to happen than the gun problem being solved. We're not a country of logic and common sense. We're a country of superstition and fear and envy."

"And the almighty dollar."

"Agreed. We can blame capitalism and big business for our gun problem as much as we can blame our lawmakers, and we need to blame ourselves, for voting those politicians into office."

"Because guns make money."

I nodded. "A lot of money. Billions of dollars."

"And not just for the gun companies. For all the places that sell guns, too. Like department stores. You can pick up a pair of sandals, a case of soda, and a semi-automatic rifle with a high capacity magazine and enough ammunition to kill dozens."

That seemed oddly specific, and then Sowa began to shake, and I realized where she was going with this. I reached for her hand, covering it with mine.

"That's what he bought," she said, voice cracking. "Richard Thomas Malkoveck. Shoes, soft drinks, a gun, and bullets. The store did a background check. He was a convicted felon, but the purchase still went through. The FBI called it an administrative error. An hour later, he came to our place of worship and killed my husband, my daughter, my son-in-law, and my fourteen-year-old granddaughter."

I answered honestly. "I can't imagine your pain, Sowa."

Her eyes went someplace faraway. Someplace horrible. "When the shooting began, none of us knew what was happening. It was so loud, but I thought it was a string of firecrackers. In a mosque … the last thing you expect … "

She choked up, and I squeezed her hand. It felt like holding my Mother's.

"He looked so calm, Jill. He walked toward us, shooting, shooting my friends and family and people in my community, he walked toward us and looked so utterly calm. Like we weren't people. Like we were a nest of rats he needed to exterminate."

I watched her tears, and thought about the loved ones I'd lost, and thought about what I'd do if something happened to Samantha.

It was beyond my comprehension.

"A neighbor pulled me out of there. Pulled me away from my family." Sowa took her hand back. "The police came. There was a brief standoff, and Richard Thomas Malkoveck was killed." She sniffled. "In some ways, the biggest tragedy came later. The killer's social media was filled with anti-Muslim rants. Hate speech. Threats. The day before, he actually wrote, 'I ought to buy a rifle and shoot as many of those camel jockeys as I can.'"

"No one reported that?"

"Oh, yes, it was reported. He was banned from the social media platform for thirty days. The police even went to his house, but they didn't arrest him. He told people he was going to do it, and they didn't arrest him."

Shit. That it should have been prevented made it even worse.

"Some people have something wrong with them, Sowa. Some vital part, missing."

"I know that. But these people with missing parts can buy weapons that can kill a dozen in seconds. And I know what you'll say. You'll say that if the guns weren't around, people like that would find other ways to kill people like me. Fires. Or bombs. But you can't buy a bomb at the supermarket, Jill."

I could have told her that making a bomb wasn't that hard to do, and that some went that route. I could have told her that racism and hate and cruelty have been embedded in our genes for thousands of years before the invention of firearms. I could have told her that the police failed in preventing the crime that killed her family, but the first responders no doubt saved lives, and they did so with firearms.

But this discussion was getting to me. Hard.

If I could snap my fingers and have all guns disappear, of course I'd do it. Just like I'd want to get rid of cancer, and hurricanes, and famine.

But if I could snap my fingers and get rid of bigotry, would I?

That one was tough. The Right to Bear Arms wasn't the only protected right in the United States. We have Freedom of Speech, which includes hate speech. We have Freedom of Religion, which encompasses many religions that despise one another. We have Freedom of the Press, but in this day and age of social media and clickbait and fake news being spread by twisted individuals as well as irresponsible professional journalists, bias proliferates our culture. And like it or not, that must include all of the ugly biases; racism, sexism, and pick-a-group-aphobia.

Without that freedom to be horrible, things could become even more horrible. Forcing people to agree with you just doesn't work.

Sowa snapped me out of my reverie by asking, "Have you ever lost a loved one to a gun?"

"Yes." More than once.

"And you've been shot."

"Yes." More than once.

"Can you tell me about how you were shot?"

"Some very bad people had some friends of mine," I said, automatically picturing Herb and Tequila. "Drug dealers. They had guns. A lot of people died. I got shot."

"Did you save your friends?"

I nodded.

"Was it worth it?"

I nodded again.

"Do you relive what happened?"

"Sometimes."

"Is it your worst memory?"

"I've got a whole pile of bad memories, Sowa. I don't know if it's the worst. But it's the most recent."

"All of these bad memories, did they involve guns?"

"Some of them." I reconsidered. "Most of them."

"And you still allow guns in your life? You still can't get away from them?"

"The guns aren't the problem. It's the people. There have always been those who want to hurt us. There always will be."

"Are you sure it isn't the chicken and the egg, Jill?"

I considered it. I carried a gun to protect myself and others from violence. But could all of the violence that I've encountered, that my loved ones have endured, be the result of my will to carry a firearm?

"That isn't it, Sowa. I was a cop. I made a vow to protect and serve. A gun is a tool I use to do my job."

"That's not your job anymore, Jill."

I had an answer. I could have asked Sowa if she would always be a mother, even though she lost her child. That would have been a horrible comparison, but a valid one.

I would always protect people. Badge or no badge.

It's what I do.

After silence, and some continued poking at the chili mac, Sowa spoke again.

"They called Malkoveck an active shooter. A rampage killer. A mass murderer. Have you ever been in a situation like that?"

I closed my eyes. "Yes."

"Can you tell me about it?"

I'd never talked with anyone about that incident. Not even Phin. "I'd rather not."

"Please, Jill. I want to hear it." She gripped my hand. "I need to hear it."

"Sowa . . ."

"This is so important to me, Jill. I've had so much counselling. I understand survivor's guilt. I understand the rage I feel. But I'm still a big, empty shell. A shell that nothing can fill. And I see that same thing in you. I see the pain. We can talk and talk about gun laws and gun safety and the Second Amendment, but that's all just talk. You have a similar experience to mine. I want to hear about it. And I want to hear how you feel about it."

This woman shared her worst tragedy with me. The least I could do was give her what she asked for.

"Fine," I said, swallowing hard. "It happened on duty . . ."

"An armed man will kill an unarmed man
with monotonous regularity."
CLINT SMITH

"If you're a terrorist, you shouldn't be able to buy a gun."
BILL NELSON

JACK

TWELVE YEARS AGO

A nd can you mega-size that meal deal?"

I reach over from the passenger seat and give my partner, Sergeant Herb Benedict, a poke in the ribs, except I don't actually feel his ribs because they're encased in a substantial layer of fat—the result of many years of mega-sizing his fast food meals.

"What?" he asks. "You want me to mega-size your fat-free yogurt?"

"No. You told me to point it out whenever I saw you overeating."

"How am I overeating?"

"You just mega-sized a triple bacon cheeseburger and a chocolate shake."

Herb shrugs, multiple chins wiggling. "So? It's just one meal."

"The mega-size french fries come in a carton bigger than your head. The shake is the size of a rain barrel."

"Be realistic here, Jack. It's only 49 cents. You can't buy anything for 49 cents these days."

"How about another heart attack? How much is that—"

My words are cut off by two quick pops from the drive-thru speaker. Though October, Chicago has been blessed with unseasonably warm weather, and my passenger window is wide open, the sound reaching me through there as well. It's coming from the restaurant.

Only one thing makes a sound like that.

Herb hits the radio. "This is Car 118, officer needs assistance. Shots fired at the Burger Barn on Kedzie and Fullerton."

I beat Herb out of the car, pulling my star from the pocket of my jacket and my .38 from my shoulder holster. I'm wearing flats and a beige skirt. A cool wind kicks up and brings goosebumps to my legs. The shoes are Kate Spade. The jacket and skirt are Donna Karan. The holster is Smith and Wesson.

As I near the building, I can make out screams, followed by another gunshot. A spatter of blood and tissue blossoms on the inside of the drive-thru window, blocking my view of the interior.

I hold up my pinky—my signal to Herb that there are casualties—and hurry past the window in a crouch, stopping before the glass doors. I tug the lanyard out of the badge case and loop it over my head. On one knee, I crane my neck around the brick jamb and peek into the restaurant.

I spot a single perp, Caucasian male, forties. I can't make out his hair color because he's wearing a black football helmet complete with face gear. Jeans, black combat boots, and a gray trench coat complete the ensemble. And under the trench coat...

An ammo belt.

Two strips of leather crisscross his chest, bandolero style. Instead of bullets in the webbing, I count eight magazines. Four more magazines are stuck into his waistband. I assume they're for the semi-automatic pistol in his hand, currently pointed at a family cowering under a plastiform table.

A mother and two kids.

Before my mind can register what is happening, he fires six times. The bullets tear through the table and into the mother's back. Blood sprays onto the children she's been shielding, and then erupts from the children in fireworks patterns.

I tear my eyes away from the horror and scan for more hostiles, but see only potential victims—at least twenty. Behind me, I hear footfalls and Herb's labored breathing.

"At least four down. One perp, heavily armed."

"You want to be old yeller?"

I shake my head and swallow. "I want the shot."

"On three."

Herb flashes one, two, three fingers and I shove through the door first, rolling to the side, coming up in a shooting position just as Herb yells, "POLICE! DROP THE WEAPON!"

The gunman swings toward Herb, I let out a slow breath and squeeze—angle up to discourage ricochets, aiming at the body mass, no ricochet because the shot is true, squeeze, the perp recoiling and stepping back once, twice, dropping the green duffle bag that's slung over his shoulder, squeeze, screams from everywhere at once, Herb's gun going off behind me, squeeze, watching the impact but not seeing blood—

Vest.

I scream, "Vest!" over the ringing in my ears and roll to the side as the gunman takes aim, firing where I was, orange tile chips peppering the side of my face like BBs.

I come up in a kneeling position behind a rectangular trash can enclosure, look at Herb and see that he's out of the line of fire, gone to ground.

I stick my head around the garbage island, watch as the perp vaults the counter, shooting a teenage cashier who's hugging the shake machine and sobbing. The back of the teen's head opens up and empties onto the greasy floor.

"Everybody out!" I yell.

There's a stampede to the door, and I glance back and see Herb tackled by a wall of people, then I take a deep breath and bolt for the counter.

The gunman appears, holding a screaming employee dressed in a Burger Barn uniform, using the kid as a human shield. Her face is streaked with tears, and there's a dark patch in the front of her jeans where she's wet herself. The barrel of his weapon is jammed against her forehead.

The perp says, "Drop the gun, Jack."

His voice is a low baritone, and it's eerily calm. His blue eyes lock on mine, and they hold my gaze. He doesn't seem psychotic at all, which terrifies me.

How does he know my name?

I stand up, adopt a Weaver stance, aiming for the face shot.

The gunman doesn't wait for me. He fires.

There's a sudden explosion of blood and tissue and the girl's eyes roll up and the perp ducks behind some fryers before her body hits the floor.

Too fast. This is all happening too fast.

I chance a look at the door, don't see Herb among the panicking people. I can't wait—there are probably more employees in the back. I dig into my blazer pocket and find a speed loader, hitting my ejector rod and jamming bullets into my revolver. When I leap over the counter, my gun is cocked.

No one by the grill. I glance left, see a body slumped next to the drive-thru window. Glance right, see a dead man on his back, most of his face gone. Stare forward, see a long stainless steel prep table. There's a young guy hiding under it. I tug him out and push him toward the counter, mouthing at him to "Run."

Movement ahead. The freezer door opens, and my finger almost pulls the trigger. It's another employee. Behind him, the perp.

The perp is grinning.

"Let's try this again," he says. "Drop the gun or I shoot."

I can't drop my gun. I'm not allowed to. It's one of the first things they teach you at the police academy.

"Let's talk this through," I say, trying to keep my voice steady.

"No talk."

He fires, and I watch another kid die in front of me.

I aim high, putting two rounds into the gunman's helmet, where they make dents and little else. He's already running away, pushing through the emergency exit, the alarm sounding off.

I tear after him, slipping on blood, falling to my hands and knees but holding onto my weapon. I crawl forward, my feet scrambling for purchase on the slickness, and then I'm opening the door, scanning the parking lot left and right.

He's standing ten feet away, aiming his weapon at me.

I throw myself backward and feel the wind of his shots as they pass my face.

"Jack!" Herb, from the front of the restaurant, voice faint because the gunfire is making my ears ring.

"He went out the back!"

My hands, slippery with blood and sweat, are shaking like dying birds. I force myself to do a slow count to five, force my bunched muscles to relax, then nudge open the back door.

The perp is waiting for me.

He fires again, the bullet tugging at my shoulder pad, stinging like I've been whacked with a stick. I scoot backward on my ass, turn over, and crawl for the counter, more shots zinging over me until the back door closes under its own weight and I climb over the girl he just killed, the scent of blood and death running up my nostrils and down the back of my throat.

I lean against the counter, pull back my jacket, feeling the burn, glancing at my wound and judging it superficial.

A soft voice, muffled, to my right.

"Hey!"

I see the green duffle bag that the perp dropped.

"Hello? Are you there, Jacqueline?"

The voice is coming from the bag. I go to it, tug back the zipper.

Gun. Another semiauto, a 9mm Dilton 76ETX. Loose bullets, more than a hundred. And a walkie-talkie.

"Jack," the walkie barks.

How the hell does he know my name?

"Can you hear me, Jacqueline?"

I pick up the radio and hit the talk button.

"Who is this?"

"I'm doing this for you, Jacqueline. For you and all the others. Do you remember Washington?"

Thoughts rush at me.

At least eleven dead so far.

He knows me.

The perp has over a hundred bullets left in his magazine bandolero.

I don't know this guy.

I've never been to Washington, the state or the capital.

He knows me.

Someone I arrested before?

Who is he?

I press talk. "If it's me you want, come and get me."

"I can't right now," the walkie says. "I'm late for class."

I race for the front doors. When I step onto the sidewalk, I see the perp darting through traffic and running full sprint down the sidewalk.

Heading for Thomas Jefferson Middle School.

I don't hear any sirens. Too soon. Look left and right, and don't see Herb.

I rush back into the restaurant, drop the radio into the perp's bag, grab the handle and run after him.

Three steps into the street I'm clipped by a bike messenger.

He spins me around, and I land on my knees, watching as he skids down the tarmac on his helmet, a spray of loose bullets from the gunman's bag jingling after him like dropped change. A car honks. There's a screech of tires. I manage to make it to my feet, still holding the bag, still holding my gun, too distracted to sense if I'm hurt or not.

The school.

I cross the rest of the street, realize I've somehow lost a shoe, my bare right foot slapping against the cold concrete, pedestrians jumping out of my path.

An alarm up ahead, so piercing I feel it in my teeth. The metal detector at the school entrance. It's followed by two more gunshots.

"Jack!"

Herb, from across the street.

"Cars in the parking lot!" I yell, hoping he'll understand. Guy in a football helmet and ammo belts didn't walk in off the street. Must have driven.

The school rushes up at me. I push through the kids rushing out of the doors and get inside, the metal detector screaming, a hall monitor slumped dead in her chair, blood pooling black on the rubber mat.

I drop the bag, pocket the Dilton and a handful of brass, hit talk on the radio.

"Where are you?"

Static. Then, coming through the speaker, children's screams.

Followed by gunshots.

I run, trying to follow the echo, trying to pinpoint the cries for help, passing door after door, rushing up a staircase, hearing more gunshots, seeing the muzzle flashes coming from a classroom, going in low and fast.

"Drop the gun," he says.

His Dilton is aimed at the head of a seven-year-old girl.

A sob gets caught in my throat, but I refuse to cry because tears will cloud my vision.

I can't watch anyone else die.

I drop my gun.

The perp begins to twitch, his face wet behind the football helmet.

"Do you have children, Jack?"

I'm not able to talk, so I just shake my head.

"Neither do I," he says. "Isn't… isn't it a shame?"

He pats the girl on the head, crouches down to whisper.

"You did good, sweetheart. I don't need you anymore."

I scream my soul raw when he pulls the trigger.

The little girl drops away, her pink dress now a shocking red, and I launch myself at him just as he turns his weapon on the children cowering in the corner of the room and opens fire.

One.

Two.

Three.

He manages four shots before I body-tackle him, both hands locking on his gun arm, pushing it up and away from the innocents, my head filled with frightened cries that might be from the children but might also be mine.

I grip his wrist and tug hard, locking his elbow, dropping down and forcing him to release the gun. It clatters to the ground.

His free hand tangles itself in my hair and pulls so hard my vision ignites like a flashbulb. I lose my grip and fall to my knees, and he jerks me in the other direction, white hot pain lacing across my scalp as a patch of hair rips free.

I drive an uppercut between his legs, my knuckles bouncing off a plastic supporter, then I'm being pushed away and he's leaping for the door.

My jacket is twisted up, and I can't find my pocket even though I feel the weight of the gun, and finally my hand slips in and I tug his semi-auto free and bury three shots into his legs as he runs into the hallway.

I chance a quick look at the children, see several have been hit, see blood on the wall covering two dozen construction paper jack-o-lantern pictures, then I crawl after the perp with the gun raised.

He's waiting for me in the hall, sitting against the wall, bleeding from both knees. I hear him sobbing.

"You weren't supposed to drop your gun," he says.

My breath is coming quick, and I blow it out through my mouth. I'm shaking so bad I can't even keep a bead on him. I blink away tears and repeat over and over, "he's-unarmed-don't-shoot-he's-unarmed-don't shoot-he's-unarmed-don't shoot … "

Movement to my left.

Herb, barreling down the hall. He stops and aims.

"You okay?" Herb asks.

I think I nod.

"Hands in the air!" he screams at the perp.

The perp continues to moan. He doesn't raise his hands.

"Put your hands in the air now!"

The sob becomes a howl, and the perp reaches into his trench coat.

Herb and I empty our guns into him. I aim at his face.

My aim is true.

The perp slumps over, streaking the wall with red. Herb rushes up, pats down the corpse.

"He's clean," Herb says. "No weapons."

I can hear the sirens now. I manage to lower my gun as the paramedics storm the stairs. Kids flood out of the classroom, teachers hurrying them down the hall, telling them not to look.

Many of them look anyway.

I feel my vision narrow, my shoulders quake. I'm suddenly very cold.

"Are you hurt?" Herb asks, squatting down next to me. I'm covered with the blood of too many people.

I shake my head.

"I found the car," Herb says. "Registered to a William Phillip Martingale, Buffalo Grove Illinois. He left a suicide note on the windshield. It said, *Life no longer matters.*"

"Priors?" I ask, my voice someone else's.

"No."

And something clicks. Some long ago memory from before I was a cop, before I was even an adult.

"I think I know him," I say.

William Phillip Martingale. Billy Martingale. In my fifth grade class at George Washington Elementary School.

"When we were kids. He asked me to the Valentine's Day dance." The words feel like stale bread crust stuck in my throat. "I turned him down. I already had a date."

"Jesus," Herb says.

But there was more. No one liked Billy. He had a bad front tooth, dark gray. Talked kind of slow. Everyone teased him.

Everyone including me.

I crawl past the paramedics, over to the perp, probing the ruin of his face, finding that bad tooth he'd never fixed.

The first body is wheeled out of the classroom, the body bag no larger than a pillow.

I begin to cry, and I don't think I'll ever be able to stop.

"*I don't think there should be more gun control.
I think there should be more education.*"
SAM BROWNBACK

"*Every gun sold should require a background check, period.*"
GARY ACKERMAN

JACK

I wiped away tears, and put my left hand over my right one and squeezed to stop the shaking.

"I'm sorry, Jill," Sowa Shadid said to me. "That's terrible you had to go through that."

When I found my voice again I said, "I'm glad I went through it, Sowa. If Herb and I weren't there, dozens more may have died."

She poked at her pizza. It no longer looked good to me.

"So that's the answer?" she asked, her voice soft. "The only way to stop a bad guy with a gun is a good guy with a gun?"

I shrugged. "I don't know if there is an answer. But I can't pretend this isn't the world we live in."

"The world we live in doesn't offer solutions, Jill. All we get is hopes and prayers. And those aren't enough."

I had no answer for that.

I had no answers for anything.

I just wanted to be able to walk again.

Sowa didn't want to discuss guns anymore, and neither did I. She took out her cell phone, showed me pictures of her niece. I took out mine, showed her pictures of Sam. We exchanged compliments on how adorable the children were, and I scanned the room for threats.

Thunder rumbled outside.

Hurricane Harry announcing himself.

"Can I tell you something I've never told anyone?" Sowa asked.

I was tempted to say no. I had too many friends I didn't keep in touch with. I didn't want to make more. Bonding with Sowa over stories of tragedy and pics of kids didn't make us BFFs.

Shit, now I was doing pluralspeak.

But, for whatever stupid reason I do things, I nodded at her.

"My husband. Kahlil. He owned a gun. He bought it after we got married. He insisted. 'To protect our home', he told me. I hated it. He wanted to teach me to shoot, but I was afraid to even touch it."

I didn't answer. I had an idea where she was going with this, and I didn't have any answers.

"Jill, I keep thinking about that day ..."

Here's proof I was no good at this relationship BS. I didn't want to stay and comfort her. All I wanted to do was run away.

"That day at the mosque ... if Khalid had brought his gun ..."

"Don't torture yourself like that, Sowa. I've played the *if only* game. It doesn't lead anywhere good."

"He had a concealed carry permit, Jill ..."

I closed my eyes, not wanting to hear anymore.

"I was the one who told him not to bring the gun to *masjid*. I told him weapons of death have no place in a house of worship."

This was my punishment for trying to win the debate. I just convinced a dear old lady to blame herself for the deaths of her loved ones.

I'm such an asshole.

"It's not your fault," I heard myself say, knowing full well that I would completely blame myself in her situation. "Even if your husband had been armed, there's no guarantee it would have ended differently."

"This haunts me, Jill. I wanted to talk with you to convince you that guns are bad. If I convinced you, maybe I could ... maybe I could forgive ..."

I lost her to sobs.

Shit. Shit shit shit.

"Sowa ..." I patted her hand. "I know about guns because they were part of my job. But my viewpoint is skewed by my experience and my opinions. Everything I said could be wrong. I'm not the one you need to be talking to. Do you know Dr. Agmont?"

She nodded.

"Have you ever met with him? Professionally?"

She shook her head.

"His office is one floor up. Why don't we go up there right now, see if he can squeeze you in?"

She nodded and stood up.

I went with her to the elevator, took her to Agmont's office, and he was so concerned about Mrs. Shadid's tears that he didn't even give me a second glance.

Dick.

I left Mrs. Shadid and checked the time.

Still an hour to rehab.

Normally, waiting around in the Darling Center had perks. I'm not ashamed to say I've killed some time in the Bingo room, open twelve hours a day. I wasn't the only moron donating her time to teach a class, so there were usually workshops, speakers, seminars, and group meetings going on in the various buildings. But I checked the schedule, conveniently posted on every floor, and almost everything was cancelled thanks to Harry.

Next to the cafeteria was an arcade, no doubt built to entertain bored grandkids. But I didn't have my leg braces and it was tough to play pinball or Ms. Pac-Man in my chair.

Of course, I had a computer in my pocket, aka my smartphone. Harry (the man, not the hurricane) had hooked me on a game called *Zombie Sugar Jackers 3: Lipsmacking Jackpacking*, but playing it any longer than five minutes required spending money, of which I had very little.

There were other cell phone games. Or ebooks, many of them free. Or I could mindlessly surf the Internet, ogling clothing and shoes that I could no longer afford or wear.

Or I could call a few more people on my squad and reconnect. That seemed the easiest way to get over the guilt from debating with Sowa.

So I went back to the cafeteria, found my table, and called Tom Mankowski, a Homicide Detective who used to work on my team and quit to live in La La Land.

"Jack! Great to hear from you. How's rehab?"

"About as much fun as you remember."

During a past case, a perp had done a number on Tom, and he'd spent many months on crutches, learning to walk again.

"My best memory is the pain meds. Why can't we buy fentanyl over the counter?"

"Because we have an opioid crisis killing fifty thousand Americans a year."

"Our country seems to have difficulties with moderation."

I considered the gun discussions I'd had with Sowa. "No kidding. How's Mrs. Mankowski?"

"Sexist, Jack. Joan didn't take my name. The patriarchal tradition of taking the man's surname is so twentieth century. You might as well ask me about her dowry."

Joan made ten times as much as Tom, so I didn't ask. "Did you hyphenate?" I tried to remember her name. "Mr. and Mrs. Mankowski-DeVilliers? DeVilliers-Mankowski?"

"No hyphen. I took her name."

I snorted. "You didn't."

"I'm Tom DeVilliers, trophy husband to one of Hollywood's most successful indie producers."

"You're so full of shit."

"Are you doubting that we're a gender progressive couple?"

"I'm doubting you'd give up your adoptive parents' surname, because I know how much it means to you."

"You got me. She stayed DeVilliers, I stayed Mankowski. Did you believe me for a minute?"

"No." But I smiled.

I watched a manager put up a CLOSED DUE TO WEATHER sign next to the register, and staff began to put away food. What they did with it, I had no idea.

Tom and I shot the shit. He talked about Joan's new movie, and his charter fishing business with Roy and some of the more unusual characters who'd hired them. I kept things light on my end, lying about rehab and my marriage and how peachy everything was.

Then Tom hit me for a loop.

"Jack … someone has been mailing me videos. Snuff videos."

My elevated mood plummeted back to ground zero. I knew a thing or two about snuff videos. It wasn't a topic I wanted to revisit.

"An old case?"

"You remember Walter Cissick?"

I winced. "The Erinyes murders."

"I think it's him. The first few vids were old. Sent on a pen drive, copied from videotapes. Clothing, hairstyles, looks like late 80s or early 90s. Six women. It's all really ugly."

I could imagine, even though I didn't want to. "Did you share with the Feebies, see if they can close some cold cases?"

"Of course."

"Is the FBI any better in LA than in Chicago?"

"No."

"You told Joan?"

"Of course. She hired bodyguards. We've got guard dogs. Crazy expensive alarm system. We both carry. Look … there's a reason I'm bringing this up. I know you're retired … "

"So are you," I reminded him.

"I know. But the last pen drive I was sent … Jack, it wasn't a copy of an old video. It looks new. Shot digitally."

"How do you know it's new?"

"She had a tattoo of the word THIRSTY."

"I don't get it."

"You know how English is always changing and evolving with new words and new meanings for old words?"

"All too well," I said, thinking of pluralspeak.

"*Thirsty* means *seeking approval*. Only been used for the last year or two. It's a new victim. He's become active again."

Terrible, but not my problem. The café began to clear out, until I was the only one left.

"I'm not a cop anymore, Tom. Neither are you."

"I know. All I want is to be able to discuss the case with you. Get your opinion. You've nailed more of these nutjobs than anyone. Your insight could help me—help the authorities—get this guy off the street."

"I can't watch any of those videos."

"You won't have to. I just want to schedule a time where I can fill you in on some details, pick your brain."

My first instinct was to say no. So was my second instinct. And third.

But for some reason I said, "I'll think about it."

"I appreciate it. I'm going to write down my notes, put together a file. Can I call you next week?"

"Sure."

"Jack … it was great talking to you. I'm glad you're doing well."

"Same here, Tom."

But when he hung up I didn't feel well at all.

At one point in my life, there was nothing more important to me than chasing monsters.

Now it was the thing I wanted least.

With a sour taste in my mouth, I scrolled through my address list and found someone who would be able to cheer me up.

Val Ryker. Another work friend from days long gone.

"The person you have called is unavailable. Please leave a message."

"Hey, Val. It's Jack. Nothing important, just calling to catch up. Hope all is good with you and Grace and Lund. Gimme a call when you have some time."

I hung up, then stared at my phone for a minute, wondering if she was screening her calls and I'd get a quick callback.

I didn't get a quick callback.

Who else was part of my squad? I knew a few spies. But, spies being spies, they weren't easy to reach. I could try to touch base with Tequila Abernathy, but as Herb had mentioned, Tequila was a man of few words. A phone conversation with him wouldn't amount to more than long silences and a few grunts.

All my other friends and acquaintances were dead.

Except for one.

I scrolled through his last few texts.

Jackie! Get in touch! Mucho important!

You still crippled? Call me!!!

CALL ME!!! DON'T MAKE ME YELL!!!!!!!!

I have work for you! Pays cray-cray $$$$$$!

Call back or I'm sending a dick pic!

Then he sent a dick pic, but the dick he sent was ten inches long, and black. My cop instincts guessed it wasn't his.

I need you on this one! The money is INSANE!

The next message was forty-seven lines of eggplant emojis. That was followed by a single middle finger emoji. Then came the latest.

I'm in Hollywood and really need your help. Please. It's not a serial killer. I swear.

The thing that caught me in that last text was the lack of exclamation points. I was used to Harry being rude and begging and yelling. Polite requests were odd.

So I gave my old dirtbag friend a call.

"We need to take the guns away from crazy people. But if you try to take my guns I'll shoot your eyes out and shove your balls in the empty sockets while they're still attached."

HARRY MCGLADE

"One must never place a loaded gun in a story if it isn't going to go off. It's wrong to make promises you don't mean to keep."

ANTON CHEKOV

GAFF

I kept getting twinges as I laid out all of my purchases on my sleeping bag.

Lit.

No FOMO here.

The Merican came in a case, with an instruction manual. I read it, cover to cover.

The GOB drum magazines didn't have a manual, but there were instructions online how to load. I put on some latex gloves and went to town. Took me half an hour to load all six, but I got faster as I went along. I also loaded the two mags that came with the gun, seventeen rounds each, and those were harder to load than the drums bcuz they didn't have a lever to hold the spring back. By the time I finished, I'd cashed my thumb from pressing in rounds.

Set.

The giggle switch—#Paperweight—also had net instructions, and I removed the backplate on the slide and installed it with some help from my Swiss Army Knife. The switch allowed me to select between SEMI and AUTO by flipping it to the left or right.

Pumped.

The laser sight fit on the underside rail and could be tightened by hand. It came with batteries—the tiny silver circle kind that looked like aspirin—and @ first it didn't work bcuz I put them in upside down. When I figured it out, and held up the Merican, aiming the green dot @ the wall, I was twinging and blinking so fast the world looked slow motion.

Fire.

The silencer-slash-compensator-slash-suppressor screwed on NP. Looked badass.

Buffed.

Valid.

I used two wet wipes to clean the weapon all over, making sure I didn't have any fingerprints on anything.

Stoked.

Flex.

When I picked up the loaded, pimped-out Merican and held it out in front of me, it felt like electricity running through my whole body.

I wanted to kill someone. Anyone.

But first, I wanted to see what I looked like, holding the gun.

I put on my black hoodie, my shooting glasses, and my rave mask. If y'all don't know, a rave mask is like a face scarf. Made of breathable nylon, it goes over your head and covers your neck and face up to your nose. You look like a bank robber. In my case, a bank robber with a giant mouth full of needle teeth.

I went into the bathroom, staring @ myself in the full-length wall mirror, and it was like I wasn't seeing me, but watching some hella ultra-violence movie. Srsly, I could almost hear the background music start to swell up right b4 I said something badass.

"I'm doing it for the lulz."

Then I whipped the gun up into shooting position—

—and totes cracked the mirror.

Fail.

#CyaSecurityDeposit.

The twinges disappeared, and I felt like I felt when I had to go see the principal or the school counsellor or my therapist.

The mirror had a big spiderweb crack in the center, about the size of a pizza, with a black triangle hole in the center where a shard of glass had fallen out. I checked the floor.

No broken glass.

I raised up my hand to touch the hole, careful I didn't cut myself, and my finger went inside. All the way in, up to the third knuckle.

WTF. Where's the wall?

I got my tactical flashlight, then went back to the bathroom and shined the light into the hole, trying to see inside.

It looked hollow, but the hole was too small to see much.

Eff it. The glass was already broken. I turned off the Powertac and held it butt first, smacking it hard against the mirror while keeping my head turned to the side.

A big chunk of glass fell into—

Holy shit. A big empty space behind my mirror.

I stuck my head through and turned on the flashlight.

The space was about a meter wide. I looked to the right, and it extended a few meters and then seemed to turn @ a corner.

When I looked down, I noticed two things.

First, there were a bunch of wadded up tissues on the plywood floor.

Second, when I looked @ the inside of the glass, I could see through it.

Someone had been watching me through a one-way mirror when I went to the bathroom.

That's why I heard giggling the other day. It wasn't in my head.

Cool as ice, I kicked out the rest of the glass, grabbed my Merican, pulled back the slide to load a round like the instructions said, switched off the safety, made sure the giggle was flipped to SEMI, and stepped into the space between the walls.

Feeling like back in middle school, roaming the halls, looking for a fight.

Chill.

It was dark, and my Powertac was bright AF, so I dimmed it down. The space between the walls wasn't quite wide enough for me to walk normal, so I had to do a sort of sideways shuffle, making sure I didn't get my feet caught on the 2x4 wooden framing boards on either side. I approached the corner turn, seeing nothing but plywood walls, occasional nails and screws poking through the plywood, and two more balls of tissue.

When I turned the corner, it was the same. Plywood, studs every two feet.

After a few yards I turned another corner and saw something shiny and bright on the wall ahead.

I turned off the flashlight and crept to it.

Glass. Staring through it, I saw someone's bathroom. Same layout as mine, with a clear shower curtain hanging above the bathtub, and a clear view of the toilet.

I shuffled around and stepped on something. Put on my light.

More wadded up tissue.

I continued down the hallway, taking a left and came to a four-way intersection.

I fished through my pocket, set down a nickel @ my feet, then kept going straight, taking right turns and left turns as the corners changed directions.

Found five more one-way mirrors, all in bathrooms, and then came up to the same intersection, my nickel still on the ground, but on my right.

I went straight, found another bathroom, and then after the next corner I found something different.

A panel in the wall between the studs, screwed on with hinges and springs.

I held my breath, listening.

Heard the faint sound of crying.

When I walked into the walls, I was all adrenaline and twinge and high key fire, so I hadn't noticed the weight of the Merican in my hand. As I listened, I realized my hand was tired from gripping it, so I changed to my other hand and wiggled my fingers.

Then, slow and easy, I pushed on the panel.

It gave a little resistance, but opened quiet. Prolly oiled. I peeked out an inch, saw a hallway with carpet. Well lit, so I killed and pocketed the flashlight and kept listening.

More crying. Sounded like a little kid. But not IRL. It had a tinny, fake sound, like speakers. A TV or computer.

I continued to push on the panel until I could slip through, then closed it softly. I was in an apartment hallway, the living room to my right, the bathroom straight ahead through a doorway. The sound came from my left.

I looked @ the panel I'd come through, saw it was a huge framed poster of a bunch of kids in black and white. On the bottom it said THE LITTLE RASCALS.

More sounds of a kid sobbing and begging *please no stop*. And other sounds.

A man. Grunting.

Grunting in real life.

I crept up on him like I'd seen spec ops guys do on YouTube, gun in front of me in a steady two-handed grip, walking in a slow and steady crouch, making sure I kept the Merican completely level.

I came to a doorway, then went through fast, and saw—

Marko. My creepy sus landlord.

He sat @ his desk in a computer chair, his back to me, about three meters away. A box of tissue was propped next to the big screen monitor showing computer porn of a little kid crying while a fat man rawdogged him from behind.

Marko had one hand in his big tub of sour gummy candy on the floor.

The other hand was in his lap, working his meat as he stared @ the screen.

#KillTheFucker.

I flicked on the laser, a dot of green appearing on the back of Marko's chair, dead center.

I put my finger on the trigger.

My blepharospasm went into overdrive, and I'd never had so many twinges in my life.

Unreal.

It all felt unreal.

It all felt so right.

But I couldn't do it like this.

I needed to look this pedo prick in the eyes.

"Hey, Marko."

Marko spun around in his swivel chair, fully naked, eyes comically wide, his legs kicking over the gummy candy, his fist still clenched on himself under the folds of his fat belly.

"Jesus! Don't kill me!"

I moved the dot up to his head, remembered that I'd never fired a gun b4 and hadn't followed the instructions to make sure the laser was properly adjusted, and switching my aim to his fat belly, aligning the dot with the fiber optic tritium sights.

He raised his hands up, palms out, his little dick waving @ me. "I'm sick. I have a disease. I need to get treatment. I never hurt nobody. I never touched nobody. All I do is look. I swear to god."

"You've been watching me in the bathroom."

"What? Who are you?"

I pulled down my rave mask, let him see my face.

"Guthrie."

"You've been jerking off while watching me."

"I would never—"

"Don't lie, you piece of shit. I know about the two-way mirrors. I saw the tissues."

He began to cry. "Please. I'll do anything. I have money. I'll do whatever you want. What do you want, Guthrie? Name it."

"I want you to be my first," I said.

"Your first? Your first what, honey?"

Honey?

I held the Merican tight with both hands and pulled the trigger.

It kicked like a cat I was trying to strangle.

The sound was crazy loud, so loud it stabbed my eardrums.

My aim was off, and instead of hitting his stomach, I hit Marko higher up, in the chest. He opened his mouth and might have yelled, but I couldn't hear him bcuz my ears were still shook.

He tried to get up, falling to his knees, his hands reaching out for me.

That's right. Come at me, bro.

I fired two more times.

The first missed.

The second hit the top of his head as he leaned forward.

His brains blurped out of his skull like I'd squeezed a plastic cup of vanilla pudding.

Sick.

OnPoint.

Lit.

Fire.

High key.

Somehow, even with half his head gone, Marko kept breathing for almost a minute.

#Curious.

After he stopped breathing, he twitched for a while.

#Wet.

After he stopped twitching, the blood continued to soak the carpet under him, stretching out slowly in an expanding oval.

I watched hard, memorizing every second.

4laterz.

4ever.

I'd remember this moment 4ever.

Maybe I stood there for five minutes.

Maybe it was an hour.

Pure sensory overload.

Everything I hoped it would be, and so much more.

Eventually, Logical Gaff nudged Emotional Gaff and told me to stop effing around.

Three shots fired. Even with the suppressor, they were loud AF. Shoulda worn my earplugs.

Someone could report it. 5-o could be on the way.

I needed to keep calm, figure out what to do.

Evidence? Did I leave evidence?

Shell casings. As I fired, the spent shells kicked out the ejector port of my Merican.

I'd loaded them while wearing gloves, so there wouldn't be prints. But maybe the cops could figure out where they came from.

I found two of them on the floor to my right.

Where was the third?

I searched around, and saw it had landed on a bookshelf, next to a copy of *A Clockwork Orange*.

We read that in high school. Real horrorshow.

Pocketing the brass, I tried to think of what the police would look for.

How'd I get in?

I didn't want them finding the hidden wall panel, bcuz that would lead to my apartment and my broken mirror. I signed the lease. It could be traced to me.

The lease had to be somewhere in this apartment.

I walked into the room, stepping around the widening pool of blood, and came to a file cabinet.

I found all of Marko's leases in the second drawer, and it only took me twenty seconds to find mine.

Into my pocket.

#Cake.

What else?

Only thing I touched was the panel when I came in, and I had on my gloves.

Shit... the cops would wonder how I got in.

I went to Marko's front door and unlocked it.

What else?

Footprints on the carpet?

I squinted @ the floor. It didn't look like I was leaving footprints, but I didn't know what sort of gadgets and gizmos 5-o had to figure out foot size and weight and shoe brand. Plus I probably had incriminating fibers all over my soles.

I need to 86 the shoes after I jet.

What else do cops look for?

Motive.

The motive was right there, on the screen. I did a quick inspection of Marko's computer, saw he was running Tor and a VPN, which would mask his browsing history.

Easy fix. I just paused the child porn video. When 5-0 showed up, they'd see what he was watching, know he was a pedo, and assume one of his victims caught up with him.

The only thing left for me to do was fix my mirror, and then there would be no evidence leading to me.

I wondered if I should search the apartment. Might be cash. Or guns. I could make it look like a robbery.

But then I'd be in deep shit if I got caught with any of Marko's stuff. #BadIdea.

I GTFO and weaved my way through the wall passage, remembering to stop and pick up my nickel @ the intersection, then made my way back to my apartment.

#ToDoList.

Clean up the broken glass.

Ditch my shoes someplace far away.

Buy a replacement mirror and hang it up.

My face felt weird. Tight. I touched my mouth.

I was smiling.

I NEVER smiled.

#GreatestDayOfMyLife.

Then someone banged on my front door.

Cops?

4realz?

Merican in hand, I crept to the door.

Can't let them take me.

Not now.

Not this fast, right after I got my first taste.

I flipped the giggle switch from SEMI to AUTO.

If they want me, they'll have to kill me b4 I kill them.

#BlazeOfGlory.

Another knock, louder this time.

I peeked through the peephole.

No shit.

Moms.

"I know you're in there, Guthrie. I can hear you."

Day-am. What do I do?

Kill her?

That would lead 5-o to me.

Ignore her?

Maybe she'll go away.

"Let me in, Guthrie. Or I'll go to the police and report my car stolen."

Day-am.

Think fast, Gaff.

Finesse.

"Gimme a sec. Gotta get dressed."

I hurried to the bathroom, put my Merican on the sink, and shut the door. Then I peeled off my latex gloves and shoved them into my pockets, and went to answer the door.

#WorstDayEver.

"Guns don't kill people; people kill people."
LAO TSE

"If guns don't kill people, why do we give people guns when they go to war? Why not just send the people?"
OZZY OSBOURNE

JACK

You've reached the voicemail of Harry McGlade, Private Eye. If you'd like to hire me for a lot of money, press 1. If you are an attractive person anywhere on the gender spectrum and would like to have sex with me, press 2."

I sighed. "I know this isn't your voicemail, Harry."

"If you think this isn't my voicemail, press 3."

I didn't press 3.

"Go ahead, Jackie. Press it."

"I'm going to hang up if you don't quit dicking around."

"Dicking around is my specialty. What made you finally call back? You broke? Lonely? Feeling guilty because you discarded our friendship just like a used condom after banging some whore with bleeding anal warts?"

I did not need that image in my head. "I've giving you five more seconds to get to the point and then I'm blocking your number."

"Testy. Rehab must be going bad."

"Rehab's going fine."

"You suck at lying. But enough about you. I'm in LA and need you on a case."

Can't stand up without braces, and hiding in Florida under a fake name, and suddenly I'm in demand. "I'm retired. And in a wheelchair."

"I knew you were lying about rehab. But the wheelchair is fine. Hollywood understands disabilities. There are ramps everywhere, wide doorways, and special seating at certain restaurants, accessible to the rear entrance in back so no one has to look at your pathetic crippled ass while you eat. Plus, you get the best parking spots."

Tolerance. That's McGlade. "I'm not chasing killers anymore, Harry."

"No killers. Simple skiptrace. I've been hired by a bunch of uber rich folks. They want me to find a guy."

"Missing person?" I hated myself for asking. Add yet another reason to hate myself.

"More like someone who wants to stay hidden."

"If it's simple, why do you need me?"

"This person has … how should I put it? This person has harmed a group of people and they'd like him found and brought to justice."

"So you want me to help you hunt down and kill someone. What is he? A rapist? Embezzler? Blackmailer?"

"None of the above. And we're not killing anyone. When we find him, we'll alert the authorities, and let the criminal justice system have him. The perp calls himself Plastic. Ever heard of him?"

"No." And I didn't want to hear about him. I was supposed to be reconnecting with my squad, not fielding job offers.

"Been in the news a few times on the West Coast. But hella more cases unreported. There's a group of fourteen of his victims who hired me, pooling together a shit ton of money. A metric shit ton."

The café had cleared out pretty quick. Staff had gone. Only me and two other tables left.

I didn't want to know what Plastic did, but at the same time, a small part of me wanted to know. Maybe I was born warped.

"What did he do to these people?"

"Various things. I'll be honest; it ain't pretty. You know how a plastic surgeon tries to fix flaws, make people look better? Well this Plastic dude is grabbing pretty people, and making them look worse."

"Torture," I said. "No way am I getting involved. I've had enough of torture."

"It's not really torture. When he does his, uh, his *procedures*, his victims are under anesthetic. They just wake up … altered."

"What do you mean, *altered*?"

"Well, one woman, he switched her hands and feet."

I wasn't sure I heard that correctly. "What?"

"He cut off her hands and feet, and stitched her feet where her hands went, and vice versa. Her new doctor said it was really one helluva complicated thing to do. He can't switch them back until she's fully healed."

I unconsciously looked at my hand and imagined my foot there. "That's horrible."

"Horrible, yes. But not as horrible as, say, Tibetan Screaming Sickness. You know, that virus that makes you scream until your throat rips itself out and you drown in your own blood."

"You made that up."

"It's a real thing. Really tough to treat, because no one wants to be around someone who screams all the time. In fact, most of the deaths are caused by care providers, who just want a little quiet. But you're getting off track. This Plastic guy, he's warped. But really skilled. He obviously has advanced medical training. The two of us should be able to track him down, no problem."

"No way in hell I'm working on a case like that."

"She was one of the more extreme ones. Other victims aren't as bad. Like one guy, Plastic turned his ears backwards. Another guy, he skin-grafted his pubic patch to his chin. I actually laughed at that one. Doesn't look too bad, either. I may do it myself."

"You're disgusting," I said, stating the obvious.

"I know. One woman, he moved her breasts to her back. Another, he removed her knees, so she can't bend her legs. But the majority are just basic disfigurement stuff. Like cutting off a nose. Or an unnecessary colostomy. Or doing lip injections until they're the size of pop cans. That one is strangely erotic, by the way."

"No."

"Let me tell you about the money. It's crazy."

Harry told me about the money.

It *was* crazy.

"McGlade, I'm hiding in Florida because I don't want psychos after me. I'm not going after some whackjob who is going to track me down and sew my labia to my forehead."

"Interesting imagery. But you wouldn't have to worry. The world thinks you're dead, so even if Plastic finds out someone is working with me—and he won't—he still won't know it's you. We catch him, he goes to jail for the rest of his life, and you go on living in anonymity with a metric shit ton of cash. It's no lose."

There's no such thing as no lose. There is always losing, and it's always me doing the losing.

"I'll think about it," I lied, to get him off the subject. "What else is going on with you?"

"Have you been following my webcast?"

"Of course."

I was not following his webcast.

"Since Heckle and Jeckle hooked up with the Cowboy, I've gotten a whole new crew. We do it once a week, in a studio. Getting crazy mad traffic. Movie and TV offers. Got a book deal. It's all good. Even cleared up my little problem with the IRS."

"So why are you going after Plastic?"

"Because that's what we heroes do, Jackie. We go after bad guys. It's who we are."

On Dr. Agmont's Jungian archetype scale, Harry leaned more toward jester than hero. And I was a wounded healer. My hero days were forever behind me.

"Dating anyone?" I asked, not really wanting to know.

"I'm a pansexual in Hollywood. I'm dating everyone. Did I tell you I was pansexual?"

Last I spoke with Harry, he'd come out as gender-blind, and decided his sole dating criteria was consent. As long as the person was willing and over the age of eighteen, Harry would bang them. Or get banged by them. Or both. Sometimes at the same time.

It was gross to think about, but also progressive in a nice kind of way.

"Yeah, you told me."

"Pansexual means I'll have sex with anything. Including pans."

He laughed at his own joke. McGlade does that a lot.

Not wanting to hear about his sexual escapades any more than I wanted to hear about my mother's, I changed the subject.

"How's your penguin?"

"Doing great. Got a great big pile of rocks in the living room. Still sleeps in the fridge. I had to give the Russian mastiff, Rosalina, back to Tequila, so I got Waddlebutt another pet friend to play with. You'll never in a million years guess what kind of animal I bought."

Harry told me, and he was correct. I never would have guessed it in a million years.

"Is that legal?" I asked.

"I dunno. Maybe. Maybe not. I'm rich and famous so I get away with shit. What's going on with you? You sucking at rehab?"

"I'm doing fine," I lied.

"How's Sammy? Harry Junior misses her."

"She's good."

"Mom?"

"Fine. Partying too much."

"No such thing. That insane cat kick off yet?"

"Not yet. He'll outlive us all."

"Phin cheating on you?"

With McGlade I never knew if he was joking or ignorant. Probably a lot of both.

"Everything's fine, Harry."

"That bad, huh?" He clucked his tongue. "Maybe it's your mental attitude. I've only been on the phone with you for five minutes, and you're already bringing me down. It's like my will to have fun is being sucked out of me."

You and me both, pal.

I changed the subject. "Had an interesting talk about gun control yesterday."

"With who? Some entitled social justice snowflake who gets offended by people protecting themselves? Or some wingnut extremist bigot who thinks you should give every cis white baby a 9mm the moment it pops out of the Christian womb?"

"All Americans aren't that polarized, McGlade."

234 • J.A. KONRATH
234 • J.A. KONRATH

"Really? Look at the news. Or social media. Or outside your window."

"It was a calm, rational dialogue."

"With a fellow American? You're kidding."

"That's the problem. It isn't *us* vs. *them*. It's all *us*. We just need to understand each other better."

"Save that crap for the commune, hippie. Wait a sec...have you gone full Brady Act just because you took a tiny little bullet in the back? Christ, Jackie, I've been shot plenty of times, and I still love guns. Hell, I lost my hand."

"Your ex-wife cut off your hand," I reminded him.

"She cut off my fingers with tin snips. But do I support a tin snips ban, leaving maybe dozens of professional tin workers unemployed? I do not. I would proudly march in any parade supporting tin workers. Especially if it was a naked parade."

The last few stragglers left, leaving me alone in the cafeteria.

"I'm not against guns. You know it's impossible to have a conversation with you that isn't defensive?"

"Stop being stupid."

"Case and point."

"You're the one that called me, Jackie."

"I called you back."

"It's still on you."

Actually, it's on Dr. Agmont. "I called just to have a conversation. Not to argue and take sides."

"Isn't that what a conversation is?"

"A conversation is give and take."

"Okay, I'll give you my opinion, and you can take it. I love guns. Love them like a mama lion loves her cubs, but with sexual overtones. I love guns so much I make up my own gun quotes and have them printed on t-shirts. Want to hear some?"

"No." Damn you, Agmont.

"People aren't dangerous because of guns. Guns are dangerous because people are dicks."

"Not very good."

"Do guns kill? Of course guns kill. That's the point."

"Can you stop?"

"If we want to keep guns out of the hands of criminals, we need to keep criminals out of the hands of guns."

"That doesn't even make sense."

"A gun in the hand is worth two in the bush."

"Now you're not even trying."

"A gun in time saves nine."

That one sort of made sense, but at this point I wasn't giving Mc-Glade any encouragement for anything.

"I gotta go."

"You'll think about LA? How are you doing on money? I know your health insurance was shit-canned, and Phin's bank robbery stash has to be running low."

"He told you about that?"

"Sure. Phin and I talk all the time."

"Bullshit."

"We have an ongoing bromance."

I rolled my eyes. "Right."

"It's true. We have nothing but brospect for each other."

"I doubt that."

"You can't deny our bro love, Jackie. You'd probably say we're bromosexual."

"That's not something I'd say. Ever. And neither would Phin."

"I'm his Pillsbury Broboy."

And we're done. "I gotta go. There's someone on fire."

"Cool. Gonna have some brotato chips. Want me to send you a *Gun In Time Saves Nine* t-shirt?"

"No."

"I'll FedEx it. Cya."

He hung up.

Did I feel better?

I dunno. A little. Maybe.

236 • J.A. KONRATH

Sort of coincidental that both Harry and Tom lived in Los Angeles, and both wanted my help.

Maybe too coincidental.

Herb also mentioned it.

Could my mother and Dr. Agmont have conspired with my squad to try and motivate me?

I wouldn't put it past Mom. And Agmont was too sexy to trust.

If that were the case, should I feel good that my fam cared enough about me to try this?

Or should I feel even sorrier for myself because I was so pitiful I needed charity?

Thunder cracked.

I flinched.

I tried to think of a happy ending to my story.

But all I could think of was guns and psychos and pain and losing my husband and never walking again.

"I have a love interest in every one of my films: a gun."
ARNOLD SCHWARZENEGGER

"I have a very strict gun control policy: if there's a gun around, I want to be in control of it."
CLINT EASTWOOD

GAFF

When I opened the door, Moms didn't rush to hug me. There was no weeping. No speech about how worried she was. Moms didn't act like any of the mothers I saw in countless TV shows and movies.

She never did.

"Can I come in?"

She threatened to call the cops about her car, and the last thing I needed was the cops coming around after I offed my landlord, so I nodded and stepped to the side.

Moms took a quick look around the apartment. I couldn't read the expression on her face, but I knew she was judging.

#Disapproval.

I regretted not bashing her face in with the cast iron pan she made me carry for years.

"Have you been taking your medicine?"

"How'd you find me?" I asked.

"Your bank."

"My bank doesn't know where I am."

"You opened your account when you were a minor, Guthrie. I was required to be a joint account holder. I logged on to your account, saw one of your purchases was for the electric company, and called them to get your address."

"I'm not going back with you."

"I'm not asking you to."

I put my hands on my hips. "So why you here?"

"Two reasons. First, I want to tell you something."

Moms never told me she loved me. If she said it now, wouldn't have mattered.

But she didn't say it.

"You were a challenging child to raise. Maybe I did some things wrong. Maybe we both did. But I want you to know that I tried. I tried my best."

"You took me to doctors that put me on meds that messed me up."

"Guthrie … I hope you keep taking your medication. When you're off it, you get … "

"I get what?"

"Do you remember when you were six and we went to a farm? We saw a steer getting dehorned. You asked why they were cutting off the tips of his horns. Do you remember what I told you?"

One more bad memory. "You said it was being dehorned so it didn't cause danger to itself or others."

"Your medication is important. So is your psychotherapy. Dr. Halforth is worried about you."

"But you're not," I said.

"I had you when I was very young. Your father … he was in a gang. I was doing a lot of things I shouldn't have, during the pregnancy. When your father was killed, I tried to straighten out. Get clean."

"Hold up. Pops was killed?"

"He was shot. Right in front of our apartment. I saw him die."

I didn't know none of that.

Dope.

"I didn't want that life for you. I tried to shield you from a lot of things. Maybe I was wrong, but I did my best."

She started to get weepy. For me, or for herself, I couldn't tell.

"That's why you came? To say that?"

"And to give you this."

She reached into her purse and handed me a folded piece of paper.

"It's the car title. I signed it over to you. You'll need to go to a currency exchange and get the title transferred, and new license plates."

"Am I supposed to say thank you or something?"

"You're eighteen. An adult. What I think doesn't matter anymore."

I looked Moms dead in the eye and said, "It never mattered."

She nodded, wiped some tears off her face. "Long drive to get here. Can I use the bathroom?"

I actually considered it. Letting her go in there. Seeing my buffed Merican on the sink. Seeing her face as I picked it up and put forty-seven bullets into her.

Bye, Felicia.

That would feel good. But it would also be stupid. I could get away with killing Marko. Killing Moms would take a lot more finesse.

I couldn't deal.

"Naw. Toilet's clogged. Been waiting for the dude to come fix it."

"A clogged toilet is easy to fix," she said, trying to walk around me.

I got in front of her and stopped her.

"I said naw."

"Do you have a plunger?" Moms did a quick look around my empty apartment. "Do you have anything at all?"

I didn't answer.

"Fine. I'll go. Good luck, Guthrie."

"My name is Gaff. You think I don't remember, bcuz I was a shawty. That's what Pops called me. Gaff. Like the hook used to snag big fish."

Moms made a snorting sound. Coulda been a laugh. "Not like the hook. He called you Gaffe. G-A-F-F-E. And I think he was right."

She left without either of us saying goodbye.

I got on the computer and looked up *Gaffe*.

A blunder, error, or mistake that causes embarrassment.

Eff her. I shoulda shot the bitch.

I thought about grabbing my nine, running out after her, spraying lead.

But I didn't.

Maybe, someday, I'd pay Moms a visit.

But I had shit to do first.

I went to the superstore, bought new boots, a different brand. Also picked up a broom and dustpan, and a full-sized mirror that looked big enough to cover the hole.

My old boots went into the trash, and I changed into the new ones.

When I got back to my crib, I circled the block three times, looking for cops. Weren't none.

Inside, I swept up all the glass, and all of Marko's nasty-ass tissues. The mirror came with some mounting screws. I didn't have no screw-driver, but I remembered my Swiss Army Knife had one. When I was finished, looked good as new.

#PerfectCrime.

I took a long walk, threw away the bag of glass in a garbage can in front of a Burger Barn, and began to think about tomorrow.

Today I popped my murder cherry.

Tomorrow I'm going to crush an all-out killing orgy.

"Violence is an evil thing, but when the guns are all in the hands of the men without respect for human rights, then men are really in trouble."

LOUIS L'AMOUR

"I believe the Second Amendment will always be important."

JOHN F. KENNEDY

JACK

Mom didn't attend my rehab.

So much for her supporting my journey to wellness.

I sweated through it alone, unconvinced I was improving, unable to ask my nurse because her full attention was focused on the window and watching the deck chairs—stacked and tied down with a metal wire—flop around like kites on a string in the 100mph+ winds.

Rather than the parallel bars, the torture du jour was a four step staircase with handrails. Over the months spent laboring through physical therapy, I'd never managed even a single step. I could get my foot up there, but the rest of my body wouldn't follow, no matter how much I strained and pushed and pulled and grunted and stretched and swore.

So the session consisted of doing the hokey-pokey. Put one foot up, put one foot down, put one foot up, and shake like a spastic clown.

After languishing in futility for an hour, my earlier prophecy proved correct; I couldn't go outside on my own without blowing over, and Phin had to come in and get me. He's a strong guy, and still had to struggle to push me into the van.

Sam greeting me with a big hug, jumping into my lap. "Daddy says we're getting a GameMaster 2 tomorrow!"

I glanced at Phin in the driver's seat, but he made no effort at eye contact.

"Aren't you happy, Mommy? It launches with City Warriors 2! It has six new characters. Maybe you'll even be good at one of them."

I looked at my daughter, still faint traces of marker on her face. "Don't you miss running around the house with mommy playing tag?"

"I miss mommy being happy," she said.

Join the club.

When we got home, Phin asked if I wanted to help make dinner. He was doing shrimp fried rice.

"You can peel some shrimp. Scramble some eggs."

I declined. Sam eagerly filled my shoes. I sat and watched some TV talk show where lowbrow people threw chairs at each other, while Sam and Phin were in the kitchen, talking and laughing.

I switched to CNN and learned Hurricane Harry was now a Cat IV, and expected to reach the coast of Florida tonight.

"Did you clean the gutters?" I called to Phin.

"Yeah. Earlier today."

"Before or after you fucked some other woman?" I asked.

I didn't really ask that.

I didn't have the guts.

I didn't want to know.

What I needed to do was turn off the TV, roll into the kitchen, and help my family make dinner.

Instead I cried. Quietly, so they wouldn't hear me.

This was officially it. The lowest point of my whole life.

I'd been in danger too many times to count.

I'd been hurt, physically and emotionally.

I'd lost loved ones.

But I'd never reached these depths of hopeless despair.

Never felt desperation this intense.

I didn't see a way out.

All I could see was life in a wheelchair, losing my husband, growing estranged from my daughter, waiting around for one of those psychos from my past to put me out of my misery.

Not a happy ending.

But an ending.

That was the only hope I had left.

"One man with a gun can control a hundred without one."
VLADIMIR LENIN

*"When in doubt, have a man come through
the door with a gun in his hand."*
RAYMOND CHANDLER

GAFF

set a wake-up alarm on my desktop app for seven am, but I didn't need it. I was up all night.

Practicing switching out magazines.

Wiping down my gun bag and contents so there weren't finger-prints on anything.

#Thinking.

#Plotting.

#Revising.

This would be the biggest day of my life, and I'd planned hard for it. Approaches and maps and routes, contingencies and potential surprises.

I was pretty solid.

But I'd already broken the first two of Gaff's Eleven Rules.

When I wasted Marko, I did a small crime b4 the big crime (Rule #1) and I killed someone I know (Rule #2).

#BadGaff.

I also broke Rule #8, don't leave evidence. Those bullets I left in Marko's body could be traced to my Merican, bcuz of the rifling marks on the slugs. I wanted to kill a whole bunch of people today, and the cops could link those deaths with Marko's, and I could be a suspect bcuz my driver's license said I lived in Marko's building.

Fail. Shouldn't have broke my own rules.

#Paranoid.

All night, as I trained, I kept waiting for the sirens and the red and blue flashing lights.

All night, I tried to divvy solutions.

The smart thing to do was call it off. Wait until the heat died down. Move to a different state. Start over.

But I didn't want to start over.

I was jonesing to kill again.

Fiending.

I considered moving Marko's body. But that was like sexing up a big sack of forensic evidence, while the public snapped me. Too easy to be seen. Too hard to get away with. Even digging the bullets out of his body would cover me with his DNA.

#LetItGo.

So @ 6 am I dressed for the biggest day of my life.

Baggy jeans. Boots. Red shirt. My black hoodie. Rave mask around my neck. Shooting glasses in my pocket. Earplugs in another pocket (my ears were still cashed from yesterday.) My gun bag containing my buffed Merican, all six drum mags, my two extra mags, gloves, my helmet, and an empty garbage bag.

Then I needed to pack. Chill, bcuz I didn't have much. Suitcase, bedroll, two garbage bags worth of food and shit. Take maybe three trips to the car to load everything.

After today, I'd move to a new state. Get a new driver's license and a passport in case I needed to go to Canada or Mexico. Stay @ a motel until the heat died down and I was sure I wasn't on the FBI's Most Wanted list. Then I could rent a new apartment, and do it all again.

And if I was Most Wanted, I could get me a BitCoin wallet, hop on darknet, and score a fake ID. They were expensive, and no guarantees I wouldn't be scammed. And even if I landed legit tags, I had no addy to send them to. But it was an option.

#WorryLater.

#FocusOnTheNow.

The first thing I took to my car was my suitcase, my body armor inside. After I locked it in the trunk I saw the black and white parked in front of Marko's apartment, lights flashing.

#WorryNow.

I considered options.

Climb into the car, take off, go back to the apartment after 5-o leaves?

Negative. I had plans for the day. Plans that involved my arsenal.

My arsenal was still in the apartment. And the countdown to kill-time was tick-tick-ticking away fast.

Ignore the cops, keep loading the car?

Risky. I didn't want to get stopped with a weapon when someone in my building was just shot.

Approach the police, ask what's going on?

Misdirection and finesse might work. But it might also draw suspicion.

Best case scenario, cops don't see me @ all.

#Stealthy.

I waited for the pigs to go inside Marko's building and figured I had maybe three minutes before back-up arrived.

I hauled ass.

Trying not to look sus was harder than I would have guessed, bcuz thinking about being suspicious made me hyper-aware and that hyper-awareness was sus. It was like stepping into a pool of boiling water and trying not to think about being boiled alive.

I practiced expressions in the mirror a lot. I could fake happy and sad and bored and interested when I was looking @ myself, but I never knew if I could pull them off when I didn't have a reflection to check on. I tried to read people's faces like they were mirrors, and match how they stared @ me, but it always felt forced and fake.

Walking back to my apartment, I tried to appear relaxed, but I was blinking more than I wanted to. I had two garbage bags of stuff, my bed roll, plus my gun bag.

The gun bag was most important. My clothes, food, bedroll, toilet-ries—all that shit could be replaced.

At the same time, if I left stuff in the apartment, it could be traced back to me. My computer had a password, but that was crackable. My prescription meds had my name on them. I shoulda thrown that shit away. My prints weren't on file, but I'd left them everywhere.

#BadGaff.

If I'd just kept a lid on my anger, like everyone had been telling me for years, I wouldn't be in this bonked scenario.

Maybe I shouldn't have quit my meds.

Maybe I shouldn't have left Ohio.

Maybe maybe maybe…

I got into my apartment without being seen, and went through my options again.

I could wait it out. If cops knocked, I didn't have to answer.

But I'd miss my killtime window.

I could try to carry everything out @ once. Super sus. It would look like I was fleeing.

I went to the bathroom, checked the new mirror I'd installed. Put on a bored face. Tried to freeze it like that.

Then I grabbed my gun bag and left the apartment.

Back-up had arrived faster than I guessed, breaking my Rule #5; no response times.

If I kept breaking my own damn rules I'd be in jail b4 breaking any active shooting records.

I watched the cops out of the corner of my eye as I made my way to my car. One of them noticed me and began to walk over.

Okurrr. Don't want him to know my car, so don't want to head that way. I swerved directions, heading for the sidewalk.

"Hold on a moment."

Here we go.

The rules for dealing with cops are all about knowing your rights, and knowing what they are legally allowed to do.

A murder has been committed. They're looking for suspects and witnesses.

Being told by the cop to hold on was a tricky area that fell somewhere between a request and an order. Requests could be ignored. But if I didn't stop to talk to him, that could give him reason to suspect me, and then reason to detain me. And if that was an order, and I didn't stop, then things could escalate.

I stood to face him, hands @ my sides, making eye-contact and trying to look curious but not guilty.

He swaggered up and stood a few feet away, chest puffed out, about five inches taller than me. Standard cop outfit; black shirt and pants and shoes, badge on chest, radio above the badge, various patches, holster with gun, mace, cuff case, spare magazines.

"Do you live around here?" he asked.

"I don't talk to police."

He puffed up a little more. "Why is that?"

"I'm aware of my rights. I don't have to answer."

"What's in the bag?"

A gun. That I bought legally. But I don't have to tell you that.

"I'm aware of my rights, I don't have to answer."

"Let me see your ID."

"South Carolina doesn't have a stop and identify statute. I don't have to show you ID."

"Are you a lawyer?"

"I don't have to answer. Am I being detained?"

"There was a murder in this apartment building. Do you know anything about that?"

I know everything about it. I did it.

But the right to remain silent applies, pig.

"Am I free to go?"

"You know I can pat you down."

"No, you can't. I don't consent to a search. You only have the right to search me if you have reasonable suspicion that I'm armed and dangerous. I was walking, minding my own business, and stopped when you asked."

#ThanksACLU.

He hitched up his belt and stuck out his chest. "Why are you being so evasive?"

"Being aware of my rights doesn't constitute reasonable suspicion. I don't have to answer your questions. You have no right to search me or detain me. You certainly don't have probable cause to arrest me."

Even though I'm going to waste a whole shitload of peeps today. If this douche brought me in, it would be the biggest bust of his life.

But the law was on my side, not his.

"What's wrong with your eyes?"

"Officer, am I free to go, or are you detaining me because I have a medical condition?"

"What medical condition?"

"Since you haven't ordered me to stop, I'm assuming I'm free to go."

He stared @ me. I stared back, thinking about the Merican and 1000 rounds of ammo in my gun case.

"Were you here yesterday? Did you hear any gunshots?"

"Am I free to go?"

"I'm just trying to solve a crime here. Don't you want to help?"

"I'll ask again. Are you detaining me?"

After a few seconds of silence, he said, "Have a good day."

I nodded and walked slowly away, turning my back on him, feeling his eyes on me.

I got lucky. This cop played by the rules. He could have abused my rights, searched me and my bag, and arrested me on some bullshit charge. My gun was legal. The paperweight wasn't.

I probably would have gotten off with a good lawyer, and the giggle switch would be inadmissible bcuz of illegal search and seizure. But that would cost money, and take time.

I was running short on time.

After walking out of the cop's sight, I circled back, making my way to my car, careful I wasn't seen. I put the gun bag in the trunk and considered my next move.

I still had stuff in the apartment. It wasn't stuff I absolutely needed, but it could possibly be traced back to me, and I was burning through my savings pretty quick and didn't want to waste money replacing everything.

My preferred move was to clear out the rest of it. But that also risked more cops seeing me and wanting to talk to me, and if those cops weren't as by-the-book as the one who just hit me up, it could lead to trouble.

Take a minute.

What the move.

#Decisions.

I decided to risk it and grab my shit. Once I cleared out, it was unlikely the cops could trace me back to this apartment. I had Marko's copy of my lease. Even if they found his hidden panel, there was no two-way mirror in my bathroom.

I walked back, keeping an eye on the cops. More arrived, six cars total. Small town, probably their entire police force. They'd call for assistance from nearby precincts, or maybe the Staties or FBI.

I managed to get back into my crib without being seen, grabbed both garbage bags and my bedroll even though everything was heavy and unwieldy, and headed back to my car with the bags slung over my shoulder, like a killer Santa Claus.

Don't mind me. Just taking out the garbage.

Nobody minded me.

#HideInPlainSight.

I loaded my car, dropped my apartment key into a nearby sewer grate, and considered my next move.

The only loose threads were the electric company, and my moms.

The electric company was easy to deal with. I drove to a nearby drug store, bought a prepaid credit card with cash, and bought a cheap cell phone where I paid by the minute. It took ten minutes to activate the phone, and I called the electric company and stated there had been a mistake. I didn't rent the apartment after all, and I wanted to cancel my service.

I was told that I had a balance of six dollars, and I paid using my new card.

Moms I'd deal with later.

It was 7 A.M.

The lines were already forming.

#TimeToKill.

*"It's better to have a gun and not need it than
to need a gun and not have it."*
CHRISTIAN SLATER

*"When a strong man, fully armed, guards
his house, his possessions are safe."*
LUKE 11:21

JACK

The wind woke me up.

A howling, screaming wind that banged on the window shutters and pounded on the roof and forced you to accept that this rock we live on is mean and deadly and doesn't give two shits about life.

Hurricane Harry had arrived.

I looked for Phin, saw the empty divot in the bed where he should have been, and then checked the time.

Bedside clock was off. We'd lost power.

We had a backup generator that ran on propane, but it only powered some parts of the house.

I checked my phone, which had managed half a charge before the electricity died. It was a little after seven.

I tried to listen to the dark house, sense Phin's presence as he made breakfast or straightened up or acted domestic in some other way.

All I could hear was the wind.

Duffy the hound, whose tubular body shape wasn't conducive to leaping up on the bed, had somehow managed to climb up and was curled at my feet, shaking.

Mr. Friskers, as antisocial an animal that ever breathed, was lying next to Duffy.

Bad weather friends.

"It's okay, guys. The storm will pass."

The words felt counterfeit the moment they left my lips.

I had a fleeting thought that Phin had gotten up early to bang the whore he'd been wasting our condoms on, then remembered it was launch day for the Gamemaster 2.

I hoped he didn't take Sam out in this storm.

I awkwardly undulated out of bed and into my chair, and rolled into Sam's room.

Gone.

What kind of unfit father takes his child out in a hurricane?

I checked the Find My iPhone app. They were a few blocks away, coming home.

Then I made my way to the kitchen, took out a carafe of cold brew, and drank straight from it. Hot coffee was my thing, but patience had become elusive and waiting for java to be made angered me, so Phin kept the fridge stocked with cold coffee, steeping grounds in a fine mesh strainer. I didn't let on how much I liked it. Because I'm a jerk.

After sucking in six ounces of caffeine while listening to Harry try to pull my roof off, Duffy ran past and began to bark.

The door to the garage opened, and Phin came in, our daughter in one arm, a large plastic bag from VideoTown in the other.

"Mommy! We got City Warriors 2!"

Sam squirmed out of Phin's grasp and bounded over to me, enthusiastic and huggy.

"Awesome," I smiled, finding the strength to fake excitement. "Is the hurricane scaring you?"

Sam frowned. "There are a lot of trees in the street. Daddy had to drive around them."

"But the Gamemaster 2 is more important than any dumb old hurricane." I eyed Phin.

Sam said, "Yeet."

Phin shrugged off his dripping trench coat. "There was a line. We saw a whole flock of sun umbrellas blowing up the road, and the rain is so bad it's like a waterfall. There was still a line around the block."

"But well worth taking our daughter along."

"Do you want Sam to face life, even when it's risky, or hide in the house when things get tough?"

Ouch. I thought of a few responses I could hurt him with, but not in front of Sam.

"Can we set it up, Daddy?"

Phin nodded, and then Sam bounced out of my lap and followed her father to the living room. They unboxed it together, and Phin spent five minutes hooking up cords and cables, and then the Gamemaster 2 logo appeared on our flatscreen and Sam squealed, clapping her chubby little hands with the kind of enthusiasm only a child could generate.

The Gamemaster 2 audibly thanked us for buying a Gamemaster 2, and then announced it required a 480 gigabyte update that would take 83 minutes to download and install.

"I can't even," Sam said.

When we moved in together, Phin and I split up household duties. Since I'd gotten shot, I'd been derelict in mine. Breakfast was usually my responsibility, but Phin dutifully got up to make some eggs, and Sam tagged along.

They didn't invite me.

I thought about showering, wondered why I should bother, which led me to wondering why I should bother with anything. Outside, the hurricane assaulted our home, but I couldn't watch the storm through the closed shutters. There was a whole world out there, loud and angry and trying to get in, and I couldn't see it.

My phone rang.

Power down, but cell service and Internet still active. Category 5's were obviously overrated.

The Darling Center. Probably calling to remind me my class and therapy were canceled.

Turned out I was way off.

"Jill? It's Dr. Agmont. Your mother was tested yesterday for TIA."

That didn't sound good. I asked the hot shrink what it meant.

"Transient ischemic attack. A ministroke that temporarily cut off blood to her brain."

Oh, shit.

I'm such a dumb ass. I thought she'd been drinking.

"Is she okay? Can I talk to her?

But I already knew the answer. If she was okay, I wouldn't have been getting a call. Or Mom would have called me on her own.

"Unfortunately, during testing, she had a full ischemic attack. We immediately began tPA to restore blood flow and destroy the clot, but she has partial paralysis on her left side, and she can't talk."

"Was she taken to the hospital?"

"She's in the clinic in Building A. We deal with strokes here faster and just as efficiently as the hospital."

In my scrambled brain a dozen questions fought for dominance. I finally chose, "She can recover from this, right? People recover from strokes."

"I've seen many people recover, some completely."

He didn't say *all*. Which meant Mom might not recover. She could die. Or be paralyzed and unable to speak for the rest of her life.

"I'll be right there."

"She's getting the medication and care she needs. Coming here during a hurricane, in your condition—"

"I'll be right there," I cut him off, then hung up.

I called a taxi service, saying I needed a van with wheelchair accessibility.

"It's a hurricane," the dispatcher told me. "Rates are quadruple."

"Fine. Just get someone here as soon as you can."

"Fifteen minutes."

I texted Phin.

Talk. Private.

A few seconds later he popped his head out of the kitchen. "Everything okay?"

I beckoned him closer and stage whispered, "Mom had a stroke."

"Jesus, Jack. Is she alright?"

"I don't know yet. I have to go to the Center."

"I'll grab Sam."

"I don't want her to know. And I don't want you bringing her out in a goddamn hurricane again."

"It's bad out, but drivable. Limited visibility, some flooded streets, gotta watch for debris, but I can get us there in twenty minutes."

"You're staying here with Sam and the pets. I'm taking a cab."

"I can take you."

"I'm taking a cab," I said, harsher. "I need some cash."

"Just use the bank card."

"I checked the bank. We're out of money."

"Use the other bank card."

"What other bank card?"

"The one I set up last month."

"What the hell are you talking about?"

"All of the money I've … *acquired*. It's in the bank."

"You never gave me a card."

"We were in bed. You put it in your phone case."

He was nuts. I checked the pockets in my leather cell phone case to prove him wrong, and there was a Visa with my fake name on it.

Rather than argue with him how it got there, I asked him how much was on it.

"Two hundred," he said.

"The cabs are charging quadruple because of the storm. Two hundred bucks might not even get me there."

Phin squinted at me. "Are you messing with me?"

"What are you talking about?"

"You don't remember this discussion?"

"What discussion?"

"There's two hundred grand in our account, Jack."

WTF?

"All the money? From the garage?"

"Everything left over after buying the house. Are you okay?"

I wasn't okay. I was the opposite of okay. How could he even ask me that?"

"You think it's the Ambien?" Phin asked. "You get kind of loopy on Ambien."

We could discuss it later. I needed to get dressed before the cab came. "Tell Sam I went to visit Grandma because the hurricane scared her."

I rolled away from Phin, into the bedroom.

Two hundred thousand bucks? And I've been worrying myself to death about money?

I wondered if my sleep meds were actually causing memory loss, or if Phin was bullshitting me.

Then I wondered if it even mattered. Our marriage was pretty much over. I hated myself, I didn't trust him, and the next big talk we'd have would be about how we divvied up child custody.

But right now I needed to get dressed and get to my mother.

Dressing was usually drudgery, but the urgency of the situation got me into pants, a t-shirt, and even socks with less effort than it had taken me since I could remember. I was wedging on my shoes when the cab texted its arrival.

"You're going to see Grandma?" Sam had snuck up on me. A pout creased her cute little face.

"I need to, sweetie."

"Will you be back soon? To play City Warriors 2?"

"I'll try. In the meantime, you can play with Daddy."

"Daddy sucks."

No shit. But instead I said, "That's not nice. Maybe you can teach him some combos."

She gave me a hug and a kiss and padded off.

I rolled to the front door, and Phin met me there with an empty garbage bag. He ripped a hole in the bottom of the bag, then stuck it over my head, smoothing it down my sides like a poncho.

It felt good to have him touch me, and I hated it.

"Is this necessary?"

"You'll see in a second."

He opened the door, and I stared into Armageddon.

Religion and I weren't pals, but Hurricane Harry looked like a circle of hell, substituting the fire with water.

The darkness.

The wind, blowing trees almost ninety degrees.

The rain, an avalanche of it, blowing sideways like it was giving the finger to gravity.

The sound of a jet engine, mixed with howling wolves in terrible pain.

Phin pushed me outside, toward the cab, and my hair was soaked within seconds, my chair so close to flipping over I had to lean into the wind. The driver had a real poncho on, not a Hefty bag, and he helped Phin muscle me up the ramp into the side of the van.

Phin bent down, kissed my cheek, and said, "You got this. You forgot how strong you are."

Then he left, slamming the door behind him.

I watched, through the window, as he stood in the rain and stared at me. Behind him, our home looked vulnerable, the roof seeming to rise and fall, making me rethink our decision to not install hurricane straps.

I locked the wheels on my chair and the driver took off, watching Phin as we pulled away, getting a sudden, terrible, hopeless feeling that it might be the last time I ever see him.

The wind shoved the vehicle side-to-side.

I watched the driver wrestle the steering wheel, fighting the wind and also the debris blowing across the road. Trees, bushes, lawn furniture, a shed; a full size, corrugated metal shed, rolling across the street like a craps die.

"You got this. You forgot how strong you are."

My husband was wrong.

Humans were fragile, temporary, borderline-helpless creatures, bound to a cruel, merciless world with only one way to escape.

And I was more fragile than most.

I felt pain in my hands, looked down and realized I was gripping my handrails so tight my knuckles were white.

Hurricane Harry chewed at the van.

If it didn't kill us, something else will. Eventually.

I closed my eyes and hoped this wretched, miserable world wasn't ready to take my mother yet.

"The Constitution shall never be construed to prevent
the people of the United States who are peaceable
citizens from keeping their own arms."
SAMUEL ADAMS

"A sword never kills anybody; it is a tool in the killer's hand."
LUCIUS ANNAEUS SENECA

GAFF

This was it.

The biggest day of my life.

I was twinging like a fiend, blinking so fast it was tough to keep my eyes on the road.

In the passenger seat, next to me, my gun bag, the Merican loaded to spray and slay.

Tweaked.

My vehicle could still be traced back to Moms, so I parked three blocks away from the VideoTown I'd Googlemapped. Paid the meter, bcuz that's how they caught the Son of Sam, and then took off my black hoodie and baggy red shirt and strapped on the body armor.

The shirt fit over it, the hoodie over the shirt.

Then I shouldered the bag and headed to the slaughter.

My expectations were surpassed.

When I got within a block of the videogame store, I could already see the line of people.

Two hundred. Maybe three.

Waiting for VideoTown to open in half an hour.

Waiting to grab their GameMaster 2 consoles on release day.

As I got closer, the twinges got stronger. Some of the people in line were cosplaying, dressing up as videogame characters.

There were even a dozen people in City Warriors rave masks.

#Can'tGetAnyBetter.

I tugged my mask up over my nose to hide my face and my smile, pulled my hoodie onto my head, and fondled the zipper on my gun bag.

When people started to run, they'd run away from me, and it was unlikely any would follow.

I approached @ a twenty-degree angle, so I had a clear view of the whole line. They were queued up alongside storefronts, most of which were closed, so they'd spread out into the street as they fled.

The nearest police station was eight miles away. Even if there were patrol cars in the area, I guesstimated response time to be @ least three minutes. I'd practiced swapping out mags last night, figured I could stand still and be able to blow through all six drums within two and a half minutes. Then I'd walk away, taking one of two pre-planned routes back to my car, taking off the hoodie and rave mask as I moved. Underneath I wore a red shirt. My gun bag would go into a garbage bag I'd brought along.

Cops would be looking for someone wearing black with a mask and a bag. I'd be wearing red, taking out the trash.

Turnt up.

On god.

Off the shits.

Worst case scenario, I ditch the gun bag. A monetary loss, but nothing could be traced to me.

#ScottFree.

#AllHailTheSecondAmendment.

#AnonymousFirearms.

#NoResgistration4Evs.

#GodBlessAmerica.

I unzipped the bag and visualized the first shots.

I was coming up on the end of the line, so I should aim @ the guys in front, furthest away. Then sweep those nearer to me as they scattered. If my arc was slow and steady, and I could keep the recoil under control, and I was fluid with reloading, I could easily shoot over two hundred, and kill @ least a quarter of them.

A respectable number for a first effort.

Both hands in the bag, I snapped on some latex gloves and pushed in my earplugs, then put on my shooting specs. I considered the helmet, figured I was okay for the moment without it, and did one more check for cops, security, and street cameras.

#AllClear.

#ReadyToRock.

#LetsDoThis.

#ItsDyingTime.

I whipped out the Merican, flicked off the safety, double-checked the giggle was on AUTO, and pointed the gun @ the jackass who had probably been standing there since midnight last night to be first in line.

I turned on the green laser dot, and could see it on bruh's side even though I was @ least fifty meters away.

This is it, Gaff.

Marko was a pedo. He deserved what he got. Kinda made me like a hero.

But killing harmless people in line is some next level shit.

I can still turn back. Still be the hero.

But where's the fun in that?

No one cares about heroes.

The bad guys get the clout.

#Gangsta4Evs.

I gripped the buffed Merican in both hands, tight.

I steadied my shaking hands.

I stood there for a moment, but no one turned to look @ me.

I was invisible.

Like always.

A nothing. A nobody.

But in a few seconds, a somebody.

Someone to fear. Someone to hate.

Someone who swoops in without any motive and kills a bunch of innocent people.

Then again, is anyone really innocent?

Nah.

Everyone sux.

Everything sux.

Eff em. Eff em all.

I could feel my mouth move under the rave mask. I was pretty sure it was a smile.

Are you ready for me, Mr. History?

Are you ready for my permanent mark on you?

#Yaasss.

I squeezed the trigger.

The Merican made a sound like a motorboat and bucked, a three second burst that felt like holding a jackhammer, throwing my shots to the right, into traffic.

Day-am.

I adjusted my aim, resetting, unsure if I'd hit anyone or how many bullets I'd fired. Some of the crowd panicked, began to run in the direction I knew they would, and they were all screaming and screeching and pointing @ me and I squeezed the trigger again, watching a few peeps go down.

It gave me feelz.

4real feelz.

Like all those net videos I seen where some kid gets ear implants and hears music for the first time, or a family buys their colorblind grandpa those glasses that let him see green and red and everyone starts crying.

I never cried @ those vids.

I was crying now.

It was beautiful.

#GaffKills100.

#Perfect.

Then the Merican stopped firing.

Out of bullets?

I pressed the button to release the drum mag, but the mag was pretty heavy. I squinted @ the spring. Still half full.

Why wouldn't it fire?

Checked the safety.

Off.

A jam?

I tried to ignore the chaos around me, the wonderful, ugly chaos I caused, to focus on the problem, dropping the drum mag in my bag, pulling back the slide a few times, trying to eject the bullet or casing that had gotten stuck.

Something resisted for a second, then the gun cleared itself.

I slapped the drum back in—

—aimed @ two thots clutching each other—

Fired—

Nothing.

I'd forgotten to load the first round. With a semi-auto, I needed to charge the slide.

#AmateurTime.

#Reboot.

I pulled the slide back, loading a bullet, and took aim again.

The thots, and the crowd, had scattered. Pretty fast, yo. I held the trigger down, spraying in an arc, catching a few of the stragglers and one gassed OG who'd stayed behind to snap me with his cell.

He went down.

Hopefully his cell was good. Hella footage.

Then my mag emptied out and I popped in a new one like I'd practiced and that's when I heard the sirens.

WTF? Like a one minute response time?

#BadLuck.

I put my gun away, took out the garbage bag, and quickly walked away from the panicking mob. When I turned a corner around a drugstore I shed my gloves, hoodie, mask, glasses, and earplugs into the gun bag, and then put the gun bag in the garbage bag.

Sirens were hella loud, seemed to be coming from multiple directions.

For a moment I got disoriented, blinking so fast I couldn't get my bearings, unable to remember my two escape routes. I just stood there like a noob.

Up the street, 5-0 roared straight @ me—

I needed to grab my Merican. Go out like a boss. But I froze.

—then the suckas rolled straight past me.

I forced my feet to move, checking my pace so I didn't run, choosing the longer path back to my car, zig-zagging the streets in case someone had eyes on me. After passing up my vehicle by fifty meters, I did an about-face and headed back.

No tails. No watchers. No cell phones aimed @ me.

From blocks away, under the sounds of the wailing emergency vehicles, I could swear I still heard screaming.

I stuck the bag in my trunk, taking it slow as I sat down and snapped on my seatbelt and used my turn signal to ease into traffic as more cops blew by.

Dope.

I chose that particular VideoTown for the GameMaster 2 Release Massacre bcuz it was less than a mile from the Interstate.

#EasyGetAway.

I dipped, cruising to I-95.

The first responders ignored me, clueless, passing by scrubs.

No one followed.

No one even looked @ me twice.

I took the onramp and headed south on the expressway.

On god.

Fire.

Lit.

I got away with it.

I actually got away with it.

I wondered how many I killed.

Double digits, I hoped.

I bet the news was blowing up.

I jonesed to check Twitter or watch TV.

But I needed to get out of town first. Far AF.

I checked myself in the rearview mirror.

Big old smile.

Face wet with tears.

No blinking @ all.

Woke. For the first time, truly woke.

It was just like Tully said.

For the first time in eighteen years ... for the first time ever ...

I knew who I was.

"I did it," I told myself.

But it was over too fast. Way too fast.

I'd made some mistakes.

Next time would be better.

And next time would be soon, yo.

"I am a 5'1" petite female. My pistol is my equalizer."
DR. GINA LOUDON

"Banning guns addresses a fundamental
right of all Americans to feel safe."
DIANNE FEINSTEIN

JACK

As the cab driver pushed me into Building A, the wind gusted hard and for a moment I balanced on one wheel, ready to topple. Thankfully, a lifetime of poor eating choices blessed my cabbie with enough mass to keep me from blowing away, and he hefted me inside.

The eerily empty lobby gave me pause, but the lights were still on. I pulled the dripping plastic bag off my body and rolled over to a garbage can, peering at the closed cafeteria.

Outside, Hurricane Harry roared, rattling the window shutters and trying to get in.

I tugged out my cell phone, saw that I still had service, and called Dr. Agmont.

"I'm in the lobby."

"We're in room 303."

"Can she talk?"

"She's stable. Her EKG looks good. But she's unable to communicate."

I took the elevator, reminding myself to ask Agmont about the Darling Center's generators, and what happens if Harry hurts the power grid. When the doors opened, Agmont was there, his GQ look at odds with his tired face and red eyes.

"Before you go in, know she's stable, and not in any pain."

That did nothing to reassure me, and as I brushed past he put a hand on my shoulder.

"Jill, your mother may be fully aware, even if she can't fully express it. Know that she's responsive, and she'll be watching how you react."

He's telling me not to fall apart.

I didn't make him any promises, and wheeled into her room.

Worse than I expected?

A whole lot worse.

At first, it looked like Mom had died. So tiny, so shriveled, so pale. Her skin, paper-thin and stretched across her face, showing the skull beneath. Hair, greasy and limp. One eye open—the right eye—dull like she'd been drugged. The left side of her face, melted wax.

I faked bravery, inside feeling like I was breaking into a million pieces, and took my mother's hand.

"You're not allowed to die," I told her.

Mom didn't respond. Didn't react.

I wanted to scream.

Dr. Agmont came in behind me to talk about tests and treatment and therapy, but I paid him little attention, instead trying to find any remnant of my mother in the sack of skin and bones lying on the bed before me.

I almost gave up. But when I moved slightly to the side, her right eye followed.

"Can you squeeze my hand, Mom?"

Maybe there was a faint squeeze. Maybe it was my imagination.

"Can you blink? Once for yes, twice for no."

She didn't blink.

I felt a sob building up in me, and I was going to lose my shit, right there, and the only thing that would shut me up was a blow to the head or forced sedation.

But before I lost myself to hysteria, Mom made a grunting sound.

"Was that for me, Mom? Do you know I'm here?"

Another grunt.

"She's not in any pain," Dr. Agmont said. "She seems aware of what's happening, and the treatment to dissolve the clots in her brain is aggressive. We'll know how she responds within the next twelve to twenty-four hours."

"No offense, but isn't there a brain specialist on staff? You're a psychiatrist."

"No offense taken. I was a neurosurgeon for many years before I switched my specialty to psychiatry."

Of course he was.

"You'll get through this," I told Mom.

Another grunt.

"Also, Jill … she's partially blind."

I whimpered.

"Sometimes, with a stroke, vision becomes impaired."

"How impaired?"

"Since the right side of her brain was damaged, the left side of both eyes has been affected. It's known as hemianopia. Because her communication is limited, it's difficult to ascertain how severe it is."

"Will it improve? Can she get glasses?"

"It's a brain problem, not an eye problem. We'll know more when we do another CT."

Another CT. "Can the Center lose power?"

"No. The entire complex has back-up generators. And we still have some of our medical staff here, and we're not going anywhere. Mary is the high-profile patient of the moment, and she's getting a lot of attention."

I covered Mom's hand with both of mine. "You'll get through this. We'll get through this. I promise."

But it didn't feel like a promise to me.

It felt like a big, fat, ugly lie.

*"I don't believe there should be any restrictions
when it comes to firearms. None."*
GARY JOHNSON

"Guns are not the problem. The species is the problem."
FORREST CARR

GAFF

When I crossed the state line into Georgia, I kept an eye out for hotel billboards. I'd never been in a hotel b4, but I knew to avoid the big chains, bcuz they might ask for ID and credit cards and license plate info. Instead, I looked for someplace privately owned.

A road sign caught my eye. Not bcuz it was big or flashy or recognizable, but the opposite. It looked hand painted and posted there without permission.

The Roosevelt Inn. Ten miles west of Brunswick.

The sign took me off the expressway, another pointed me down some side roads, and after two more I was thick in the woods. After a few kilometers of nothing but trees, I realized I must have taken a wrong turn.

Then the inn appeared.

It looked like one of those motels out of a low budget horror movie. Creepy one-story building from the 1950s with no cars in the parking lot and a VACANCY light that had a short in it and blinked spastically. The kind of place where some indestructible and possibly supernatural serial killer prowled the hallways to gruesomely murder teens who were having sex.

I pulled in, knowing no one would look for me here. Plus, written under the CHECK-IN sign was CABLE TV and WIFI.

#JustWhatGaffNeeds.

I parked in an empty lot and walked up to the front door, entering a small office. No one sat @ the desk, and a nameplate on top read CHESTER B ARTHUR ROOSEVELT, OWNER.

A bell on the desk could be rung by tapping on it. I tapped.

I tapped again.

I tapped again.

After a minute, a gnomy-looking bruh with a weird-shaped head limped through the side door. He wore denim bibs and his nametag said FRANKLIN.

"I need a room."

"How many days?" Franklin sounded scratchy, like he didn't use his voice often.

"Just one."

"You alone?" He looked behind me, squinting @ my car through the window.

"Yeah."

"From Ohio?"

Impressive he knew my license plate design, especially from thirty yards away.

I turned on the finesse, not wanting to answer questions or be in any way memorable.

"How much a night?" I dodged.

"Sixty, plus eight dollars tax. We got cable." His eyes narrowed as he grinned. "All the dirty channels, whether you like girls or boys."

I handed over seventy bucks.

"Also need Driver's License and a credit card for the security deposit."

"I don't have any of that. Wallet was stolen."

He stared @ me. I stared back.

"Sorry to hear it," Franklin eventually said. "But we still need a security deposit."

"For what?"

"In case you break the TV. Or steal towels."

I wasn't sure if that was normal, but it sounded legit. "How much?"

"An extra hundred. You get it back when you check out."

I fished out another hundo, and Franklin opened up a desk drawer and handed me a key. His hands felt like a cold package of lunch meat, and he had body odor. A weird body odor, kinda sweet.

"Room 8, just around the corner."

"Am I the only guest?"

He didn't answer.

"What's the WiFi password?"

"ELEANORLIVES. All caps."

"How do I spell that?"

"E-L-E-A-N-O-R. It's the name of our sainted mother."

No doubt she was a saint, putting up with this creeplord.

"Check out at 10 A.M. Ice machine on the other side of the motel, near the vending. Have a nice stay."

He grinned, missing teeth, giving me a whiff of rotten fish breath.

I left the office and unloaded my car, wanting to take everything inside bcuz I didn't like Franklin, this hotel, or being this deep into the woods with nothing else around.

Happily, I still had 900 rounds of ammo left.

#Ready4Trouble.

The lock to my room stuck and I had to jiggle the key. Inside smelled like an old closet that hadn't been opened in a while.

I flicked on a light switch, saw a bed and an older model TV—one of the thick ones made b4 flat screens—and a small desk and chair not much bigger than the ones @ my high school.

I found a remote for the TV, flipped on a news station, then made three trips to my car to bring everything inside.

The news was all about a hurricane in Florida, so I flipped to another station.

More hurricane footage.

Fail.

I set up my laptop, punched in the password, and viddied social media.

#VideoTownShooterSC.

Hells yeah. Trending.

I quickly scrolled down, looking for stats.

Seventeen injured.

No dead.

That's it?

That's all?

WTF?

The smile left my face like a guy jumping off a bridge.

There were half a dozen videos. I hadn't expected that many, but when I watched one I realized people had already been recording while in line to capture the hype around the GM2, and then turned on me when the shooting began.

The first image of myself, shooting, brought my grin back.

Then, watching myself trying to unjam the Merican, I felt my neck and ears flush.

I looked like a noob. A scrub.

I watched another video as I reloaded my magazines.

Then another.

And another.

#Amateur.

#Embarrassed.

#DoOver.

But I couldn't stop looking.

Facebook already had a fan page for the shooting.

The YouTube vids had hundreds of comments.

Someone set up a GoFundMe to help with medical bills for the survivors.

SJWs on Twitter demanded stronger gun control laws.

4chan and 8chan and gab were buzzing with speculation. With my rave mask and hoodie, no one could divvy my race. Was I Al Qaeda? ISIS? A neo-Nazi? Antifa? CIA false flag? Anarchist? Fake news?

One enterprising channer even shopped a pic of me, Merican blazing, with a halo over my head, dubbing me The Line Cutter.

Others weren't so kind.

Zero fatalities. Fail.

Dude is a bitch.

Women shooterz are like women driverz; suck.

Didn't kill no one ran like a pussy.

I left the shitposting boards and went back to Twitter and YouTube. Two hours later, I was still watching. Still reading comments.

Still feeling salty.

No dead.

No one even critically wounded. All superficial shit.

And I told Tully to watch CNN.

#TotalFailure.

My Moms used to say that every cloud had a silver lining. That made no sense. Literally. But I knew what it meant. Even when things are bad, there can be some good.

So I thought it out.

On the plus side, no one had a clue who I was. South Carolina, and the Internet, was in full freak-out mode. Lots of crying eyewitnesses and survivors and family members of victims, lots of tough talk from 5-0 and the mayor of Katydid, lots of protestors whining for stronger gun laws.

Dope.

On the minus side, some fake news asswipe actually called it a "failed attempt at a MoshMania-style mass shooting", one survivor said, "The guy seemed really inexperienced," and someone made a gif of me trying to unjam the Merican, repeating it over and over, with the word MERP underneath me, and it got over six thousand views.

Then I actually got pushed off the trending screen by that stupid Florida hurricane.

#Fuming.

I needed to regroup.

To think.

To plan.

What did I do wrong?

Break it down Gaff.

#MakeAList.

I should have practiced with the gun first. I hadn't shot it on full auto b4, and it was harder than I thought.

I should have anticipated a faster first response since every damn person in line was an early adopter tech-head with a cell phone. Some of them had even been streaming.

I shouldn't have picked such an open area. I had gone for a Mosh-Mania-style massacre, shooting into an outdoor crowd. But I didn't have long guns and scopes, I hadn't barricaded myself in a high vantage point, and the crowd wasn't contained in a venue and bottlenecked by exits.

I should have gone the Rathlin Massacre route, getting inside a building, killing people room by room.

So what did I need to change?

#Here'sMyList.

My next attempt would be indoors.

Far from the first responders.

I needed to target a group that couldn't run so fast, or call the police so fast.

I needed to practice fully auto.

I went back to the TV, flipping from news coverage to news coverage, looking for me.

All I saw was that damn hurricane, pounding away @ Florida.

Canceled.

Dumbass storm stealing my clout.

FOMO.

Hold up.

Right now, Florida was getting the shit kicked out of it.

Electricity out in many areas. Cell towers down.

Emergency services maxed out.

If I picked the right spot in Florida to do #GaffKills100Round2 there would be no cops on me. They'd be too busy doing other stuff.

I could pick a big place indoors. Take my time.

What was open during a hurricane?

#Hospitals.

Not a bad idea. Patients couldn't fight back or run away.

But hospitals had security. They also had an endless stream of cops coming and going.

What else?

School?

Closed. Same with museums, amusement parks, beaches.

An apartment or condo?

That might work. A big one. Start @ the bottom, work my way up, floor-by-floor, killing as I went.

I got online again, tracking Hurricane Harry.

Supposed to batter Florida for the next twelve hours.

I searched for big apartments in Ft. Myers, where the storm was hitting hardest.

The first thing that came up was something called the Darling Center.

A retirement community and rehab clinic. Only admitted people over age sixty.

Over eight hundred residents.

Residents who wouldn't fight back.

Luddites, who prolly didn't even have cell phones.

Old people, who might not even be able to hear the shots being fired, or be too demented to know what was happening.

I could take my time. Not waste any rounds.

Fire.

I took a moment to study the layout of the facility. Eight buildings. Six floors each. All of them pretty much identical.

Hell, they even had an Alzheimer's ward and a hospital.

I mapped it out.

About a six hour drive. By the time I got there, most of them would be asleep.

High key.

It's on.

#WhyDidn'tIThinkOfThisSooner?

I spent a few minutes loading up the car, then on a whim I did a quick walk around the motel.

No other vehicles. Whole place seemed empty.

No security cams.

No traffic driving past.

Nothing around but woods.

I went back to my trunk, hung my gun bag on my shoulder, stuck my hand in the open zipper with my fingers curled around the Merican, and walked into the check-in office.

It took four rings of the bell b4 Franklin showed up.

"I'm checking out."

"No refunds."

We stared @ each other.

"Fine. Gimme my security deposit back."

"I need to inspect the room first. Make sure it's all in order."

More staring.

Eff it.

I pulled out the gun and shot him over a dozen times in less than two seconds, only stopping bcuz the noise was excruciating.

#ForgotEarplugsAgain.

Franklin twisted around a few times, twirling little bloody spirals, and fell to the floor as I rubbed my ears and stretched my jaw, trying to get the pain to stop.

Water. I should have used water in the suppressor.

#RememberTheAblative.

I also forgot the gloves.

Messy. I was acting on instinct and emotion, instead of cold equation planning.

Making mistakes.

Begging to get caught.

I needed to slow my roll.

I walked around the desk, to make sure the little toad was dead.

Franklin lived. His eyes wide, and every time he tried to gasp in some air, blood burbled from the holes in his chest.

Hype.

I checked the floor, making sure I wasn't stepping in the widening pool of blood.

"Where's my hundo?"

He didn't answer. Blinked, like a lizard, one eye then the other.

I put on some latex gloves and picked up a small garbage can. Then I set it on his ribcage and leaned on it, asking again.

He whined hard, and the bubbling blood made a rattling sound.

"Drawer," he croaked.

I followed his gaze and saw a drawer under the desk.

"Losing ... blood ... so ... much ... *precious* ... blood ... "

The drawer had a little keyhole in it. I guessed Franklin had the key on him, but I didn't want to pat him down bcuz I'd get his DNA all over me. So I kicked it with my heel until the wood splintered. It hung open like a mouth, and I spied guap inside. I pulled the drawer out and set it on top of the desk.

Cash. Bands. A few hundred bucks, maybe more. And about a dozen credit cards.

I knew credit cards could be tracked, so I left them alone. But I took the mad stax.

Franklin wouldn't be needing it.

I fished my earplugs out of my bag and stuck them in, then flipped the giggle switch to SEMI.

Walking to the other end of the office, I aimed @ Franklin's head.

He looked @ me and began to laugh. "You can't ... can't end my bloodline."

I shot.

Missed.

Put on the green laser and shot again.

Another miss. Too low.

"Immortal ... bloodline is immortal ... Eleanor ... lives ... "

The laser had an adjustment screw on it, and I used a hex wrench to give it half a turn.

Franklin began to giggle and wheeze and twitch. I noticed he had a hard-on.

I aimed the dot @ his ear and pulled the trigger, blowing half his head off.

Tight.

Not as much twinging and blinking and euphoria as b4, but still a feeling I liked a lot.

#Addicted.

Then I switched from SEMI back to AUTO and aimed @ a file cabinet across the room.

I tried a short burst. The gun kicked to the right.

I adjusted my grip, leaning into it, and tried again.

After putting the remainder of my fifty round drum into the cabinet, I needed to practice with something farther away. I walked through the rear office door and found myself in a hallway about ten meters long.

After swapping out mags, I aimed @ a framed painting in the distance.

Squeeze.

Adjust.

Squeeze.

Adjust.

Then I went back to SEMI, turned off the laser dot, and found I was able to hit what I aimed at.

Lit.

#FortMyersHereICome.

"Gun violence is not something that appears just in a bad neighborhood or in another part of the world. It appears right here, right outside your door."

STEPHEN YOUNG

"The true soldier fights not because he hates what is in front of him, but because he loves what is behind him."

G. K. CHESTERTON

JACK

The tissue plasminogen activator therapy seemed to be working. Mom's next CT showed the clot had broken up, and her MRI revealed minimal brain damage.

But she still couldn't talk, her movement still severely compromised.

I read to her, from the Kindle app on my phone. An old Travis McGee mystery that I'd gotten in paperback three decades earlier. Travis reminded me of Phin in a few ways. Not the criminal history, the drug use, the cancer, or the infidelity. But the quiet strength and unwavering determination.

And the core of loyalty.

That's why cheating on me was so unlike Phin.

My fault. Had to be.

Once upon a time, I had a quiet strength. It had been usurped by mewling weakness. Doubt and self-loathing had done a hostile takeover of my determination.

Phin had battled cancer. More than once.

Travis McGee never gave up, no matter what obstacles author John D. McDonald threw at him.

So what the hell happened to me?

Why did I decide to stop fighting?

The lights flickered, then went out. I faced my cell toward my mother, to see her face.

"Dr. Agmont says there are generators. It'll be okay."

Mom moved slightly. It might have been a nod.

A few seconds later, the lights came back on.

I got through another chapter, Travis digging deep to find some inner strength reserves he didn't know he had, and then overcoming overwhelming odds, and I was ready to put the book down without finishing because it was bullshit.

When the gas tank is empty, there are no reserves.

I asked Mom if she wanted to watch some TV.

A grunt.

"Can you hear this, Mom? Should I turn it louder?"

Grunt.

"Louder?"

Grunt.

I cranked the volume up until it rattled my fillings.

Hurricane Harry, all over the news. It sounded bad from indoors, but the outdoor footage bordered on surreal.

Trucks tipping over.

Boats in the middle of the street.

Houses blowing to pieces.

Trees and furniture rolling through parking lots.

Emergency services maxed out.

A meme-hopeful reporter, doing the obligatory standing-in-waist-deep-water bit, might wish-fulfill and go viral because he got sideswiped by a floating car.

I switched the channel.

Another news station had reports of a shooting in South Carolina. Some nutjob opened fire on a line of people. He'd been dubbed The Line Cutter, and wore one of those balaclavas on his face with silkscreen printing on it, giving me unwelcome memories of The Cowboy.

The Line Cutter had shot at people waiting outside a VideoTown for the GameMaster 2 launch.

I got a panicky spike in my gut about Phin and Sam, and called them.

"How's Mom?" my cheating bastard husband asked.

"Not good, but stable. You guys okay?"

"Generator still working. The house is shaking hard. Mr. Friskers is clinging to my leg. Roof sprang a few leaks."

"Bad?"

"Not good, but stable. Making due with pots and garbage cans catching the water. No flooding. Not ready to run yet."

Phin had the same problem I did. Neither of us knew when to run. We never took the multiple obvious hints.

"Maybe you should go to the neighbors." I tried to remember their name. "They have hurricane straps for their roof."

"The Patels. If it gets bad, we will."

"Promise me."

"I promise."

In the background I heard Sam squeal, igniting all my mother cells. "What happened?"

"New leak. Big one. Gotta go. Love you."

He hung up before I could dispute that.

I flipped through channels, and actually found a *Columbo* marathon. Coincidence much? Mom and I watched a few episodes.

I remember liking the show as a kid, thinking Peter Falk an uncanny genius able to figure it all out. But as an adult, and a former cop, I was way ahead of every mystery and found it depressing.

Real life didn't work like that. It didn't have obvious clues and obvious villains and all loose ends tied up in a neat bow. Real life was messy, and sometimes there were no answers, and sometimes the hero didn't win the day and bad guys got away with it.

A nurse came in with food, and I fed Mom applesauce and thickened water; H2o with some sort of ingredient that made it the consistency of a milkshake. When Mom tried to drink regular water her throat muscles couldn't swallow right and it went into her lungs and she choked.

I didn't want Mom to see me cry, so the nurse had to finish feeding her.

After that, more TV. *Columbo* had ended, and the next timeslot featured another 70s sleuth, *Ironside*. I had less-than-zero desire to watch Raymond Burr play a former cop who got shot and became paralyzed, confined to a wheelchair.

Should have called it *Ironyside*.

I switched off the TV and went back to reading, getting through the ending where Travis McGee's totally unrealistic access to his hidden strength reserves won the day.

Bullshit.

When I put the book down, I knew I'd run out of things to distract myself with, so I managed to summon up enough guts for the Big Talk.

There were things I had to say, and I wasn't sure if there would be time later to say them.

I took my mother's hands, the skin translucent and paper thin and so cold, and remembered when her hands were young and mine were small.

"You're going to make it, Mom. I know you are. You're a fighter. This is … it's just a bump in the road. You'll be back to normal, swimming with Sam, in no time."

She grunted once.

"I … I know that … that I haven't been the best daughter."

Mom grunted twice and tried to shake her head.

"Lemme finish. I've … made a lot of mistakes. I've brought harm into the lives of people I love. I should have quit my job sooner. I haven't been giving this rehab thing my all, and to be honest, I don't even care about myself anymore."

Again, she grunted twice, a tear forming in her right eye. I kept going.

"I know I've been in my own way, stuck in my own head. But … for once … this isn't about me. This is about you. I need you to know something, Mom." I took a deep breath, felt it jiggle in my lungs. "I need you … I need you to know … I need you know that you are the best mother, ever."

I couldn't hold in the sobs, so I quit trying.

"I'm so lucky and so, so proud to be your daughter. And … and I'm … I'm sorry that I'm not as strong as you are, but you've been everything to me."

I gripped her hand, crying so hard it was tough to see.

"You've been everything, Mom. Lately…lately I don't know how much I have left in the tank. I feel empty. But that isn't your fault. Every bit of good I have left, every bit of strength I have left, every bit of fight I have left…is because of you. Thank you. Thank you for raising me. Thank you for always being there. Thank you for everything you've ever done. I…I appreciate it more than I can express. I love you so much."

I wanted Mom to say something. I needed Mom to say something.

But all we could do was cry as I held her hand.

I killed half a box of tissue on my face and nose, used a few on her, and put on a happy face.

"TV?" I asked.

A grunt.

I channel-surfed for something funny, couldn't find anything recognizable, and wound up on the Home Shopping Network, featuring walking shoes for the elderly.

Ten minutes into the show, seconds away from using my new credit card to order matching pairs for me and Mom, I got a text from Phin and noticed it was past one in the morning.

Safe @ neighbor's with Sam and pets.

I texted back, WTF happened?

Lost roof. Blew onto van.

A picture came next. A picture of the house we paid cash for. The house without homeowner's insurance, because that was something I was supposed to do and kept putting off. Harry had torn the entire roof off, and it had pancaked our van.

My cell rang a moment later.

"Mommy our house blew away like Wizard of Oz!"

Sam didn't sound traumatized. She sounded excited.

"Are you okay, peanut?"

"I'm good. We all went to Mr. and Mrs. Patel's house when the shaking got bad. Daddy saved the GameMaster 2."

"Can you put Daddy on?"

"Sure. Daddy, Mommy wants you."

If only Daddy wanted Mommy just as badly.

"The Patels have roof straps," Phin told me. "We should be fine. How's your mother doing?"

"We don't have insurance, Phin."

"It'll work out, Jack. It always does. How's Mom?"

"How can you say that?"

"Because we always get through it. No matter what happens. We always get through it."

What didn't he understand?

"How are we going to get through this, Phin?" I noted an edge creeping into my voice, and stared at my mother to see if she'd noticed. "The house looks totaled. Do we have enough to repair it?"

"It'll work out."

Hysteria peaked and took over. "How can you say that? I'm crippled. Mom can't talk, can't move. And I know you're cheating on me. Maybe you're wrong this time. Maybe we don't get through this one. Maybe this ends with everything going to shit."

Phin didn't answer.

"Did you hear me? This is where you talk me down off the ledge. I need you to convince me we're going to be okay."

Phin didn't talk me off the ledge. He didn't convince me we'd be okay. He didn't say a damn word.

I looked at my cell.

NO SERVICE.

I glanced around for a land line, and wheeled over to the phone, my mother following my movement with one eye.

The Patels next door. We'd only met them a few times. Nice people, but not friends. I didn't have their number in my cell, so I picked up the room phone to call information.

"All circuits are currently busy. Please try your call again later."

"Goddammit!"

I slammed the phone down. Then I did it a few more times, for good measure.

Mom eyed me.

"The roof blew off our house, onto our van," I said. "Phin, Sam, and the pets are at the neighbors. The neighbors have a hurricane roof, so they should be fine."

Mom stared.

"Phin and I haven't had sex in months. The other day I found an empty condom box in the garbage. It's my fault. I don't blame him. My sex drive has been zero lately. Nothing. I feel dead. But I could have taken care of him. We're partners. I could have taken care of him."

I shut off the TV, reached for my mother's hand, and began to sob, surprised I had any tears left. "I don't know how much more of this I can take, Mom. I keep screwing up. This is it. This is officially the lowest point in my entire life. And that's saying something, because I've had some really low points. I've bottomed out. For the first time ever, things cannot possibly get any worse."

And then I heard it. A rapid *BBBBRRRRRRRRRRRRRRRTTTTT-TTTTTT!* like a string of fireworks going off.

But it wasn't fireworks.

I knew what it was.

So did Mom, her good eye wide with fear.

Gunfire.

Sounded like it was coming from the floor below. I had no idea how long it had been going on, because we had the TV cranked up loud.

Run. We needed to run.

But neither of us could run. We couldn't even walk.

Hide. Second option was to hide.

Hide how? Each patient room had windows facing the hallway. And the only thing to barricade the door to Mom's room was Mom's bed.

That left the only option.

Fight.

The door burst open, scaring the crap out of me. Dr. Agmont hurried inside.

"He's on the second floor." Agmont panted, his expression pure disbelief. "A masked man with a gun. He's … he's … killing everybody."

I reached under my wheelchair, pulled out my leather pouch, took out my .38, then looked for the key to the trigger lock.

No key.

I tried to remember where I put it, and recalled my mother was the one who locked the gun last, during my rehab session.

"Mom, where's the key?"

Mom stared, unable to answer.

"Where's her clothes?" I barked at Agmont.

He opened up a drawer and we both pawed through her things, checking every pocket, rifling through her purse.

No key.

"Where's the key, Mom? In your room?"

Mom grunted once.

More pops of gunfire, so fast it had to be a fully automatic weapon.

"We need to get to another room and hide," I told Agmont.

Agmont's dark complexion had lightened by ten shades. "Windows," he said, pointing at the privacy curtains that blocked out the hallway. "Every room on this floor has windows. And the shooter has tools on his belt. A hammer. A crowbar."

Shit. Premeditated.

"What kind of gun does he have?" When Agmont didn't immediately respond, I rephrased. "An assault rifle? A machinegun?"

"He held it in one hand. It had a long front, and the bottom was curled."

Sounded like a modified semi-auto with an extended mag.

"He also had a bag with him. A large gym bag."

Filled with ammo and more guns, no doubt. This kept getting worse and worse.

"Body armor?"

"A bulky vest. A helmet. Yellow glasses. Latex gloves."

Gloves?

Holy shit.

In just about every active shooting situation I'd heard of, the killer expected to get caught or taken down. Usually they knew it was a one-way trip. A suicide mission.

This guy played by different rules. Worse rules. Automatic weapon and lots of ammo. Ballistic armor. Tools to get into rooms. Choosing a retirement home during a hurricane. Gloves so he didn't leave prints, and a mask to hide his face.

I looked at my mother for confirmation. "He's expecting to get away with it."

She grunted once.

We needed to move. Fast.

"911 won't pick up," Agmont said, his voice squeaky. "I tried the clinic phone, I tried my cell—"

"How many people are in this building?"

He blinked.

"How many people?" I repeated, louder.

"People. Right. Clinic staff, eight people, including me. Sixteen patients. Ten on the floor below. They're ... I don't see how any of them can get away. I have eight patients on this floor, plus a nurse and an orderly. I told them all. They're getting out now."

"Out? Where? Into a hurricane?"

"The basement has service corridors that connect all of the buildings. It's how we move patients and residents without drawing attention."

I'd wondered about that. The Darling Center was a retirement home and rehab facility. Invariably, people die, the elderly sooner than most. But all the time I'd been here, I never saw any dead bodies being carted around. They must have been transporting them underground.

"How about maids? Laundry? Janitors? Maintenance?"

"Sent home because of the storm."

BBBBRRRRRRRRRRRRRRRRTTTTTTTTTTTTBBBBRRRRRRRRRRTTTTTTT!

The gunfire sounded closer.

"The key to my gun lock has to be in my mother's room. B65. She also has a gun safe with another firearm and ammo, and a bulletproof vest."

Agmont had already unplugged Mom's bed from the wall and released the brakes. "He's on the east side of the building, moving west. We'll take the east elevator, hope he doesn't notice."

I rolled out into the hallway, looking in both directions.

BBBBRRRRRRTTTTTTT! from the floor below.

Agmont pointed. "To the right. Go."

I rolled right, the doctor pushing my mother's wheeled bed behind me. The corner of the hallway seemed to distort and expand, getting further away, like in Hitchcock's Vertigo. Since hearing the first gunshots, I'd been on autopilot. But now, trying to get away, thoughts and doubts began to override training.

We can't protect ourselves.

We're going to die.

All my experience, all my preparation, undone because of one stupid key.

Homeland Security was wrong. I'd been right all along.

All we could do was hope we got lucky.

We turned the L shaped corner, and I saw a handful of people ahead of me, waiting for the elevator, three in wheelchairs.

I knew how big those lifts were.

I knew we all wouldn't fit. Not with my mother's bed.

As we approached, the elevators doors opened, and panicked people shoved their way in.

"Hold the door!" I yelled, then slowed and turned to Agmont. "Put my mother into my lap."

He hesitated, then nodded, getting a grip under her armpits.

In the elevator I heard an argument, and turned to see an orderly and a male nurse in a shoving match. Several patients got involved, and I realized what was happening.

The orderly was jamming on a button, trying to close the doors.

"Not enough room! They can take the next one!"

"We have to wait for—"

And the nurse was pushed to the floor, and the orderly smashed the button over and over, but I knew we had time, knew those buttons were placebos and didn't control the mechanism, knew we had a few more seconds to—

The doors closed.

One more thing I was wrong about.

The other elevator was at the opposite side of the L shaped building. Which, according to Agmont and the last gunshots we heard, was the direction the active shooter headed.

In the middle of the L was a staircase. Agmont could carry Mom, and I could slither down on my hands and ass, but that left me without a wheelchair.

Still, beat dying.

"What do you want to do?" the doctor said.

"My lap. Put her in my lap. We'll go to the stairs."

BBBBRRRRRRRRRRRRRRRRRTTTTTTTTTTTTTTTTT!

Louder than before. I realized why when I heard the screams.

The shooter was directly beneath us. Killing everyone in the elevator.

"Hurry."

My mother, dead weight, awkwardly dropped onto me, and I cinched my hands around her waist like a seatbelt.

Below, the gunfire and screaming stopped.

For a moment, silence. Dr. Agmont tried to push the chair, and one of Mom's legs dragged and she began to pitch forward.

I held her, but Agmont couldn't keep us level, and the chair toppled sideways.

Agmont appeared terrified, and I would have told him to run and save himself but I couldn't leave Mom like that.

Dr. Agmont, however, showed the same grit he must have employed climbing Everest, because he muscled the chair upright and set Mom back in my lap, this time making sure her feet were on top of mine on the footrests.

Then I heard a *BING* and we all watched, horrified, as the elevator began to ascend to our floor.

"I do not accept that we cannot find a common sense way to preserve our traditions, including our basic Second Amendment freedoms and the rights of law abiding gun owners, while at the same time reducing the gun violence that unleashes so much mayhem on a regular basis."

BARACK OBAMA

"You've got to have defense, too. You can't just be sitting ducks."

DONALD TRUMP

GAFF

EARLIER

A hurricane.

A real live hurricane.

Lit.

When I rolled into Florida, the rain rained upwards, bruh.

Literally.

No shit.

WTF.

Wind so thic it blew water into the air, like mashing the rewind button. I had to keep both hands on the wheel because I kept getting pushed around by gusts that got under my car and made it bounce and skid.

Shook.

Literally.

Unreal sound. Like demons screaming.

Crap visibility.

#UnsafeConditions.

It was so hard to see that I almost gave up and turned back, but I pulled over at a truck-stop to fill up and buy a hammer (actually found a schweet 10lb sledge and a one-meter crowbar) and gas station bruh told me to put water repellent on my windshield. I bought a bottle for ten bucks and it hella worked. I could drive above the speed limit, water bouncing off my window like little BBs, while noobs pulled over on the side of the road, freaking out.

Long day, lots of driving, cray tired, but I tweaked on energy drinks, sucking down so many that when I stopped @ a rest area my piss fizzed.

Some roads were closed and blocked, and I had to use the car GPS to get to the Darling Center, which still worked even though my cell phone lost its signal. Wasn't worried about Moms tracking me via GPS satellite, because she gave me the car.

Real hard to see, but the retirement complex still had its lights on. Eight buildings, with six floors each. I knew from the website that one of those buildings was the hospital clinic where all the sickos were, one was the memory care unit for the demented, and the others were apartments.

I decided to start with the hospital, then kill my way to the Alzheimer's folks. Working my way through the alphabet, A through G. Pregame with some sitting ducks, get bonked AF with the door-to-door condos, then chill with the braindeads, and donezo.

#ShouldBeFun.

#GaffTripleDigits.

The Center was one of those gated communities, with a keypad entrance for the fence stretching across the driveway. But Hurricane Harry had done me a solid, the iron-barred door wide open. Didn't even need to eff around with the crowbar.

I drove up to Building A, the clinic, looked around for a parking space, avoiding the handicapped spots bcuz I didn't want to get in trouble, and found one near the back of the lot.

Then I dressed for success.

Gloves: check.

Vest: check.

Hoodie: check.

Helmet: check.

Rave mask: check.

Glasses: raining, so I'd put them on inside.

Earplugs: hells yeah check. My ears still hurt from killing Franklin.

Merican: check. Full drum mag, one in the spout, giggled to AUTO.

Gun bag: check. Five full drums, two full mags, and a few hundo rounds for reloading.

I got out of the car and stuck the sledgehammer and crowbar on opposite sides of my belt, which I loosened to accommodate their width.

Then I flicked on my green laser dot, shouldered my bag, and walked through a sick poppin fire high-key hurricane.

#TotesWindy.

Having to crouch so I didn't get blown off my feet, I managed to get to the front door of Building A.

Not even locked.

According to the floorplans I saw on line, all eight buildings had the same layout. They were L shaped, elevators on either side, staircase in the middle @ the juncture. In Building A, the security office was 2 the right of the cafeteria, on the first floor.

I put on my shooting specs and headed there to say hello.

I walked past the empty café, looking for people and cameras, seeing neither. Through an office window I saw a security bruh, feet up on his desk, watching TV.

He didn't notice me until I walked in.

The twinges got me all shook.

"Hands up."

Dude immediately raised his mitts. White guy, chubby. Nametag said EARNEST.

"Gun on the desk."

"Only got a taser."

"Put it on the desk, Earnest."

He did.

"How many security guys on duty?"

"Two. Justin is making rounds."

"He armed?"

"A taser, like me."

"Got any cameras?"

"What?"

"Security cameras."

"No. No cameras."

Dope.

"Can you contact Justin?"

Earnest nodded. "Radio."

"Tell him to come here, quick. Some old guy acting crazy. Say that exactly. If you say anything else, any number codes or shit like that, I'll kill you."

He picked up his radio and said, "Justin, come here, quick. Some old guy is acting crazy."

"Put the radio on the desk."

He did. Like the best game of *Simon Says* evah.

"Where's the vault?" I asked.

"What?"

"The money, with all the gold."

I couldn't read his expression, but it was probably funny as hell.

"There's … there's no gold. This is a retirement community."

"I know, bruh. Just messing with you."

I shot him about twenty times.

Much quieter with the suppressor all wet from the rain.

#AblativesRule.

Earnest didn't cling to life like Franklin. Security bruh str8-up died. Caught him in the mouth and his jaw split in half like a *Predator*.

Lit.

By the time I got my blepharospasms under control, Justin showed up. Another white guy. Apparently this place didn't comprendo diversity.

He walked in, saw his dead partner, and I stepped out from behind the door and shot him until my mag ran out.

Epic.

The blood didn't look like movie blood. It was darker, and there wasn't as much as I expected. Also, people died ugly. Earnest had both eyes open, his mouth exploded, arms and legs bent all weird, and for some reason the scrub had a hard-on. His buddy Justin pissed and shit himself, stank AF, and his hand continued to twitch even though his chest stopped moving.

#Freaky.

I stared for a moment, twinging.

#Wet.

After I memorized every detail, I grabbed both their taser guns, and took a minute to reload the drum I emptied.

Going through rounds too fast. I switched back to SEMI.

Then I hit the reset button on my legacy.

Marko? A warm-up.

The Line Cutter shooting? A test run.

Franklin? Practice.

Time to go for the high score.

Darling Center Massacre Total: 2.

So far.

#JustGettingStarted.

I walked back into the hall and checked out the cafeteria. No one around, so I went through a door labeled EMPLOYEES ONLY.

I twinged when I did.

Going somewhere off-limits, somewhere I could get in trouble, provided a thrill similar to murder.

I was doing something I shouldn't. Which was something I did a lot.

But never with this sense of liberation. This sense of pure independence.

No authority could stop me. No adult could control me.

For the first time evah, there were no consequences.

For the first time evah, I was master of my world.

I went into the kitchen, didn't see any employees, and opened up one of the coolers. Seeing bins of frozen bagels made me realize how hungry I was. I grabbed two, sticking one in my vest and gnawing on the other, and left the café to explore the rest of the first floor.

No one around. Deadzo.

#Disappointing.

I checked out an arcade. Lots of cool retro games, including a *Hunt Master 7* cabinet with a plastic rifle.

Schweet. But I got the real thing, yo. And I ain't shooting deer.

I passed an empty meeting room, a few empty offices, then found an elevator. I took it to the second floor, and immediately saw a male nurse in blue scrubs.

When he noticed me, he froze.

#Doubletap.

The gunshot got the attention of a few other staff members, and three came into the hall to see what was going on.

I switched to AUTO.

BBBBRRRRRRRRRRRRRRRTTTTTTTTTTTTTTTT!

Dropped two, missed two.

I chased them and one screamed as I caught her in the back. The other, a tall good-lookin' dude, took off so fast I missed. Bruh moved like his life depended on it, which it did. I considered tracking him down, but another nurse poked her head out of a door right next to me, and I lined up the green dot perfectly with the center of her forehead.

BBBRRRTTT!

She went down in a poofy blood cloud, and I retraced my steps as I changed drums, putting a few into the ones still breathing.

Darling Massacre Total: 7.

Hype.

Then I did a door-to-door, checking on patients.

Paging Dr. Gaff. Code Lead.

First guy was a bajillion years old, on oxygen, didn't even find the unravelling events exciting enough to try and defend himself. Bruh just stared at me, all sad-like.

But points are points. I switched to SEMI not to waste rounds.

Next room, an elderly woman was struggling to get up.

Struggle no more, grandma.

After her, I moved on to a room where the guy actually managed to push his bed against the door.

Barricade. Smart.

But I watched him do it through the room window. Stupid.

Rather than fuss with the door, I flipped to AUTO and let him have it through the glass.

He did a funny little dance, like he'd been electrocuted, b4 he went down.

The gunfire had gotten louder. In the next room I took a bottle of water from the patient's bedside, poured it on and into the compensator.

"Why?" the old dude asked me.

He wouldn't understand, but I didn't try to explain it. I wasted him, forgetting to switch back to SEMI and making a real big mess.

#CallHousekeeping.

The other patients had managed to get out of their rooms, four of them shuffling down the hallway, a few of them whimpering.

A gaggle of old prunes in hospital gowns, flashing their wrinkled asses, lumbering for their lives.

I went through the rest of my drum, taking them all down. Then I walked over to check.

Darling Massacre Total: 15.

Double digits. We're getting there.

The channers couldn't beeatch about me missing this time. Fake news couldn't call this massacre "failed."

And I was just getting started.

I exchanged magazines, and some little voice in my head told me to turn around, look back @ the elevator.

Stopped on floor 3.

The same hunch that made me look made me go back and press both call buttons.

Then I took a few steps back and raised the Merican.

About thirty seconds later, the elevator stopped and the doors opened.

Eight sitting ducks. Three literally sitting, in wheelchairs.

They screamed when they saw me.

I laughed when I shot them.

Actually laughed.

#GreatestDayEvah.

Darling Massacre Total: 23.

On another hunch, I pulled out the bodies blocking the elevator door and then stepped inside.

The 'vator took me back to Floor 1, then I hit the button for Floor 3.

Had a feeling there were more patients in the building.

Be a damn shame to leave stragglers behind.

"Guns are our friends because in a country without guns, I'm what's known as 'prey.' All females are."
ANN COULTER

"There's no question that weapons in the hands of the public have prevented acts of terror or stopped them."
SHLOMO AHARONISKY

JACK

Dr. Agmont hauled ass.

We were going so fast when we hit the L corner in the hall that I didn't think we'd make the turn without crashing. But Agmont knew some kind of wheelchair-fu and barreled us through without knocking us over or letting go, and I managed to hold my mother without either of us slipping out of the seat.

In our wake, I heard the elevator *BING* once again.

The shooter. On our floor.

Agmont raced for the opposite elevator, and I tried to brace myself best I could for the burp of the automatic fire, the irony not lost on me that if I got shot, once again it would be in the back.

We reached the lift, and though Agmont came to an abrupt stop and I kept a grip on Mom, her knees bumped the elevator doors and I heard her moan in pain. The doctor hit the down button, and I craned my neck around, watching for the killer's inevitable approach.

Agmont stepped behind me, ready to push, his eyes focused ahead of him, on the elevator.

My eyes focused behind me, waiting to see the shooter turn the corner.

Seconds crawled past like drunk turtles, and then I heard the *BING!* the same moment I saw the killer.

The first thing I noticed was the balaclava, and my first instinct was; The Cowboy had come for me.

But the shooter was shorter than the Cowboy, and stouter, and instead of a skull face mask, this mask had pointy teeth; a character I recognized from the game *City Warriors*.

I also recognized the killer from television. The Line Cutter. The one who shot up the line at the VideoTown in South Carolina.

He didn't manage to wrack up a body count there, so he came to hide in Hurricane Harry.

Smart.

And horrifying.

Agmont hit the gas, ramming us into the elevator, hitting the B button. It didn't light up, because beneath it was a keyhole.

The basement was apparently key access only.

I pressed 1 to get the lift moving, and the first shots came, so loud and sudden and terrifying that I almost pissed myself. The shots went high, hitting the ceiling of the elevator, blowing out a lighting fixture just as the doors closed.

I wasn't hit. Mom wasn't hit.

Agmont didn't appear hit either.

"Key!" I yelled at him.

He turned to me, his face slack, and then he figured out what I meant and dug a key out of his pocket, jabbing it under the B button.

The lift stopped on 1, and the doors opened, and I held my breath, knowing the shooter couldn't have run down the stairs that fast, but also not knowing if this was a lone wolf, or if more than one player was in the game.

The doors closed, and again we descended, coming to the basement level.

Agmont pulled us out of the lift and turned us around. We were in a service hallway.

"Can he get down here?"

"What?"

"The shooter. You used a key. Can he get to this level without a key?"

"Not in an elevator. There are stairwells. Locked. But he's got a crowbar. What do we do?"

A damn good question.

"Is there any sort of announcement system? Any way to alert all of the tenants what's happening?"

He shook his head. "No. No intercom. We'd have to call each of them, or knock on every door. I could run to each building, pull the fire alarms."

"Bad idea."

A bunch of old, confused people, all gathering in their lobbies, would be like shooting fish in a barrel. And where were they supposed to run? Into a hurricane?

But what were the alternatives?

The killer had a crowbar and a sledgehammer. Locks wouldn't stop him. But if we could warn everyone, they could barricade their doors.

How long would that take? There were seven more buildings, hundreds of tenants.

Agmont tried his cell phone again, but I guessed Emergency services already had their hands full with Harry. Even if the lines weren't busy, it would be a while before help arrived.

"Do you have a car?" I asked.

"Damn line is still busy."

"Dr. Agmont, do you have a car?"

"Yes. But I can't leave all these people here."

"You can take my mother. Go directly to the police station. Driving there will be quickest."

Mom grunted twice. No.

"What about you?" Agmont asked.

"My gun lock key is in my mother's room, and she has another gun, and bullets, in her safe."

"What are you going to do?"

An important question. One I'd been asking myself a lot lately.

I'm crippled. What am I going to do?

My husband is cheating. What am I going to do?

My mother had a stroke. What am I going to do?

But, in this case, there wasn't any uncertainty.

I was going to do what I needed to do. I was going to do what I was born to do.

Harry McGlade was right. We were the good guys. We needed to act like it.

I squeezed my mother tighter.

"I'm going to stop him," I said.

"Background checks, waiting periods, reports of transfers, and access to mental health records have not stopped the legal sale of firearms to legitimate buyers."

COLLEEN HANABUSA

"The bad guys, the criminals, don't follow laws and restricting more of America's freedoms when it comes to self-defense isn't the answer."

SARAH PALIN

A swing and a miss.

I approached the elevator, watched the lights as it stopped on Floor 1, and then on Floor B.

The basement. Interesting.

I pressed the down button, waited for the 'vator to come, and took a look @ the button panel.

Button B had a keyhole beneath it. Employees only.

So I pressed 4 and went up.

The floor contained offices. All empty.

#BadNews.

But good news, I got to the other elevator in less than 2 minutes.

I didn't know yet how long it would take me to get inside a locked door, but I bet some residents would answer when I knocked, so I did the maths. If I averaged ten minutes a floor, seven buildings with six floors each, I should be able to kill between 400 and 600 people in about seven hours.

#WorldRecord.

I just needed to make sure I didn't waste any more ammo. Who coulda thunk 1000 rounds wasn't enough?

Floor 5, empty board rooms.

Floor 6, a gym. Empty.

No prob. I had a different kind of workout in mind.

I moved to the center of the hallways, where the staircase was, and went down a flight of stairs to a 180 degree angle landing, then turned and took another flight down to the basement B level.

Door was locked. Heavy duty.

I checked the time on my cell and went @ it with the sledge and pry bar.

Savage.

Banged that shit open in under a minute.

If they were all that easy, I'd be outtie b4 sunrise.

I paused in the hallway, listening.

No sounds.

The floors were concrete and the walls were white painted cinder block. Florescent lights overhead. No doors that I could see. I followed the corridor to the right, took a turn, and it ended @ an elevator. I backtracked, passed the stairs I came down, and found another elevator and a hallway. Painted on the wall, a red arrow and the words BUILDING B.

#Lucky.

I wouldn't have to stumble through a hurricane to get to the next building.

#BestPlanEvah.

When I came to the locked Building B stairwell, I had to pry the door rather than bang it open, and that took a lot longer. Five minutes, maybe more. It had one of those steel panels over the lock so I couldn't get the crowbar in, and using the sledge made it worse, bending it all to hell.

Hardo. Extra AF.

I'd almost given up, and then I decided to give the hinges a try.

Three whacks each.

Cake.

When I got the door open I saw another staircase. I stopped and listened.

Nada. Not even the hurricane.

I went upstairs, and the first floor door wasn't locked. There was also a door leading outside, with a small square window at eye-level.

Now I could hear the hurricane roaring, and I peeked out and saw a palm tree get torn from the ground and cartwheel out of sight.

Lit.

I entered Building B, walked to the right, and found apartment B6. I knocked.

A moment passed, then, "Who's there?"

I yanked down my mask so I didn't look scary through the peephole. "Exterminator."

#BestJokeEvah.

"It's late."

Finesse. "The hurricane has riled up the rodent population, ma'am. We think the rats are trying to get into your room."

That did the trick. I heard the door unlock, and when it cracked open I stuck in the suppressor.

#OneShot.

#OneKill.

Darling Massacre Total: 24.

And I haven't even hit my stride.

I popped into the old lady's place to see if she had an old man.

Nope.

But she had bottled water in the fridge, and there was half an apple pie on the counter.

I grabbed a fork and gobbled down some pie.

Bitch deserved to die. Pie was str8 trash. I almost OD'ed on cinnamon. Wished I could resurrect her so I could kill her ass again.

I drank half the water, poured the rest on my suppressor, and washed the fork and bottle because my saliva was on them.

#DNA.

Then I went to B7.

No one answered the knock. But these doors were a lot easier than the security doors leading to the basement. One good whack with the sledge, and it burst inside.

Old guy, one door over from B9, stepped into the hall, wearing an undershirt and whitey-tighties.

Bruh had a handgun, pointed at me.

I raised my gun ultrafast, and we both fired a few times.

He went down.

I did not. But getting shot effen *hurt*, dawg. For a few seconds I couldn't catch my breath, and I thought the vest didn't work and the bullets got through. Like getting whacked with a bat in the chest three times. I reached up, felt my trauma plate, felt the dents in it.

Worth every penny.

Old bruh fared worse. He fell into the hall onto his back, his white underwear all red and getting redder. He tried to raise his gun again, but I stepped on his wrist and took it away.

Old POS revolver, prolly older than my Moms.

"I'm a veteran," he wheezed. "I fought in Cambodia. I'm not afraid of you, you nasty little bitch."

I pointed his own gun at his face. "You should be."

I fired his gun three times into his face.

His dentures came out, all bloody and spitty.

#OldPeopleRGross.

His old ass gun worked pretty good. Much easier to hold and control than my Merican. But the shit was empty, so I dropped it. I went into his room to see if he had a bae, found an old woman in a bathrobe, holding one of those old-fashioned phones with a cord on it.

"Where's Charles?" she said.

"Where you think, old lady?"

She stuck out her chin, all defiant-like, but she was quivering all over. "I told him to stay inside."

"Wouldn'ta mattered. I woulda gotten in anyways."

I raised the Merican and she said, "Hold on a moment. I have a question."

"You gonna ask me why?"

She nodded.

Other dude earlier wanted to know why, too. Like shit had to have a reason.

"You think I got some sort of cause. Like I'm political. Or hate certain kinds of people. Causes are bullshit. Just BS to justify doing what you want to do anyway. It's an excuse. I don't need no excuses. Why am

I doing this? Dumb question. Why do snakes bite? It's what they're born to do."

I shot her twice. When she fell she let go of the phone, and I picked it up and pulled out an earplug to see if anyone was listening.

"—ARE CURRENTLY BUSY. PLEASE TRY YOUR CALL AGAIN LATER."

#Sweet.

I caught movement, something black dashing past.

Charles and his bae had a cat.

I put my earplug back in and wasted three bullets trying to hit the salty thing, but it moved fast, and funny as it would have been to see a news graphic that said *238 Dead Plus A Cat* I couldn't waste any more time.

I went back to B7. Dark inside. I found a light switch, heard snoring, followed it to a bedroom.

Another old lady. Sleep mask on. Earplugs in.

Killing her in her sleep seemed...I dunno...wrong for some reason.

So I woke her up.

My bad with expressions, but I bet her expression was pretty funny when I put the gun up to her nose.

#MessyUpClose.

Dumb move.

Her DNA was everywhere, and I probably had some bits on me. And spray. Maybe when I went out into the hurricane it would cleanse me, but just to be safe I'd ditch the outfit and buy a new one.

The twinges were coming so often that feeling good was becoming my new baseline. Is this how human beings lived? Is this what being happy felt like?

I had such a buzz, such a high, that it felt almost sexual. Maybe sensual was the better word. My body and me weren't friends. Didn't get along, mentally, physically, or emotionally. But feeling tingly made me want to take off my clothes and rub on things.

Also, it was getting hella hot. The vest I bought was supposed to wick away moisture, but I was feeling the sweat in my pits and on my belly. I unzipped the hoodie, which didn't help much. My hands felt all wet and pruned in the latex gloves, and my shooting specs had begun to fog.

I wiped them on my hoodie.

Where was my high score @?

Darling Massacre Total: 27.

Yurrr.

Needed to step up the pace.

#NoSleepTillTripleDigits.

I got back to it.

B8. No answer. Empty when I busted in. Same with B10.

#Disappointing. Both apartments looked lived-in, so maybe the occupants left ahead of the hurricane.

I reached the 'vator and had to double-back.

Knock-knock on B5. A dude answered without even asking who it was.

#StrangerDangerYo.

I shot him in the face.

#DarwinAwardsYo.

Really, if you gon live your life without ever paying attention to the threats around you, y'all deserve what you get.

No one else in the room, onto B4.

Knock. Sledge. No one home. Found some juice boxes in the fridge, drank one, rinsed off the straw and threw it in tha garbage.

B3.

Knock. Sledge. Completely empty. Not even furniture.

The windows had no drapes or blinds, but there were shutters on the outside. I couldn't see nothing, but heard Hurricane Harry cheering me on.

Props back 2U, Harry.

I used the sink, soaking my suppressor, and moved along.

B2.

Knock. Sledge.

I busted the lock out of the doorframe, but the door only moved an inch. Blocked by something.

I put my weight on it, managed to open it far enough to squeeze through the crack, and was climbing on top of the sofa that had been pushed there and some old bitch hit me on the head with a golf club.

#Triggered.

She hit me in my ballistic helmet, and it didn't hurt nothing, but it sure pissed me off. I flipped the giggle to AUTO and emptied the rest of my drum, knowing it was a waste of ammo, not being able to stop myself. I took a minute to calm down, to stop blinking so fast.

Chill.

Went to the bathroom. Pissed. Flushed. Watered my suppressor in the sink. Popped in a new drum.

Checked on B1. Knock. Sledge. Empty.

That's all, yo.

Checked my phone.

Took seven minutes to complete the level, even with a pit stop.

Five more floors. Figure forty minutes to wrap it up, then on to Building C.

#KillingIt.

I headed for the elevator.

"If you can't take something down in 10 bullets, you probably shouldn't even own a gun."
CAROLYN MCCARTHY

"When a lady accessorizes here in Texas, she's selecting caliber, not color."
RON BRACKIN

JACK

We made it to B65 and couldn't get inside because we had no apartment key. We'd forgotten Mom's purse back at the clinic.

Unbelievable.

"I can kick the door in," Dr. Agmont said.

I shook my head. "No. We want to be able to lock it if we have to."

"I'll run back to Building A. Grab her purse."

The thought of Agmont leaving us in the hallway, my mother in my lap, defenseless and unable to move, terrified me.

But what was the alternative? Pick the lock?

Why did that sound familiar?

Mr. Fincherello. He'd mentioned working as a locksmith before retiring. He might actually have some tools. And he was in this building. B31, three floors down.

He'd also said something else during my last gun class. That the locks in the Darling Center were rinky-dink. You can get through most of them by loiding with a credit card.

"Hold on," I told Agmont. "Got a credit card on you? I can use it to try to pop the lock."

"You can do that?"

"Maybe. If the deadbolt isn't on. Mom, did you put on the deadbolt when you left?"

Two grunts. No.

Agmont reached into his slacks, took out a wallet. "Do you take American Express?" he asked me.

Handsome. Heroic. And a sense of humor in the face of danger.

I kept hating him more and more.

I rolled my eyes and he handed me his AmEx—of course it was Platinum—and then scooped up Mom. I slid the card into the jamb.

The door swung inward, so the curved end of the bolt opposed me. I had to come at it from the top, try to get behind the latch, then pull it forward.

The latch didn't want to cooperate. I wondered if it had one of those little security plungers on in, preventing loiding. But if it did, why would Mr. Fincherello say it was rinky-dink?

After I left the Job, I worked with Harry McGlade in the private sector for a bit, and he had all sorts of tools to illegally breach doors. Mc-Glade, I was loathe to admit, could break into Fort Knox with a library card and a screwdriver. During down time, I played with a few of them, including a flat bar called a shove knife. It had a notch on the end, making it easier to catch the bolt.

I dug into the compartment under my seat, taking out my prepper box and removing my Swiss Army Knife.

"You mind if I cut up your credit card?" I asked Agmont.

"Do whatever you need."

I used the scissor attachment, and cut a notch into the plastic.

"Fingers crossed."

After some wiggling and pulling I caught the latch and pushed the door open.

I went in, Agmont following. I heard Hurricane Harry through the window storm shutters, trying his best to get in.

"Put her in bed," I told him, wheeling toward the second closet. "Then check around for my gun lock key."

The second closet was even worse than the crammed one I'd gone through the other day. Who needed this many towels? Seriously, there were enough to dry off every person on Ft. Myers Beach during peak season.

I started pulling them out, caused a minor towelalanche, and then pawed through shelves looking for Mom's bullet proof vest and her gun safe. In the other room, I heard Agmont gently interrogate my mother.

"Did you put in in your pocket?"

Grunt.

"What were you wearing? Pants? Shorts?"

Grunt.

"Where are your shorts, Mary? Do you have a hamper?"

Two grunts.

Agmont continued to ask questions in his mild-mannered, patient way, and I ignored them and concentrated on the closet.

Nothing on the lower shelves.

Okay then. I had to go high.

That meant standing up. On my own.

No leg braces. No crutches.

Without thinking about it too hard, I took my feet off the chair rests, then grabbed onto both sides of the closet doorway—

—pulled—

—pulled even harder—

—and then I was standing.

My legs didn't want to hold my weight, the atrophied muscles trembling, my back spasming in pain.

I told my body to shut up, and used one hand to explore the top shelf.

I found a stack of jigsaw puzzles—when did Mom ever do jigsaw puzzles?—and took them down, one-by-one, throwing them onto the floor behind me, reaching deeper, stretching for it—

Kevlar. I knew that feeling well.

I pulled down the vest, collapsing back into my chair, panting with effort as I hugged it to my chest.

Still smelled like Mom. And I still remembered when she got it, when I was young, being so proud of her and marveling how strong she looked in it and wondering why Barbie didn't have body armor but GI Joe did.

We've come a long way, baby.

Now for the gun safe. For Mom's birthday, decades ago, I'd bought her a small, steel safe with a combination lock.

"Combinations are best," I'd told her, "because you don't want to be in an emergency situation and can't find the key."

Great advice. I should have listened to myself when it came to my trigger lock.

Once again I had to stand, and once again my legs wanted to disobey me.

"I'm sick of your whining," I said, teeth clenched. "I'm sick of you being weak. I'm sick of you not getting better. Now work, goddammit."

I didn't know if I was talking to my legs, or to myself, but I managed to get upright once again, and as my whole body trembled I felt around for the safe.

There. Wedged in the back.

I got a hand on it—

—pulled it a few inches—

—and let go, once again collapsing back into my wheelchair.

I considered calling for Agmont. But then my mother's voice came into my head. Something she'd said while phubbing me at a rehab session.

"The woman I raised wouldn't ask for help. She'd help herself."

And she was right.

She was always right.

I grabbed the doorway again, sweat beading into my stinging eyes, and stood for a third time.

My legs wanted to give up.

My back wanted to give up.

But I wasn't just the sum of my parts.

I was stronger than that.

My mom raised a fighter.

I reached up again, getting my fingers on the gun safe—

—and pulled it off the shelf.

When I fell back into my chair, the fifteen pound safe in my lap, I heard Dr. Agmont say, "Your mother thinks your gun key is in her shorts, and laundry service picked it up."

He was right behind me, and I startled at his voice. "You were there the whole time?"

"Just a few seconds."

"You could have helped."

"You did fine on your own."

Even in a crisis, Agmont still couldn't stop being a shrink.

Not having my trigger lock key was irritating, but I still had a good chance of stopping the shooter with my mother's pistol. I dialed the combination—my birthday—and opened up the safe, staring at her old service revolver.

The .32 Colt Police Positive.

Nickel-plated, older than I was, but Mom kept it in excellent shape. Though a smaller caliber than my .38, this had a longer barrel, which improved accuracy. Mom also had an open box of .32 wadcutters; bullets with a flat lead head that were commonly used for target practice because they punched clean holes in paper silhouettes.

They also devastated soft tissue.

I checked the gun, unloaded, and counted 10 bullets in the box.

"Will that be enough?" Agmont asked.

"It has to be."

The alternative was unthinkable.

I tucked the gun and box of bullets into my seat compartment.

"Help me put on the vest. And don't tell me I need to do it myself."

"A good psychiatrist always listens to their patient."

I leaned forward and lifted up my arms, and Agmont placed it over my head and pushed down the back panel while I tightened the side straps.

While I dressed for the showdown, I argued with myself in my head.

I wanted Agmont to stay here with Mom, push the refrigerator in front of the door after I left, and guard her with his life.

But the best chance for the survival of the several hundred people at the Darling Center was for Agmont to get to the nearest police station and bring in SWAT.

I remember being asked a similar question, a long time ago, by none other than Harry McGlade. We'd been working a prostitute sting, me in heels and a micro mini and a mic in my push-up bra and earpiece hidden behind gigantic puffy 80's hair, and while waiting for johns Harry entertained himself by asking me deep philosophical questions,

342 • J.A. KONRATH

like would I drink a cup of my own urine every day if I was guaranteed to live to a hundred. My answer was no. Harry's answer was hell yeah, he did it anyway.

The question that stood out, the question that seemed just as fanciful at the time but turned out to be wildly prophetic, was if I had to decide whether to save five hundred strangers, or one person that I loved, which would I choose.

A terrible decision to make.

But that's exactly what I had to do.

I just needed to clear it with the boss.

I rolled into Mom's bedroom. Her eyes pinned me, and she must have noticed the vest because she grunted twice.

"I have to," I told her.

Another double grunt.

"I know. I was there for my gun talk. Run/Hide/Fight. But you said it yourself. You didn't raise a runner. You didn't raise a hider." I reached over, grabbed her hand. "You raised a fighter."

Her good eye teared up. Both of mine did, too.

"I want Dr. Agmont to stay here with you and protect you while I'm gone. He'll move something heavy in front of the door. You'll be safe."

Two more grunts.

"It's a no-brainer, Mom. I can't lose one more person I love. If he went for the cops, maybe it would save more lives. But I care about you. You're the one I want to save."

Mom's lips moved. She was trying to say something.

"You're not changing my mind. I'm going to try to stop this guy. I'm going to try my best. And maybe I will. And maybe I won't. But I can't leave you alone. I don't care what you say."

Once again, she tried to speak. It came out garbled, but I heard just enough to know what it was.

"Pussy."

And I knew what she meant.

Mom wasn't calling me weak.

She was reclaiming that word.

My mother was saying I was strong.

My eyes hurt from all the crying I'd done, but they'd never hurt like this.

"Please, Mom. Please don't make me leave you alone."

But I saw the resolve on her face. And I knew my mother.

"You're an even bigger pussy than I am," I told her through all the tears.

I gripped her bedrail and pulled myself to my feet.

Then I kissed her on the cheek.

If I stayed any longer I'd lose my resolve, so I sat back down and wheeled into the kitchen, finding her spare apartment key. Then I gave instructions to Agmont.

"Get out of the building, get to the police station. Tell them everything about the shooter. And tell them I'm on their team and to watch for me."

"You're going to face him? Alone?"

"It's our best bet. I'll take the elevator. You take the stairs. Give me the key to the basement."

He handed it over. "Are you sure this is the best course of action?"

I nodded. "Get to your car. Bring help."

He nodded, then held out his hand. I shook it.

"Good luck, Jill."

I made a face. "You're my shrink, right?"

"Insofar as you want me to be."

"So there's a doctor/patient confidentiality."

"Yes. Of course."

"Then stop calling me Jill Johnson." I took my mother's .32 Colt Police Positive out from under my seat and set it on my lap. "My name is Jack Daniels," I told Dr. Agmont. "And I'm going to take this fucker down."

"I truly believe that firearms in the hands of law abiding citizen's makes our families and our communities more safe, not less safe."
MIKE PENCE

"For an unarmed man may be attacked with greater confidence than an armed man."
THOMAS JEFFERSON

GAFF

I hit the call button on the elevator, and when it came I almost stepped inside.

Almost.

A thought stopped me.

Hella chances that other people—even old people with bad hearing one floor above me while a hurricane raged outside—heard the gunshots.

If I used the elevator, I'd be warning them I was coming, and telling them exactly which direction I was coming from.

So I let the 'vator doors close, and went back to the stairwell in the middle of the building.

On god.

I opened the door, slowly, and took out an earplug so I could hear.

Nothing. Just Hurricane Harry, so loud and angry I could hear the storm through the walls.

I walked up the stairs, slow and easy, and when I made it up two flights to the second floor I heard a noise.

Footsteps. From above. Coming down.

I got down on one knee, holding the Merican in both hands, aiming at the top of the stairs where the angle landing was.

The footsteps got louder, getting closer…louder, getting closer…and—

They stopped. Right above me.

I waited, holding my breath, finger on the trigger and death on the brain—

—and then I realized my mistake.

My green laser dot. On the stairwell wall.

Dude saw it and knew I was there.

#MyBad.

I rushed up the stairs just as the door to the third floor almost closed, and I breezed through it and looked left, then right, and saw a man running.

Not an old dude. The doctor, from Building A, who got away from me before.

This time he wouldn't get away.

I chased him all the way to the elevator, sprayed full auto and hit him in the back just as he pressed the call button.

He dropped, moaning and writhing, and I took my time walking over.

Bruh was a snack, even with his pain face on.

"Y'all had a chance to get away. Why'd you stay?"

"I'm … I'm a doctor. I … I … "

"You what? Spit it out. I'm on a tight schedule."

#GaffTheStoneColdBadAss.

"I … help people."

"I wasted 29 people so far. You didn't help any of them."

"Maybe … maybe … I can help … "

"Help who? Help me? You a shrink?"

He nodded.

Wrong answer, bruh.

"I hate shrinks," I said. "All my life, you scrubs been putting me down. Saying I was messed in the head. Putting me on all sorts of meds and shit. You know what I think of shrinks?"

I squeezed the trigger, aiming for his stomach.

A single bullet hit home, but then the slide stayed open.

#EmptyDrum.

As Hot Dr. Shrink moaned and clutched his belly, I reached into my bag—

—and then heard the elevator *BING*.

I watched as the doors opened, and saw some lady in a wheelchair. Looked younger than all the old people around here and was she wearing a bullet proof vest? and HOLY SHIT SHE HAS A GUN!

The first round hit me in my helmet and the second caught me on the side of my face and then I was running fast AF down the hall and three shots hit my back and one more caught the edge of my hip.

I turned the corner, threw my shoulder against the wall, and felt my face, my ear.

Where my ear used to be.

Nothing there but a hole. My glove came back all bloody.

Then I touched my hip, which hurt even more, and saw more blood.

Someone started to scream, and I realized it was me.

All the beautiful, sensual tingling vanished, the happy gassed zone I'd been rocking turned dark, and rage took over. White-hot hate-filled lit woke rage, and I changed my drum mag to a full one as I blinked like a fiend and yelled, "YOU BITCH! YOU'RE DEAD YOU BITCH!"

And then the wheelchair bitch yelled back.

"Come and get me, asshole!"

Don't do me dirty, chica.

I quickly stepped around the corner, and she shot me right in my effen gun.

I went back to hiding, checking my weapon for damage.

The suppressor. She hit the goddamn suppressor from thirty meters away.

WTF? Who the hell was this trash?

The silencer had a bend in it, so I grabbed the base—the blood on my glove sizzling from the heat—and then I unscrewed it and dropped it in my bag.

My ear started to hella ache, and my hip throbbed even worse. I looked down, saw a bloody crease in my pants.

Super Wheelchair Bitch had fired seven shots, and all of them had hit home.

So ... what do I do?

Take the L? Run?

My high score was 29. Maybe 30, if the hot doctor kicked.

A solid effort. Enough to make me viral. Enough to impress Tully.

Should I get away, go bigger next time?

#Indecisions.

#MakeAChoice.

I reached up, felt my ear again—

—and realized my rave mask was off.

Shit. Super Wheelchair Bitch had seen my face. So had Hot Dr. Shrink.

They saw me.

They knew my secret.

They would tell 5-0. There would be police sketches all over the news, all over the net.

Plus I was bleeding DNA evidence all over the place.

I'd be caught. I'd be convicted.

I'd do time. Life. Or maybe death. Florida had the death penalty.

But prison didn't scare me, yo.

Neither did lethal injection.

Nothing scared me. I didn't have the fear gene.

But I didn't get triple digits yet.

I wasn't going out until I hit 100.

That meant Super Wheelchair Bitch and Hot Dr. Shrink had to die.

#Going4It.

I thought about sticking my gun around the corner, spraying blind, but I didn't want Super Wheelchair Bitch to shoot my gun again.

So I changed my plan, pulling my mask on, sitting down, gritting my teeth against the pain in my leg. I'd shoot from the floor, on my side. Maybe that would surprise her just enough for me to take her out.

I needed to go for the head, because of her vest. But if I kept my hands steady, aimed good, and emptied a whole drum at her, I think my chances were dope.

Bouta bang 30s.

I took a deep breath and laid down, aiming around the corner—

—and Super Wheelchair Bitch shot me once in the helmet and twice in the chest and I sprayed the ceiling while retreating around the corner.

"Next one is going in your face!" Super Wheelchair Bitch yelled.

I felt my vest, felt the bruises. Her shots came within an inch of my bare neck.

WTF? Did she shoot in the effen Olympics?

Think, Gaff.

#HowDoIBeatHer?

I got hundreds of rounds and an automatic weapon. She got that old ass revolver.

But she also got hype mad skills. When Super Wheelchair Bitch said she'd shoot me in the face, I believed her.

#GrrlPowerYo.

Take a minute.

What the move.

Move …

I could move.

I could move faster than her.

I had fifty rounds in the drum.

Her revolver only had six.

If I could run at her, zig-zag, make her waste bullets, I could get to her before she could reload.

As long as she didn't get the kill shot, I was home free.

I took out my current mag, pulled the spring, and put in more rounds until I filled it back up. Then I stuck it back in the Merican and flipped the giggle to SEMI.

No spraying and hoping.

I finna make every bullet count.

Not bouta catch a fade, yo.
Clap back in three … two … one!
I ran around the corner—
—and saw the elevator doors close.
Super Wheelchair Bitch and Hot Dr. Shrink were gone.
I watched, saw the elevator stop on the fourth floor.
Then I limped back to the stairs fast as I could.

"The two most important things to do for self-defense are not to take a martial arts class or get a gun, but to think like the opposition and know where you're most at risk."

BARRY EISLER

"If guns are outlawed, only outlaws will have guns."

ANONYMOUS

JACK

I fired ten shots, unsure if I killed the shooter or not.

My guess was not.

Which horrified me, because I had no bullets left.

"Next one is going in your face!" I yelled over the ringing in my ears.

Then I reached down for Agmont. He'd been shot several times, bleeding everywhere, but his breathing seemed steady. Somehow, he and I managed to get him up onto my chair, his arms around my shoulders, and I called for the elevator, pressing both the UP and DOWN call buttons. The doors opened, and I managed to back us up inside, and I pressed the CLOSE DOORS button again and again, hoping it wasn't just a placebo.

The doors closed just as the shooter came running around the corner, and I had to make a quick choice.

I could go down to the basement level. But I was limited in my ability to wheel around with Agmont awkwardly holding on. And once we got there, where could we go? Into the hurricane, to his car? He couldn't drive. Neither could I.

Maybe we could get away, but there was still an active shooter in the building.

Which meant I still had a job to do.

A job to protect and serve.

There were a whole lot of people who needed protection.

But how could I protect them with no bullets?

I had an idea. I pressed the 4 button.

"Is the shooter ... ?" Dr. Agmont mumbled, his voice trailing off.

I knew what he meant. "Yeah. I think so."

When the elevator doors opened on the fourth floor, I managed to wheel us into the hallway. Luckily, stupidly luckily, B41 was the first door I came to.

I banged on it, hard, yelling for help.

After fifteen seconds, the door opened. Mr. Fincherello, in his robe, Mrs. Fincherello in a night gown standing behind him, her hand clutching her collar.

Mr. Fincherello pulled us inside and shut the door.

"My God! What's going on?" Mrs. Fincherello asked.

"There's an active shooter downstairs, coming up. Help me get him on the floor."

Both of them eased Dr. Agmont off my lap, and I dug into my seat compartment and pulled out everything.

"Mrs. Fincherello, this is my first aid kit. Inside you'll find packets of QuikClot. It's a blood clotting powder. Pour them on Dr. Agmont's wounds to stop the bleeding."

She took the case and went to work.

I turned to Mr. Fincherello and handed him my leather pouch. "Please tell me you have lock picks."

"I'm a locksmith. What's a locksmith without lockpicks? It's like a whore without a hoo-ha."

"The trigger lock on my gun. I need you to open it."

He took the pouch and hurried away. I turned my attention to Agmont. "How bad is it?"

"Got ... got one in each shoulder blade ... one in my arm ... one in my gut."

"Can you make it?"

"I need ... I ... a hospital. Stomach acid ... it'll eat through my organs ... "

His eyes fluttered and I thought he died. Mrs. Fincherello felt his neck. "He passed out."

"Keep pouring on the powder. Then bandage him best you can."

Mr. Fincherello came back, my gun in his hand. "Took me three seconds. These fingers are nimble as ever." He handed me the Colt, butt-first like I'd taught him. "I loaded it for you. But, naturally, I expect you to check for yourself."

I swung open the cylinder and checked. All six rounds were in place. I snapped it closed.

"Do you have a car?" I asked.

He nodded.

"I need you to drive to the police station. Get them here. Tell them it's the Line Cutter from South Carolina. Get every damn cop in the state here, along with medics. Make sure to tell them about me, that I'm a friendly. Can you do that?"

Mr. Fincherllo turned to look at his wife. "What do you say, hon?"

"Do it," she told him. "And when you come back I'll suck your ding-dong so hard you won't be able to walk for a week."

I finally understood how Mrs. Fincherello put up with Mr. Fincher-ello. She was just as crude as he was.

He went to her, gave her a quick kiss on the lips, and then grabbed his car keys.

BBBBBBRRRRRRRRRRRRTTTTTTTT!

It came from the hallway, by the stairs.

"Get to the elevator, I'll cover you."

"Good luck," he told me. Having known him for months, it was the first time I'd ever seen him serious.

"You, too."

He opened the door, and I wheeled out and turned toward the shooting, aiming my Colt, as Mr. Fincherello called the elevator. It ar-rived, he gave me a squeeze on the shoulder, and then I heard it close behind me.

The Line Cutter was in someone's apartment, looking for me.

Killing someone, looking for me.

I needed to yell. To draw the shooter out.

But my adrenaline reserve was gone. And it was taking my bravery with it. Taking my strength with it.

When this whole shitstorm started, I'd reverted to my training. Everything happened so quickly, I didn't even have time to think about it. I just reacted.

Now, sitting there alone in the hallway, I began to calculate my odds.

And my odds weren't good.

Behind me, an elevator. I could go back up to Mom's floor. Stay there and protect her until the police showed up.

Ahead of me, a stone cold killer. Younger. Faster. With untold hundreds of bullets and an automatic weapon against my six double-action rounds.

I needed to yell. To draw the shooter out.

I stayed silent.

I needed to yell.

No yell came.

Maybe I wasn't a fighter.

Or maybe I was, once. But not anymore.

Maybe I was what Dr. Agmont said. A wounded healer.

Wounded healers didn't save the day.

Wounded healers didn't take down the bad guy.

Maybe I'd done enough.

Not just tonight. But over my whole life.

How many monsters did I have to stop?

How many times did I have to risk it all?

I thought of Mom upstairs. Alone. Probably worried to death.

I thought of Sam. Of her growing up without me.

Was facing this shooter worth the risk?

I thought of Phin.

Jesus … Phin.

My husband. The man I loved so much it hurt.

And what was the last thing he said to me?

"You got this. You forgot how strong you are."

No, Phin. I'm not strong.

"You got this. You forgot how strong you are."

Not anymore. I'm scared. I'm weak.

"You got this. You forgot how strong you are."

I'm not the woman you think I am. I can't even keep my marriage together.

"You got this. You forgot how strong you are."

I can't even tie my own goddamn shoes.

But I kept hearing the son of a bitch.

"You got this. You forgot how strong you are."

I pictured Phin, kissing me goodbye.

I pictured Sam, with marker all over her face.

I pictured my mother, calling me a pussy.

And I pictured me.

But when I pictured myself, I didn't see myself in a wheelchair.

I pictured myself standing up. With a gun in my hand. Facing anything and everything life threw at me.

"You got this. You forgot how strong you are."

Maybe Phin was right

I forgot how strong I am.

And then I spoke. Aloud. To myself. To my family. To the whole damn universe.

"I got this."

Then I yelled, loud as I could, louder than the hurricane outside, louder than the gunfire, louder than anyone had ever yelled anything in the history of humankind.

"I'M HERE!"

"When seconds count, the cops are just minutes away."
CLINT SMITH

"You can have my gun when you pry it from my cold, dead fingers."
ANONYMOUS

GAFF

Darling Massacre Total: 31.

After painfully climbing to the fourth floor, I looked down both hallways and didn't see Super Wheelchair Bitch or Hot Dr. Shrink.

I squinted at the elevators on either side. Neither seemed in motion.

So where did they go?

Maybe the woman had a room on this floor.

Without thinking about it 2 hard, I freed my sledgehammer from my belt and whacked the first door I saw, B46, half-expecting to get shot when it burst inward.

Spoiler: I didn't get shot. I switched on the light. Another unrented apartment.

I hit B47 next, found an old man in his bed.

My gat spit death in his old-ass face.

Darling Massacre Total: 32.

But where was Super Wheelchair Bitch?

I did a quick count of my ammo. I'd gone through all my drum mags, and I sat on the dead guy's bed and spent a few minutes loading up two of them. I was filling a third when I heard the yell.

"I'M HERE!"

Super Wheelchair Bitch.

I felt a twinge. But it wasn't like a normal twinge.

Normal twinges made me feel good. Sensual. Immortal. Lit.

This twinge made my mouth get dry, and my palms get wet.

WTF?

I stood up, but didn't immediately walk into the hallway.

She was out there. Waiting for me.

Calling me.

I needed to rush out there, pop some caps, waste her ass.

But my legs wouldn't move.

Mood.

Salty.

Was I...was I actually scared?

That didn't make no sense. Nothing scared me.

So why wasn't I going out there?

"She's in your head," I said aloud. "She's just some old lady in a wheelchair. I got a high score of 32. She can't stop me. No one can stop me."

#Unstoppable.

But I still didn't move.

"YOU HEAR ME, YOU CHICKENSHIT?! I'M RIGHT HERE!"

Day-am, chick was loud.

And my hip hurt.

And the side of my head hurt, where my ear used to be.

And I didn't want to go out there.

"I KNOW WHO YOU ARE! YOU'RE THE LINE CUTTER FROM SOUTH CAROLINA!"

I wondered if she was 5-0. She had that vibe.

I wondered if more cops were on the way.

I wondered if I should GTFO and drive out of state and lay low for a few months until I healed, and then try again some other day.

"I'VE SEEN YOUR FACE! THROW DOWN YOUR WEAPON AND I WON'T KILL YOU!"

Actually, prison didn't seem so bad. I'd have my memories from the last few days. I could see myself kicking back, chillin' in a cell, remembering everyone I killed, over and over and over. Even if they executed me, that shit took years to happen.

#Tight.

A memory zapped into my dome. My Pops face.

Weird.

So many counsellors asked me about my pops, but I could never remember nothing. Just that he called me Gaff.

But now I could picture him. Picture him perfect. His hair. His eyes. All the tatts he had on his arms.

I could remember his voice. Low and rough.

I could remember him talking to Moms.

Yelling at Moms.

"Are you fucking high again, bitch? You 'spect me to take care of the fucking mistake while you zone out?"

"Guthrie's not a mistake."

"Biggest fuckin' mistake of my life. Shoulda worn a rubber. Look at that kid, staring like some kinda freak. That ain't normal. Other kids cry. Other kids laugh. All that fucking kid does is stare."

Pops picked me up and shook me. Hard.

"Stop it!" Moms yelled.

"I should chuck this fucking kid out the fucking window. Biggest fucking mistake of my life."

Moms tried to grab me, but Pops wouldn't let me go. He kept shaking and shaking, like he was trying to shake my head off.

"I got a better name than Guthrie. How about Gaffe? When I was a kid and I fucked up, my Moms said I made a gaffe. That's what we made. We made the biggest fucking gaffe ever!"

So Moms was right.

I wasn't Gaff.

I was Gaffe.

A blunder. An error. A mistake that caused embarrassment.

So why did I remember it now?

Why now, after all the years of therapy, all the counselors and psychiatrists, all the meds, why now did I remember my Pops and what he said?

I had an answer.

I had the perfect answer.

My answer is: who gives a fuck?

Like I said at the beginning of this story, the problem isn't movies or music or games or the internet or porn or immigrants or Muslims or the poor or the rich or drugs or whatever political party isn't yours.

But it also ain't a meth addicted mother who didn't love me, or an abusive gangbanger father who got shot when I was two, or the school system that gave up on me, or the community who shunned me, or the doctors who force-fed me pills to stop me from being me.

There's no one to blame.

Bcuz I'm not a mistake.

I'm not Gaffe, with an *E*.

I'm Gaff.

I'm death AF, and I'm never gonna stop, and don't try to tag me or label me or understand me or diagnose me because I'm here, and I know I'm not the only one, and we all don't care what color you are or what religion you are or what you believe in bcuz we're going to burn your world down.

If I died today, I'd inspire ten more like me to do the same thing.

You scared?

You should be.

Givin' up was str8 trash.

And my score's not high enough.

Would I ever have another chance like this?

#PerfectOpportunity.

The only thing standing between me and double-digits was this wheelchair bitch.

And she wasn't even standing, yo.

I made sure I was giggled to AUTO.

Then I ran into the hall, twinging like a fiend, the good kind of twinging, fiending to make Mr. History my bitch.

"Sometimes if you want to get rid of the gun, you have to pick the gun up."

HUEY NEWTON

"If you haven't hit the deer with three shots, you're a pretty lousy shot, that deer deserves to get away."

MICHAEL BLOOMBERG

JACK

I was ready to yell out another taunt when the shooter came running down the hall, fast and erratic and spraying bullets everywhere.

I was so surprised I missed my first shot.

The second hit home, but too low, drilling center of the vest.

The third caught a leg, and the Line Cutter went down.

The fourth hit the helmet.

The fifth, a shoulder, covered by body armor.

One shot left.

Then, blinding green light.

The Line Cutter's laser sight, right in my eye.

I pushed forward off my chair, barely standing in time for a barrage of bullets to beat against my Kevlar, knocking the breath from my chest, driving into me like a speeding truck, and I fell forward and hit the floor and I looked up and met the killer's eyes, dead-even with mine, and I saw nothing there.

Emptiness.

Oblivion.

I brought up my Colt.

I took careful aim.

I fired my last round.

PING off the helmet.

A miss.

I screwed up.

The Line Cutter reached into the gun bag, going for a fresh drum magazine.

I was in serious trouble.

I tucked my empty Colt into the back of my pants and crawled around my chair, managing to get a knee under me, somehow managing to barely reach the elevator call button. The doors opened, and I pulled myself inside as the gunfire tore through the hallway and into the lift.

Up or down?

I didn't have my wheelchair.

I could stand, but I couldn't walk.

I could barely crawl.

I was unarmed. Again.

Unless…

I pressed 6, hoping my hunch was right.

The doors closed. The elevator went up.

I crawled on my hands, pulling my legs behind me, reaching B62.

Then I banged on the door. "Mrs. Shadid! Mrs. Shadid! Sowa! Open up!"

Seconds passed.

The elevator doors closed, and the elevator descended.

"Sowa! It's Jill! Open the damn door!"

The door cracked open the width of a security chain.

"There's an active shooter," I told her as she peered down at me. "Let me in."

She didn't let me in.

"Sowa, please. There isn't any time."

"There's really a shooter?"

I glanced back at the elevator, the number stopped on 4. The Line Cutter was getting on it. I could feel it.

"There's really a shooter. You told me your husband owned a gun. Do you still have it?"

The elevator climbed to 5.

"Dammit, Sowa, we're going to die!"

Sowa closed the door.

Then she opened it just as the elevator doors opened. I dragged myself inside her room and shut the door and realized why Sowa had been reluctant to let me inside. It was the same reason she'd stood in the hallway and hadn't entered her apartment until I'd gone into Mom's.

The Darling Center staff gossip had been correct. The building had a hoarder.

A hoarder named Sowa Shadid.

I laid on the floor, doing a yoga cobra pose, trapped between two huge piles of stacked stuff. Stacked almost to the ceiling. It was like being in my mother's closet, but with a thin aisle in the center. Cardboard boxes, mostly. But also loose clothing, books, shoes, papers, all crammed together like a vertical yard sale.

"When they died, I couldn't bear to throw anything away," Sowa said.

I couldn't tell if she were half-asleep, terrified, or just in a daze because I'd discovered her hoard.

"I understand, Sowa. Did you keep the gun?"

Banging, on the door.

The Line Cutter.

"I know you're in there!"

"If you try to come in, I'll shoot you!" I turned back to Sowa and lowered my voice. "Your husband's gun. Do you still have it?"

"I didn't throw anything away."

"Find it, Sowa. Find it or we're both going to die."

Sowa walked off, in no hurry at all. Was she drunk? Sleepwalking? So depressed she wanted to die?

More pounding on the door.

"You used a different gun the second time." The Line Cutter's voice was alto and sing-songy, like a pre-pubescent boy taunting on the playground. "I bet you're out of ammo."

"I have boxes of ammo. Come in and I'll show you."

I quickly looked around for something to barricade the door, and remembered Mr. Fincherello from the gun class.

I needed a wedge of some kind. A tube of lotion or toothpaste or—

A magazine.

I snagged a catalog out of the nearest pile and rolled it into a tube. Then I smashed the tube flat and folded it in half lengthwise.

I jammed it under the door, pushed it hard, just as a BANG! shook me to the core.

The sledgehammer.

I dragged myself away, through a labyrinth of stuff, cherished memories of Sowa's dead family reminding her of her loss every minute of every day.

After two meters, the hoard forked. I took the left path, trying to use my legs to go faster, knowing I couldn't hide anywhere.

"Sowa! Did you find it?"

She didn't answer.

Another *BANG!* How long would a magazine hold up to a sledgehammer?

I needed to do something other than lie on the floor and wait around for The Line Cutter to bust in and shoot me. But there was no-where to run. No place to hide. And I couldn't find anything to fight back with. Everything was boxed up, except for some old mail, random kitchen utensils, assorted toys, neatly stacked furniture, towels; just piles and piles of endless stuff, none of it useful to me.

BANG!

I had no idea what to do. But I was clear on one thing.

I wasn't giving up.

I'd wasted months. I'd ruined my marriage.

I was done skinny dipping in the self-pity pool.

If today was the day I died, I was going out fighting.

I looked around, trying to will a brilliant idea into my head.

BBBBBBBRRRRRRRRRRTTTTTTTTTTTTTTTTTT!

The Line Cutter had given up on the sledgehammer, and was now shooting the door.

Think, Jack. What will happen next?

The Line Cutter will get in, and search for me, expecting for me to be crawling on the floor.

What if I wasn't on the floor?

What if I was somewhere The Line Cutter wouldn't expect? Wouldn't even think to check?

I stared at the massive hoard on either side of me. Difficult to climb, even with two good legs. In the shape I was in, impossible.

But I can do impossible.

I pulled myself up on a sofa buried in old clothes, and got one foot under me. Then the other foot.

I'd seen TV shows about hoarding, and they usually involved piles of garbage and old food, so haphazardly thrown together that tip-overs were inevitable.

But Sowa had taken great care with her collection. The stacks were orderly. Clothing and towels folded. Boxes labeled and sealed.

I pushed against some boxes, hard, and managed to shove some back. Then I pushed on the boxes stacked on those boxes—

—making a big, cardboard staircase.

Stairs. My nemesis.

But an even bigger nemesis was outside the door, trying to get in.

BANG!

BBBRRRRRTTTT!

BANG!

Could I lift my foot high enough?

I had no idea.

But I also didn't have a choice.

I leaned on the boxes with one hand, then raised my knee, grabbing my Velcro gym shoes with my other hand—god how I hated those shoes—and placing it on the sofa.

Now the hard part

Reaching up for the boxes, finding one with some weight to it, I palmed the sides and then tried to lift myself up, pushing with both legs, fighting to stand on the sofa.

My muscles trembled. My whole body hurt. Every breath was hell, probably because I had cracked ribs under the Kevlar.

But I would not give up. I could not give up.

I took all of the effort I'd wasted during months of rehab, and put it into that one task.

Get up on the sofa.

Get up on the sofa.

GET UP ON THE DAMN SOFA!

And my foot left the floor, and my body shook, and my muscles screamed NO! but I wasn't listening to them, and then there I was, on the damn sofa.

I repeated the process, lifting my foot, grabbing my shoe, putting it on the first box of the makeshift stairs. It should be easier, because rather than climb vertically, I was moving up and over, on a 45 degree angle.

It wasn't easier.

This height was too much. I couldn't get my foot on the box.

Okay. A setback. Not a finale.

I needed to revise and adapt.

Couldn't get my foot high enough? Fine.

I could get a knee up there.

Then, pushing and pulling and straining and lifting, the other knee.

BANG!

"Why haven't you shot me yet, wheelchair lady? I'll tell you why. No bullets. But I have lots and lots of bullets. And I'm coming in."

One more box to go, this one labeled POTS & PANS. Heavy. I got a good grip on it, ignored the tremors in my legs, ignored the all-over pain, ignored the fear, and I focused and heaved and stretched and got my knee on it.

Almost there.

BANG!

No failure. It wasn't an option.

Five plus decades of life all came down to that moment.

Get up onto that last box, or die.

BANG!

"Almost got it, wheelchair lady! You ready for me?!"

Bitch, I was born ready.

I thrust my body upward, getting on top. My forehead grazed the ceiling.

Eat your heart out, Dr. Mount Everest.

BANG!

And the shooter was through the door.

I belly-flopped onto the box, pulling myself across the top of the hoard, and my hand broke through the top packing tape and hit something cold and solid. I shifted my weight and pulled it out.

A cast iron frying pan.

I had the height advantage.

I had the element of surprise.

And now I had a viable weapon.

"What the eff is going on in here? Are you a hoarder, wheelchair lady? How can you even fit your chair in here?"

I watched The Line Cutter's head bob down the main aisle, to the fork in the hoard.

I'd gone left. Sowa had gone right.

The Line Cutter turned right.

Thinking quick, I shoved a box to my right, hard, sending it tumbling to the floor.

The Line Cutter stopped and changed direction, coming my way. Quick.

I held my breath.

The shooter came closer.

I knew what I had to do.

All during rehab, gravity had been my enemy. Struggling to walk. Struggling to stay on the parallel bars. Struggling to climb the stairs. Struggling not to fall.

But today, gravity was my BFF.

The Line Cutter walked directly under me, not thinking to look up.

Big mistake.

I pushed off with one hand and both legs, going over the edge of the boxes, falling on The Line Cutter while swinging the cast iron pan, aiming for the face.

I connected. Hard.

Then I connected with the floor, even harder.

Gravity ceased being my bestie, and my forehead bounced off the carpeting.

Seeing stars, unable to breathe because my cracked ribs got cracked even more, I turned onto my side and watched The Line Cutter's nose bleed like a faucet had been turned on.

I took the opportunity to swing the pan again, aiming for a knee, but the shooter stepped away and raised the modified semiautomatic and fired just as I was able to get the pan in front of my face.

Bullets stitched across my vest, and pinged against the cast iron, and then before I could even focus on a last thought, the gunfire stopped.

I chanced a look. The gun had jammed.

Luck.

I jack-knifed into a sitting position and dropped the pan, stretching for the weapon, grabbing the drum magazine, and we played tug of war for a few seconds before I pulled it away—

—momentum taking over and the firearm flipping through the air, into the hoard.

For a moment, we stared at each other. The Line Cutter made a sound. A harsh, barking sound.

Laughter.

"Look at that pan. Stopped four bullets. Moms was right."

"It's over," I said, watching the noseblood soak the City Warriors mask.

"Nah. Not yet. Gaff's Rule Number Eleven. Always have a back-up weapon."

The Line Cutter jammed a hand into the gun bag and came out with a small semi-auto.

"I haven't fired this one yet. I'm fiending to try it out."

I stared into the barrel.

Not the first gun I ever stared into.

But it would be the last.

My luck had run out.

And then Sowa Shadid came up from behind and placed the barrel of a forty-five caliber 1911 against the shooter's neck—

—and pulled the trigger.

The Line Cutter dropped, falling next to me, a fountain of blood squirting my face. I took the weapon, threw it to the side, and pulled off the balaclava, pressing it to the chunk missing from the young girl's neck.

But there was no way I could save her. Sowa had severed the carotid. Or the jugular. Or both.

I watched the life drain out of The Line Cutter's eyes, and her lips moved, saying something.

It sounded like, "for the lulz."

Then she was still.

I glanced up at Sowa.

"I kept everything," Sowa said. "I didn't throw anything away."

Then she put her husband's gun to her temple.

"No! Please, Sowa, no!"

Sowa stared at me, tears in her eyes.

"Too many people died today, Sowa. Please don't do this."

"I want to be with my family."

"I know you do, Sowa. But not like this."

She closed her eyes. "I've taken a life. I've used a gun to take a life."

I tried to sit up, but pain prevented it. "You saved lives, Sowa. My life. Dozens, maybe hundreds, more. So did your husband. His gun just saved hundreds. He'd be so proud of that. But would he be proud if you used his gun on yourself?"

She didn't answer. I saw her trigger finger begin to flex.

"Please, Sowa. I'm begging you. No more deaths today. Please."

Her hand shook. "When will this stop, Jill? We can't solve this with thoughts and prayers. How many people have to die before somebody actually does something?"

The question of questions. One I didn't think I could ever answer.

But right then, I had an answer.

"Maybe we shouldn't be waiting for somebody to do something. Maybe *we* should be doing something. But you can't do anything, you can't help anyone, if you kill yourself. You can't help solve the problem if you're gone, Sowa. And this is a problem we need to solve."

"You really think I can make a difference?"

"I think you can make all the difference, Sowa Shadid. But only if you make the right choice."

Long seconds passed.

Sowa opened her eyes—

—and lowered the gun to her side.

I managed to sit up, managed to reach for it, managed to take it away from her, and then she knelt down and put her arms around me and we cried and cried and cried and cried until the police finally came.

"I ain't afraid to love a man. I ain't afraid to shoot him either."
ANNIE OAKLEY

*"Nothing we're going to do is going to fundamentally alter
or eliminate the possibility of another mass shooting…"*
JOE BIDEN

JACK

I sat in my wheelchair in the lobby, a rescue blanket wrapped around me, watching as the paramedics brought Dr. Agmont out on a gurney.

"Who's the wounded healer now, Doc?" I asked him.

He smiled, somehow managing to look dazzling even with a bunch of bullets in him. "That would be me. But I have to say, Jack, that you're the first patient in years who proved me wrong."

"How's that?"

"Your archetype. I've never been so wrong in my entire career. You're not the wounded healer."

"What am I, then?"

"You're the hero, Jack Daniels."

Agmont's wife—who did look like a supermodel, even in a hurricane—hurried up to us and kissed him all over his face until his complexion was the color of her lipstick.

She rode with him to the hospital, and another in an endless stream of ambulances pulled up just as they were bringing down my mother.

I told the medics to wait and I rolled over to her gurney and held her hand. "You okay?" I asked.

She grunted once. Then she raised her right eyebrow, just a little bit.

"Yeah," I said. "I'm okay, too. I need to talk to a few more responders, but I'll see you at the hospital later."

A grunt.

I got up out of the chair, kissed her forehead.

"Pussy," she whispered.

Wow, did I love that woman.

I sat. First responders asked me questions. Second responders asked me questions.

I remembered something Mr. Rogers said. Whenever something scary happened, look for the helpers. There were always helpers.

Someone eventually figured out that I was injured, and I was ordered to the hospital, which was fine with me. A reporter came over, followed by a camera crew, and I kept my head down and feigned sleep. They moved along to Mr. and Mrs. Fincherello, and Mr. Fincherello told them what he'd told the other eight reporters.

"I did it all for the love of my life, my dearest, sweetest wife. Because she promised me a blowjob."

I'd asked a few cops to get in touch with my husband at our neighbor's house, but cell towers were still out, and land lines still busy, even though Hurricane Harry had been downgraded to a Category 1 and was expected to die out within a day or two.

So far, the death toll was at 32, including The Line Cutter. She had no ID on her, but a car from Ohio was found in the parking lot.

Her story would come out. There would be thoughts and prayers. There would be outrage and demands for change. Maybe Sowa Shadid would be part of that change.

And maybe, this time, something would actually be done.

"You're not fooling me, Jack."

I turned. Phin, standing there in that bomber jacket I bought him. My heart melted.

"Fooling you how?"

"You did it again. You saved everyone. Like you always do."

I didn't answer.

"Am I right?" Phin asked.

I didn't confirm it. But he knew me so well I didn't need to.

"Where's Sam?"

"With the Patels. They let me borrow their car."

"Did the police call you?"

"No. Saw it on the news. Figured you were doing your thing again."

"Is this my thing? Bringing death wherever I go?"

"You don't bring death, Jack. You go up against it. Over and over. And you always come out on top. I gotta say, you're the most impressive person I ever met. I love you so much."

I was completely out of tears by that point, so when I cried nothing came out. "Really? So why are you cheating on me?"

Phin made a face. "What are you talking about?"

"The empty box of condoms, Phin. You're not using them with me, so who are you using them on?"

He didn't reply.

"Do you want to leave me?" My lower lip was trembling. "I gotta be honest here. I don't think I can live without you. You're a guy. You have needs. It's my fault. But I can try harder."

"Are you messing with me?"

"I know, since I peed on you, you don't want anything to do with me."

"You're not messing with me. You think we stopped having sex because you pissed a little? You think I'm that shallow?"

"I don't blame you for cheating."

"And you really think I'm cheating."

"I saw the condom box."

"Jack, we used those. Together. We have sex a few times a week. We just had sex a few days ago."

We stared at each other.

"When?" I asked.

He grinned. "Holy shit. All this time, you really thought I was cheating?"

"Why do you think this is funny?"

"I knew Ambien made you horny. But I didn't know you wouldn't remember it the next day."

My sleeping pill?

Oh, shit. I was having blackout sex.

"We're sleeping together?" I asked.

"Yeah. You take your pill, and about an hour later, you attack me. We've been doing this for months. You seriously don't remember?"

"Do I pee on you?"

He laughed. "No. It's fine. It's great, actually. The best sex of our marriage."

"We've been having the best sex of our marriage and I don't remember it?"

Phin shook his head. "This is hysterical. McGlade is going to love this when I tell him."

McGlade? Harry McGlade?

"You're talking to McGlade?"

"Sure. We got this bromance thing going on."

I don't know what surprised me more, that my marriage was solid, or that my husband was actually friends with Harry.

"I need two favors from you," I told him.

"Name them."

"First, next time we make love, I want to do it without any sleeping pills."

"Done. And the second?"

I pushed myself up out of my wheelchair and stood, facing him. "Kiss me so hard you take my breath away."

He did. And it was so good that maybe I peed a little bit.

And neither of us cared.

"Gun control is like trying to reduce drunk driving by making it tougher for sober people to own cars."
UNKNOWN

"Firearms manufacturers usually find themselves playing defense."
BOB BARR

EPILOGUE ONE
SOMEWHERE IN MONTANA

As he addressed the board of directors, Merican Gun Company CEO Wilson Tedley pressed the remote button to bring up the next PowerPoint graphic, which showed steadily declining sales.

"As you are well aware, this is our seventh consecutive quarter loss since our country elected a Republican President. When no one is worried about their Second Amendment rights being taken away, the whole industry slumps. But we just got some news that can't possibly be any better. Ladies and Gentlemen, a round of applause for our Team XQR recruitment leader, Barney Zapadow."

Cordial applause. But Tedley knew that would change after Barney spoke. He shook Barney's hand, the one with all the gold rings, and then handed him the remote.

"Good afternoon, all. You're all well aware of The Line Cutter shootings in South Carolina and Ft. Myers. It has just been leaked to the press that the suspect, eighteen-year-old girl Guthrie Slessinger, was using a Merican XCQ-TER9."

This time, the applause was stronger.

"Better yet, the 9mm was modified with parts from our sister company, Good Ole Boy Incorporated. Silencer, giggle switch, drum magazines, and laser sights. We expect there will be public outcry for a ban on giggle switches, but that will take several weeks. In the meantime, we can sell our remaining stock to dealers at ten times current retail value."

More strong applause. Barney hit the remote button.

"As you can see from this slide, we're predicting next quarter profits to be quadruple over last quarter, with a 700% rise in female buyers."

That resulted in huge applause, and several board members, most of them women, stood up to clap.

Tedley smiled, and walked up to Barney with a small box. "Great work, Barney. As you no doubt expected, I'm honored to be presenting you with your eleventh MGC recruitment ring."

He handed over the box and shook Barney's hand again. When the applause died down, Tedley asked, "Anything new on the recruitment circuit?"

"My team and I have been to eleven gun shows in the last week, and have sold Mericans to twelve new prospects, one of which is a woman. We know that a Level 5 active shooter scenario always spawns copycats, so I wouldn't be surprised if there is another incident within the next few days."

More applause, and Tedley joked, "If you keep succeeding like this, you may run out of fingers for more rings."

Belly laughs all around.

Tedley leaned in and whispered. "Nice work, Barney. You're getting the funding you asked for. By next month, you can quadruple your staff."

"I appreciate it, Wilson. You know there are over two thousand gun shows per year. We're missing a whole lot of opportunities."

Tedley motioned to the doorway, and staff brought in a tray of champagne. When everyone had been served, Tedley raised his hand and began to speak his usual toast. After the first four words, they all joined in, rising in volume until everyone in the room was yelling.

"…being necessary to the security of a free State, the right of the people to keep and bear Arms, SHALL NOT BE INFRINGED!"

"After a shooting spree, they always want to take the guns away from the people who didn't do it. I sure as hell wouldn't want to live in a society where the only people allowed guns are the police and the military."

WILLIAM S. BURROUGHS

"When the Constitution gave us the right to bear arms, it also made us responsible for using them properly. It's not fair of us as citizens to lean more heavily on one side of that equation than on the other."

JESSE VENTURA

EPILOGUE TWO
TWO WEEKS LATER

JACK

"Seriously?" I said to my husband as we pulled into the parking lot.

"Sam's sleeping over at Taylor's, I figured we could have a night out."

"I'm all for that. But Cowlick's?"

"They have pool tables. Or, if you want to, we can go back to our complimentary apartment at the Darling Center and binge Netflix and chill."

I was sick of the Darling Center, and TV. I wanted to be on the town.

But this felt less like a fun night out on the town, and more like Phin trying to prove some point.

Since Hurricane Harry totaled our house, and we didn't have insurance to rebuild, we had to sell. Happily, real estate in Florida was worth a lot, even with a wrecked house on it, so we'd be able to start over somewhere else.

Somewhere without tropical storms.

I already had my leg braces on, set to spring assist, and managed to get out of our rental car by myself and make it to the front door with only a cane.

Phin went for drinks. I found a free pool table.

We played four games of nine ball, Phin beating me three to one. But I felt my mojo coming back as the beers kicked in, and I was ready to make my comeback.

Then two guys came in and took the table next to us.

Two familiar guys. One with a handlebar mustache. One wearing some denim bibs.

"You planned this, didn't you?" I asked Phin.

He spread his hands out. "It's just dumb luck. I swear."

But it wasn't dumb luck that made Phin walk up to them.

"Sorry, guys. This table is reserved."

The handlebar mustache guy puffed out his chest, protesting that there was no table reserves. Then he noticed me and grinned. "Oh, yeah. I remember you two. You bought us drinks last time."

He and his buddy guffawed.

"And now you can buy us some drinks," Phin said. "And then get out of here."

"Really? Is that what we're going to do?"

"That's what you're going to do." Phin jabbed him in the chest with his finger. "If you want to keep your teeth."

I got a little chill up my spine. Dammit if I wasn't enjoying this way too much.

"You're acting all tough in front of your cripple bitch, pal. How about we go and settle this out in the parking lot?"

"Jill? You want to feed these guys their teeth out in the parking lot?"

I'm not proud of myself, but I said, "Why not?"

The four of us went outside, Phin being gracious enough to wait for me because I took a little longer.

The mustache guy took off his jean jacket. "So how you want to do this?" he asked Phin. "One at a time?"

"Two at once is fine," Phin said.

Mustache guy lost some of his cocky, but he blustered anyway. "You think you can take on both of us at once?"

"Asshole, I *know* I can take on both of you at once. But this isn't my fight. I'm just here to give emotional support to my wife."

I handed Phin my cane. Phin handed me his beer. I threw the liquid in mustache guy's face. "You owe me for that one as well," I told him.

The bully called me a name that rhymed with *punt*—yet another word women needed to take back—and he moved to shove me. But I moved with him, grabbing his hand, getting him in a wristlock, and introducing his face to the pavement.

His buddy in the bibs raised a fist and came at me, and I blocked, pivoted, and then rammed the heel of my hand into his nose.

He bent over, gripping his face, and I grabbed his ears and bounced his chin off my knee brace.

My balance, as Sam would say, was on fleek.

Mustache managed to get up on his knees, and Phin made good on his promise and punted him in the teeth.

And that's when we saw the flashing red and blue lights.

"Seriously?" I said to Phin. "You didn't check for cops first?"

His smile was so big and bright it could be seen from space. "Too busy watching my lady kick ass."

We spent the night in jail, courtesy of our fake names.

Got out the next day in time to pick up Sam at Taylor's.

Best date night ever.

"The fascination of shooting as a sport depends almost wholly on whether you are at the right or wrong end of the gun."
P.G. WODEHOUSE

"Guns made us free and have kept us free, one side says; the other side rejects guns as instruments of domination, lawlessness, and terrorism. The conflict rages on because both sides are right."
JAN E. DIZARD

EPILOGUE THREE
SOMEWHERE IN NEBRASKA

The walnut balanced on an empty beer bottle, forty meters of prairie away.

The Cowboy squinted at the nut, hand poised above the hip-holstered Ruger Bisley Vaquero.

It took .455 seconds to draw, fire, and shoot the walnut off the bottle.

The bottle remained untouched.

Not the Cowboy's fastest. But getting better every day.

Heckle and Jeckle walked through the brush, toward the Cowboy. Heckle carried a laptop.

The Cowboy waited.

"We found them," Heckle said.

"Actually, our spider did," Jeckle said.

"Facial recognition software scanning police databases. She was arrested in Ft. Myers. Assault and battery charge reduced to disorderly conduct. Using the name Jill Johnson."

The Cowboy squinted at the mugshot on the screen.

It was Lieutenant Jack Daniels. No mistaking it.

"Her husband was arrested at the same time." Heckle pressed a button and another mug shot appeared.

The Cowboy's stomach clenched.

"Ft. Myers PD ran his prints, but he isn't in the national database. But we cross-checked with Chicago. His name is Phineas Troutt."

"Where are they?" The Cowboy asked.

"They had a house in Ft. Myers, but it sold yesterday. Cash. We don't know where they went," said Jeckle.

"But we found someone who might know," said Heckle.

"We have to go to Illinois," said Jeckle.

The Cowboy holstered the Vaquero.

"I've been waiting a long time to find these two. When's the next flight?"

"Four hours," said Heckle.

"We already booked three tickets," said Jeckle.

"Nice work, boys."

The Cowboy offered a rare smile.

After more than a year of searching, revenge was finally within reach.

And it was going to be beautiful.

"In the myopic world of the liberals, guns are responsible for evil instead of the perpetrator of evil. But criminals are not bound by our laws. That's what makes them criminals."

RICK PERRY

"Enough with all the gun quotes. What happened to the good old days, when you could settle a playground disagreement with your fists?"

HARRY MCGLADE

"Also, there wasn't enough of me in this book."

HARRY MCGLADE

"Seriously, I better have a really big part in CHASER.*"*

HARRY MCGLADE

"You will."

J.A. KONRATH

"Promise?"

HARRY MCGLADE

"I promise. SHOT GIRL *was dark. I need to do a fun one next."*

J.A. KONRATH

"Hell yeah!"

HARRY MCGLADE

EPILOGUE FOUR
SOMEWHERE IN CALIFORNIA

JACK

"Phin! Jack! It's been too long!"

Harry McGlade, wearing so much aftershave that TSA shouldn't have allowed him inside of an airport, gave us a bear hug as we walked into baggage claim.

Then he squatted down to Sam's height and held up his prosthetic hand for a high five. She smacked it.

"Hi, Uncle Harry. You smell like the stuff Mommy uses to clean the toilets."

"Good to see you too, sweetheart. Glad you could all come out to the coast and spend some time with me and Harry Jr."

"We needed the money," I told him.

"And the money is cray-cray, Jackie. You guys check any bags?"

"All our stuff blew away," Sam said.

"Good. I hate waiting for bags." He ruffled Sam's hair and stood back up. "It's about an hour drive to my hacienda. I got a limo."

"Where's the Crimebago?" Phin asked.

"That tank is a bitch to park at the airport. Limo is easier. Also, slight change of plans, Tom Mankowski is joining us tonight."

Warning bells went off in my head.

"I'm happy to see Tom, but you're the only one I'm helping, Harry. I have no interest in getting involved with Erinyes."

"Actually, Jackie, I don't think it's up to you."

Harry motioned me aside. I gave Phin a silent signal to distract Sam, and followed McGlade to a phone charging station. I did a quick check of the crowd, but the only one who looked suspicious was the guy I was talking to.

"So what's the ugly ass leg braces? I thought you were all healed."

"Did you pull me over here to insult my leg braces?"

"Partly, yes. Christ, they're hideous. How does Phin even get an erection with you wearing those. When I saw you hobble over my dick shrunk three sizes."

"You want to see what these leg braces feel like when I kick you in the balls?"

"Strangely, yes. Maybe later. But I want to talk to you about Tom and Erinyes."

McGlade pulled a cell phone out of his inner suit jacket pocket. "You know Erinyes is sending Tom snuff vids."

"Yeah. He told me."

"Well, Tom's also been monitoring a few darknet snuff sites. He was hoping that maybe Erinyes was just stealing footage, rather than creating it. But he found this. Brace yourself. It's awful."

I shook my head. "I don't want to see it, Harry."

McGlade stared at me, as serious as I've ever seen him. "You have to."

He pressed play. A video started, a close up of a woman's bare breasts.

Then a hot branding iron came into frame.

"Harry, I can't."

"Keep watching."

There was branding. There would have also been screaming, but thankfully McGlade had the sound off.

"Why are you making me—"

"It's right here. Watch."

The camera tilted up, to show the woman's face.

My face. Wracked with pain.

"Jesus," I said. "She looks just like me. What the hell is this, Harry?"

"Tom will explain it when he comes over. But for now, look at the bright side."

Another serial killer fixated on me? Another chance to put my family in danger? Another chance to be stalked by a psychopath? "This has no bright side."

Harry grinned, wide as a zebra's ass. "Sure there is, Jackie. We're getting the whole gang back together. I can already feel it. This is going to be the adventure of a lifetime..."

AUTHOR AFTERWORD

I'm not a fan of the author afterword. A book should stand on its own without the writer having to explain himself. So feel free to skip this. I would.

Still here? Okay, then thank you for indulging me while I yap for a bit.

My usual goal is to entertain, and I try to create books with fun characters and some laughs and some scary situations, and it is all firmly in the land of make-believe with larger-than-life heroes and super-evil villains and a few dumb jokes.

I do escapism. I leave social commentary to better writers.

SHOT GIRL is different. I wrote it with a purpose in mind.

If you managed to make it through the whole book, you were force-fed a lot of information about firearms. I touched on gun safety, gun laws, active shooting situations, buying guns, shooting guns, and the infamous gun show loophole.

But I didn't offer any answers. Because there are no answers.

I was purposely ambiguous when it came to Gaff's motivation. I purposely didn't take a side in the gun debate.

I wrote the book to inform and arouse and provoke. I wrote it to stimulate conversation. With your family. Your friends. Your neighbors. In person, on forums, and even in the comments sections of book websites.

As a nation, we need civil discourse about firearms. We need to listen to one another. Especially to the people we don't agree with.

Us vs. them isn't going to solve anything. The only way we can get better is by coming up with solutions that everyone can live with.

Live is the key word.

People like Gaff exist. Active shooters are becoming an epidemic. The system failed to help these people get the mental health treatment they needed, and then the system failed to protect the innocent.

As a country, we need to take care of each other. We need to respect each other. We need to work together to make things better.

So let's stop being enemies and talk.

Joe Konrath

Preview of CHASER

by J.A. Konrath

The Cowboy stared at the giant of a man on the other side of the glass, and marveled how tiny the phone looked in his huge hands.

"She was living in Florida, living under a fake name. I've got two cyber guys trying to find her. I'm planning to kill her, and her husband, Phineas."

"Why do you want Phin dead?" His voice was so low it rumbled.

"Personal reasons," The Cowboy answered.

"I know how to find him. But I need you to do something for me first."

"What?"

Hugo Troutt placed his massive palm on the glass and said, "Get me the fuck out of here, and I'll help you kill my brother and his bitch wife."

The Cowboy smiled. "I was hoping you'd say that."

JOE KONRATH'S COMPLETE BIBLIOGRAPHY

JACK DANIELS THRILLERS
WHISKEY SOUR (Book 1)
BLOODY MARY (Book 2)
RUSTY NAIL (Book 3)
DIRTY MARTINI (Book 4)
FUZZY NAVEL (Book 5)
CHERRY BOMB (Book 6)
SHAKEN (Book 7)
STIRRED (Book 8)
RUM RUNNER (Book 9)
LAST CALL (Book 10)
WHITE RUSSIAN (Book 11)
SHOT GIRL (Book 12)
CHASER (Book 13)
OLD FASHIONED (Book 14)
LADY 52 (Book 2.5)

JACK DANIELS AND ASSOCIATES MYSTERIES
DEAD ON MY FEET (Book 1)
JACK DANIELS STORIES VOL. 1 (Book 2)
SHOT OF TEQUILA (Book 3)
JACK DANIELS STORIES VOL. 2 (Book 4)
DYING BREATH (Book 5)
SERIAL KILLERS UNCUT (Book 6)
JACK DANIELS STORIES VOL. 3 (Book 7)
EVERYBODY DIES (Book 8)
JACK DANIELS STORIES VOL. 4 (Book 9)
BANANA HAMMOCK (Book 10)

KONRATH DARK THRILLER COLLECTIVE
THE LIST (Book 1)
ORIGIN (Book 2)
AFRAID (Book 3)
TRAPPED (Book 4)
ENDURANCE (Book 5)
HAUNTED HOUSE (Book 6)
WEBCAM (Book 7)
DISTURB (Book 8)
WHAT HAPPENED TO LORI: THE COMPLETE EPIC (Book 9)
THE NINE (Book 10)
CLOSE YOUR EYES (Book 11)
SECOND COMING (Book 12)
HOLES IN THE GROUND with Iain Rob Wright (Book 4.5)
DRACULAS with Blake Crouch, Jeff Strand, F. Paul Wilson (Book 5.5)
GRANDMA? with Talon Konrath (Book 6.5)

STOP A MURDER PUZZLE BOOKS
STOP A MURDER – HOW: PUZZLES 1 – 12 (Book 1)
STOP A MURDER – WHERE: PUZZLES 13 – 24 (Book 2)
STOP A MURDER – WHY: PUZZLES 25 – 36 (Book 3)
STOP A MURDER – WHO: PUZZLES 37 – 48 (Book 4)
STOP A MURDER – WHEN: PUZZLES 49 – 60 (Book 5)
STOP A MURDER – ANSWERS (Book 6)
STOP A MURDER COMPLETE CASES (Books 1-5)

CODENAME: CHANDLER SERIES
(CO-WRITTEN WITH ANN VOSS PETERSON)
FLEE (Book 1)
SPREE (Book 2)
THREE (Book 3)
EXPOSED (Book 4)
HIT (Book 5)
NAUGHTY (Book 6)
FIX with F. Paul Wilson (Book 7)
RESCUE (Book 8)

OLD FASHIONED

Former Chicago Homicide Lieutenant Jacqueline "Jack" Daniels has finally left her violent past behind, and she's moved into a new house with her family.

But her elderly next door neighbor is a bit… off.

Is he really as he appears, a kind old gentlemen with a few eccentricities?

Or are Jack's instincts correct, and he's something much, much darker?

And what is it he'd got in his basement?

Jack Daniels is about to learn that evil doesn't mellow with age.

OLD FASHIONED by JA Konrath
How well do you know your neighbors?

STOP A MURDER

This is unlike any mystery or thriller book you've ever read before. You play the sleuth, and try to follow the clues and solve the puzzles to prevent a murder from happening.

In this five-book series, you'll be tasked with decoding the mind and motivations of a nefarious killer who is plotting to commit an unspeakable crime.

Each book contains an epistolary collection of emails, texts, and letters, sent to bestselling author J.A. Konrath, by a serial killer. This psychopath is leaving detailed, cryptic hints about who will be murdered, why, when, where, and how. Some of the hints are easy to figure out. Others are much more devious.

Do you like solving mysteries? Do you enjoy puzzles or escape-the-room games? Are you good at spotting clues?

Only you can stop a murder.

Are you smart enough?

Are you brave enough?

Let the games begin…

#1 STOP A MURDER – HOW: Puzzles 1–12

#2 STOP A MURDER – WHERE: Puzzles 13–24

#3 STOP A MURDER – WHY: Puzzles 25–36

#4 STOP A MURDER – WHO: Puzzles 37–48

#5 STOP A MURDER – WHEN: Puzzles 49–60

TIMECASTER

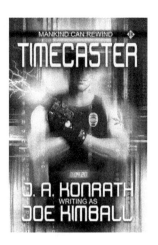

FUNNY! SEXY! ACTION PACKED!
Chicago, 2064: Mankind Can Rewind

Talon Alalon is a timecaster—one of a select few peace officers who can operate a TEV, the Tachyon Emission Visualizer, which records events (most specifically, crimes) that have already happened.

With crime at an all-time low, Talon has little to do except give lectures to schoolkids—and obsess on his wife's profession as a licensed sex partner.

Then one of her clients asks Talon to investigate a possible murder. When Talon uses the TEV to view the crime, the identity of the killer is unmistakable—it's him, Talon Avalon.

Someone is taking timecasting to a whole new level and using it to frame Talon. And the only way he can prove his innocence is to go off the grid—which in 2064 is a very dangerous thing to do.

Time is not on his side.

Featuring all of the action, thrills, and humor of other Konrath books, but set in an outrageous never-before-seen future, the TIMECASTER series is ecopunk on super steroids. Add in healthy doses of sex, some characters from Konrath's previous books (Talon is Jack Daniels's grandson), and a lot of outrageous ideas about technology, society, and politics, and Timecaster is a book that will appeal to anyone who likes to be entertained, even if they don't dig on sci-fi.

Sign up for the J.A. Konrath newsletter. A few times a year I pick random people to give free stuff to. It could be you.

http://www.jakonrath.com/mailing-list.php

I won't spam you or give your information out without your permission!

CPSIA information can be obtained
at www.ICGtesting.com
Printed in the USA
LVHW080215230221
679704LV00021B/162

9 781099 020421